THE SEER'S SISTER

PREQUEL TO THE MAGIC EATERS TRILOGY

CAROL BETH ANDERSON

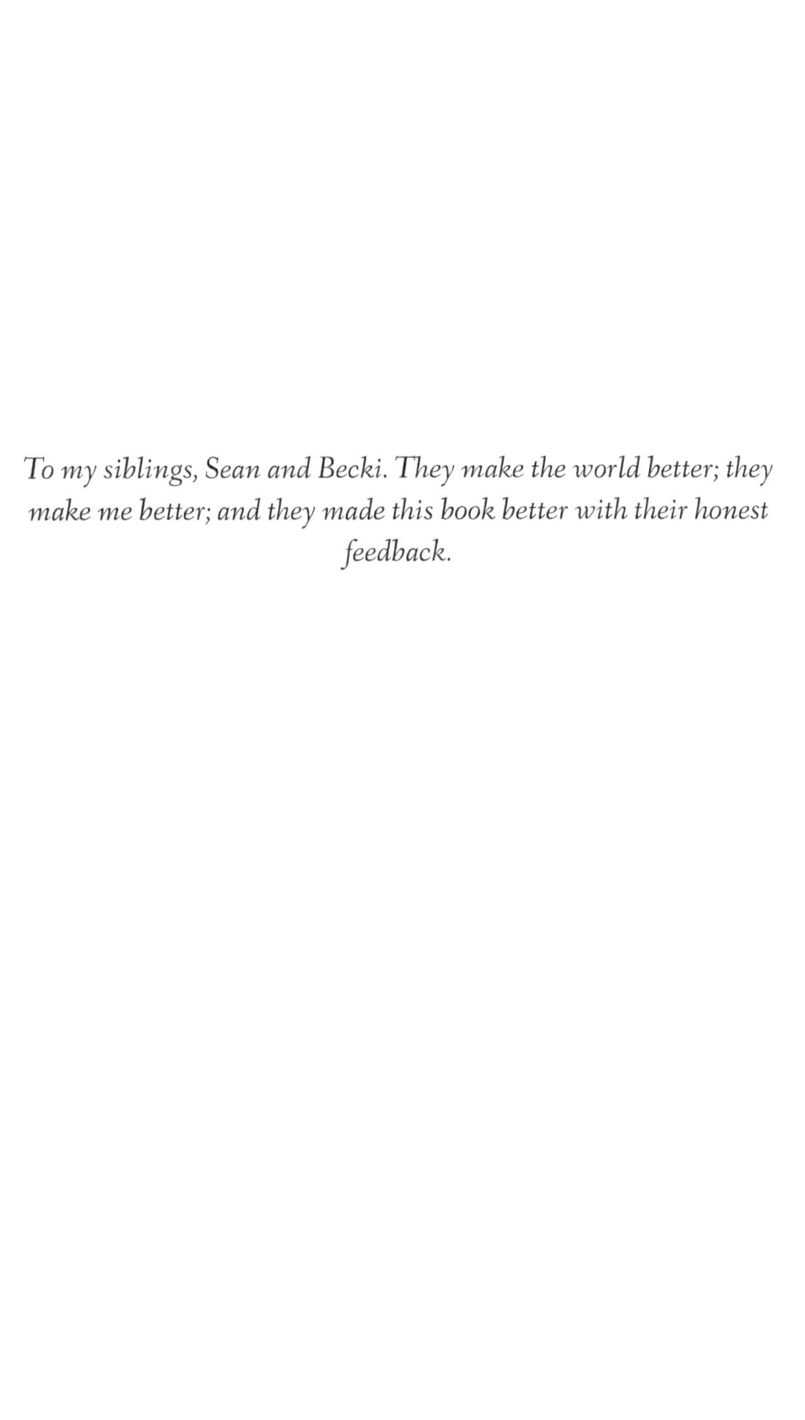

To my siblings, Sean and Becki. They make the world better; they make me better; and they made this book better with their honest feedback.

CHARACTERS AND PLACES

Characters

Rena Abrinan (uh-BRY-nan), a seer

Ellin Abrinan, Rena's sister

Kizha (KEE-zhuh), Rena's friend

Trett Stelios (STEE-lee-ose), Ellin's boyfriend

Alvun Merak (AL-vunn MARE-ack), owner of Merak Technologies

Arisa (uh-REE-suh) Merak, Alvun's wife

Tereza (terr-AY-zuh), works for Merak

Jovan (JOE-vin), works for Merak

Dr. Efren Rouven (ROO-ven), Merak researcher

Dr. Nomi (NO-mee) Anson, Merak researcher

Dr. Septimus (SEP-tih-muss), known as *Sep*, Merak researcher

Places

Anyari (ann-YAHR-ree), a planet settled by human colonists

Vallinger (VAL-in-jer), a country in Anyari's northern hemisphere

Stollton (STOLE-tun), the city in Vallinger where Ellin, Rena, and Trett live

Amler (AM-ler), a city in Vallinger, home of Merak Technologies' headquarters

Therro (THAIR-oh), a country in Anyari's southern hemisphere

Cellerin (SELL-err-in) Mountain, in Therro

Krenner (KREN-er), a city in Therro

Immerse yourself in the story by listening to the audiobook of *The Seer's Sister*. Get it on Amazon or Audible.

1

WEDNESDAY, QUARI 3, 6293

THE END, Rena wrote on the calendar square.

Ellin stood behind her sister's chair and glanced at the words. "End of what?"

"Humanity. Most of us, anyway." Rena's shoulders lifted in a little shrug.

Ellin had entered the room to discuss their dinner plans. All at once, her appetite fled, and her thoughts blurred into a thick haze. She stared at the whorl of short hair on the crown of Rena's head.

At last, one thought wriggled free from Ellin's sluggish brain: *Rena shrugged.* Mind sparking back to life, Ellin scrambled to interpret the gesture: *She was joking. Or she's not sure what she saw.*

She opened her mouth to voice her suspicions, but nothing came out, because she knew the truth: Rena was a seer. She didn't joke about her visions. And her certainty was only matched by her accuracy.

Ellin drew a deep breath and turned away. It didn't help. In her mind's eye, she still saw Rena, pen in hand, her prophecy scrawled in stark, black ink on the white page. Gritting her teeth, Ellin spun back around. She grasped her sister's shoulder and squeezed it hard. "I'm going to stop it."

Rena looked up. Her eyes, unblinking and calm, met Ellin's. "Please do."

After getting a large glass of water, Ellin returned to the kitchen table and sat across from Rena. Countless questions raced through her mind, and she blurted out the most urgent ones. "How's it going to happen? What do you mean by *most of us*? What can I do?"

Rena's pale-brown eyes locked onto Ellin, and she spoke in a low, flat voice, relating what she'd seen and ignoring the other questions. "I was at the indoor produce market, and I felt a vision coming on, so I stepped between a couple of stalls. I saw the same market in my vision, but it was full of dead people. One man was standing there, looking down at all the bodies, screaming."

Ellin took a deep breath and blew it out. "Could you tell how they'd died?"

"It looked like something had bleached their skin and hair. They were as white as paper, and they had blood coming out of their mouths, noses, eyes, and ears." She blinked twice. "It was as terrible as it sounds."

It took a lot for Rena to admit such a thing. Ellin ran her fingers through her wavy, brown, shoulder-length hair, waiting for her sister to continue. After several seconds, she prompted, "What happened next?"

Folding her arms tightly across her chest, Rena said, "I could tell I hadn't seen the whole vision, and I didn't want to put off the rest of it. So I came home and lay on my bed. I saw scenes from all over the world. Every continent and island on Anyari will be affected."

She picked up Ellin's glass and took a drink, seemingly unaware it was her sister's water. "I saw thousands of people. All but three were dead. When the vision stopped, I picked up my calendar and brought it to the table. It fell open to the right page, and I knew the day it would happen."

"That's when I walked in?" Ellin asked.

"I heard you walk up, and I couldn't think of a better way to tell you than to write what I did."

"*THE END.*" Ellin released a short, awkward laugh. "Pretty melodramatic, don't you think?"

Rena remained stoic. "When I wrote those words, I knew they were true. They wrapped up the prophecy. Our world is ending." Her forehead crinkled, and she covered her mouth with her hands before releasing a sob.

Ellin froze. Rena didn't cry. She hadn't even shed a tear eight years earlier when their parents had died in the Skytrain crash. Or if she had, she'd done it alone.

"I'm sorry." Ellin reached out tentatively toward Rena. Then she thought about all the times she'd come to her sister for comfort after the crash and received blank stares in return. She pulled her glass back across the table, like that was what she'd intended.

Rena's jaw flexed, and she breathed deeply through her nose. Once she got her emotions in check, which didn't take long, she said, "It's immutable."

Ellin brought one hand up to her mouth and let out a high-pitched "Oh." An immutable prophecy was set in stone. The whole world working together couldn't prevent it from coming true. "Then how . . . how can I stop it?"

"I have no idea, but you're supposed to try."

"How do you know that?"

"The same way I know it's going to happen."

Ellin shook her head. She was in the kitchen where she ate every day, sitting in one of the padded chairs they'd used for as long as she could remember, hands resting on their old, scratched table. Yet everything felt different—surreal and wrong. "I don't get it," she said softly.

"Neither do I, but it's all true." Rena stood, like she thought the conversation had reached a satisfactory conclusion. "I'm going to take a shower."

It wasn't until she was gone that another important question occurred to Ellin: *When?* She hadn't looked at the date as Rena wrote her dire message. Her gaze darted to the calendar. Curiosity and dread warred inside her, freezing her in place for several long minutes.

Probing tendrils of panic began to squeeze her lungs. Ellin forced life back into her arms, reached out, and touched the calendar's closed cover.

The connection with a physical object was just what her reeling mind needed. She ran her hand across the cover, allowing its smooth texture to anchor her to the present, then brushed her fingertips across the slight indentations where her sister had written her name: *Rena Abrinan.*

Ellin shook her head, pulling her hand and eyes away from the thin book. She'd never understood Rena's insistence on paper calendars. They were exorbitantly expensive due to environmental regulations. Digital calendars on flexscreens had more features, but Rena liked writing with a real pen on paper pages.

Well, if Rena wants to spend her limited money that way, it's her prerogative. Ellin had learned not to argue such points. Rena was twenty-six and was convinced she always knew better than her seventeen-year-old sister.

Ellin's pounding heart and rushing breaths brought her back to the present. *The world's ending, and I'm criticizing what kind of calendar my sister uses?* A laugh burst from her chest, and she covered her mouth with both hands. *What the hell is wrong with me?* Dragging her eyes back to the table, Ellin sent herself a single, silent command: *Focus!*

Her mind was too scattered, her body too frenzied. One thing was clear: she couldn't do this alone.

Ellin grabbed the calendar and rushed to the front door. She threw on a light jacket and slipped the calendar in her pocket, then exited the small house.

She stopped before she reached the street. Her rapid breaths were making her lightheaded. Standing under a fernfrond tree, she closed her eyes and forced herself to take deep, slow breaths of the cool, early spring air.

Within a couple of minutes, her heart rate was below panic range, and she was confident she could walk without passing out. She opened her eyes, stepped onto the sidewalk, and turned right.

"Good evening, Ellin!"

Ellin turned. Her next-door neighbors were eating dinner on their patio. "Nice night to eat outside," she called.

"Sure is," one of the men said. "How's school? Still aiming for the top?"

"It's going well."

The other man laughed. "I'm sure that's an understatement."

"Have a great night." Ellin waved again and continued down the street. A solarcar passed her, followed by a young woman on a hover scooter, or *hov*. Everything was so pleasant and normal—the vehicles, the neighbors, the safe streets and crisp air. Rena and her doomsday promises were just a few dozen steps away, but out here, worldwide destruction felt impossibly distant.

Ellin put her hand in her jacket pocket, touching the little calendar book. The questions roared back into her mind: *When? How? Why? Can I stop it? CAN I STOP IT?*

She pulled her hand out and shook it off, like the book had burned her. The calendar held the answer to the *when* question, but even with the pleasant, normal world surrounding her, she couldn't look at it alone. It could wait a few more minutes, until she was with Trett.

A sudden fear hit her: *What if he's not home?* She had no idea what his plans were for the evening. It was Wednesday, and other than seeing him at school, she hadn't communicated with him all week. She'd been busy studying, as usual, and he'd been patient, as usual. She could pull out her flexscreen and send him a quick message to make sure he was home, but she knew what she'd find if she opened her messages: ems from him she'd forgotten to respond to, despite her best intentions.

Why do I always do that? One of these days, his patience will run out. It was a frequent worry Ellin battled with—but not as often as she worried that she'd lose her ranking at the top of her class and the university scholarship she'd been promised.

I should be studying right now.

No, I should be with Trett, making sure he remembers I exist.

Ellin's arm brushed against the edge of the calendar sticking out of her pocket, and awareness of the horrid prophecy reentered her mind, bringing her internal debate to a halt. She had no idea how to properly cope with an impending apocalypse, but she was pretty sure it was counterproductive to obsess about her boyfriend and scholarships.

She forced herself to focus again on Rena's unthinkable descriptions of the future. *White skin and hair. Bleeding faces. Death everywhere. No escape.*

Ellin's hard-fought calm fled as two horrifying words—*THE END*—dug their claws into her consciousness, turning into a rhythmic, internal chant. The terrible refrain brought her all the way to Trett's house. Even the double-tap of her knuckles on the pale-yellow door resonated in her mind not as knocks, but as a two-word harbinger of Anyari's destruction. *THE END.*

She stared at the door, begging it to open.

2

WEDNESDAY, QUARI 3, 6293

RENA STEPPED out of the shower, dried off, and dressed in her favorite sleepwear, a pair of ultra-soft, yellow pants and a matching tank top. It was time for dinner, and while her brain told her she was hungry, her stomach hurt. In a post-vision state, or *PVS*, she'd get sick if she tried to eat. Today's PVS felt more severe than any she'd experienced in years. Just thinking about food brought on a wave of nausea.

She got in bed and had just quieted her mind enough to doze off when the flexscreen on her nightstand buzzed, waking her. She sat up and grabbed the wadded-up device, then pressed its corner. The thin, pliable screen flattened and firmed up. The pinch also activated a fingerprint scanner, and the screen lit up, having confirmed her identity.

Her message icon was glowing, so she tapped it. An em from Kizha read,

How's your day going?

Rena typed,

Just fine, yours?

Then she deleted the message, shaking her head. *I can't lie to her like that.* Instead, she typed,

Vision today. PVS.

She sat back, waiting for a reply.

Kizha was the only person Rena had ever told about her gift. They were both accountants, and they'd met through an online conference five years earlier. They'd gradually become close friends, the only such relationship Rena had ever had.

It was impossible to cultivate normal friendships while living such an abnormal life. Rena had been four years old when her parents realized she was a seer. Even then, she sensed how strange she was. Later, she learned there hadn't been a seer in over a hundred years.

Historical seers had played prominent roles in Anyari's major societies. People had generally treated them well as long as their prophecies were positive, then ridiculed and rejected them when the news turned bad. Some seers had been killed by frightened governments or angry vigilantes.

Rena hadn't known all that at four years old. All she knew was that she had to keep her visions a secret. When she was a little older, her parents explained why.

"We live in a good world," her mother said, "but there are still mean people who hurt others, just because they're different."

When she was older, Rena's parents told her about their other fear. Seers of the past who had survived to old age invariably lost their minds. Their visions stopped coming true, and in time, their sanity disintegrated completely. At the end of a seer's life, prophecy, imagination, and reality became indistinguishable.

Perhaps if no one knew about Rena's gift, her parents reasoned, she'd avoid rejection and violence. If she was free from the pressures of being a famous seer, maybe she could even retain her sanity. Her parents had schooled her at home, keeping her away from other children who might witness her having visions.

Rena had no doubt her life would have been difficult if everyone knew about her gift. She wasn't cut out to be a public figure; she wouldn't have handled the scrutiny well. Was her solitary life a worthwhile trade-off, though? She tried not to think too much about that question.

By the time Ellin was born, nine-year-old Rena had learned to keep not only her visions to herself, but most of her other thoughts too. It never occurred to her to befriend her sister; she was accustomed to only interacting with her parents. As Ellin grew, she asked questions about Rena's odd behavior. When the sisters were nine and eighteen, their parents at last shared the family secret with Ellin, and she vowed to protect the information.

Weeks later, the sisters' parents died in a Skytrain crash the likes of which the country of Vallinger hadn't seen in decades. After losing the only people she really trusted, Rena was expected to turn into an instant adult and care for herself and her sister. She barely managed it.

A few years later, Rena met Kizha. For the first time in years, maybe for the first time ever, Rena felt alive. She didn't tell Ellin about her new friend. What would a girl with a normal life think of her pathetic big sister's flexscreen-based socializing? Rena and Kizha quickly became close, and in a moment of weakness, Rena revealed her gift. Kizha hadn't given her any reason to regret it.

Like Rena, Kizha worked from home, and she, too, had a secret. She was a talented hacker. Countless times over the last few years, she'd helped Rena act on her prophecies. Kizha had hacked into emergency response systems, sending out warnings for earthquakes and tsunamis before scientists could predict them. And several corrupt politicians had been outed, thanks to Rena's visions, Kizha's not-quite-legal research, and a few well-placed messages to the press.

Rena's flex vibrated again, and she read Kizha's message.

Sorry, I had to answer a call. Can you tell me about the vision?

Pressing her lips together, Rena considered the question. A spike of pain entered her brain.

"Oh no," she murmured. A certain *full* sensation in her head often signaled an oncoming vision, but when she was in a severe PVS, that fullness turned into outright pain.

The sensation intensified. Rena fell backward. Her head struck the pillow, and she closed her eyes as a deep groan emerged from her chest.

A vision entered her mind. It started out dark and blurry but soon clarified into the image of a person. Her first feeling was relief—not only because the pain was subsiding, as it often did once a vision got started, but also because the person was moving. She'd seen enough dead people to last her a good, long while.

Then she recognized the person. Black, curly, shoulder-length hair. Stunning, bright-green eyes.

Kizha.

Oh no. After her earlier vision, the last thing she wanted was a prophecy about someone she knew. *Please, God, make this a good one.*

In the vision, Kizha wore a blue, short-sleeved shirt and black leggings. She was lying on her bed, propped up by a mound of pillows, typing on her flex. Rena's perspective shifted so she could see the screen of Kizha's device. She'd typed an em to Rena reading,

Of course, I'll help you however I can. I hope everything's okay. Are you sure you don't want to talk about it?

Rena's response soon popped up on Kizha's screen.

I wish I could. I'll let you know soon what I need.

The scene faded out, but the vision wasn't over. The same scene returned to Rena's mind. This time, however, Kizha read something on her flex, and her eyes widened. She continued to stare at the screen, and one smooth, tan hand came up to cover her open mouth.

Again, Rena's perspective shifted. On Kizha's screen was an em from Rena, describing her apocalyptic prophecy.

Rena watched as Kizha's fingers danced across her device. A few seconds later, Rena's face appeared on the screen. She was sitting on her bed, wearing the same comfy pajamas she was in now, backed by the same old, green headboard with its chipped paint. She greeted Kizha, who interrupted her, asking, "Is this real, Rena? Is it immutable?"

"Yes and yes." Her vision-self nodded, her short, brown hair quivering with the motion.

There was a long pause, and then Kizha said, "I'm coming there. If we don't have much time left, I'm spending as much of it as I can with you."

"Kizha, we've got to try to stop it."

The vision zoomed out as Kizha stood and began pulling clothes out of drawers. Her wide eyes glanced back at the flex she'd left propped against her pillow. "We can't stop it; you said it's immutable."

"It is. But something tells me Ellin's supposed to try to stop it. We can help her."

"I'll help once I get there. I have to pack, Rena. I'll call you when I've got a flight lined up." Kizha reached over and pressed the corner of her flex, collapsing it.

The scene transitioned into another, then another. They were all flashes from the coming weeks, just a few seconds each time. Kizha and Rena finally meeting. Eating meals, taking walks. Eager lips and hands. Every flash was filled with joy and passion, colored with extra intensity from knowing how little time they had together.

Rena saw herself reminding Kizha they needed to help Ellin. Then she saw Kizha hushing her with a kiss. They were lost in each other, at last surrendering to feelings they'd stifled for years. Yes, they made some effort to save the world, but they were halfheartedly checking tasks off a list, knowing they'd never reach their goal.

The last scene, of Kizha holding Rena, faded away gradually. Rena sat up, even more drained than before. Needing a drink of water, she reached over to her cluttered nightstand. All three cups sitting there were empty.

A string of ems from Kizha waited on her flex, all variations on *Where did you go?* and *Everything okay?* Rena wanted to answer, but first she had to process what she'd seen.

This vision wasn't a sure thing, like the one from earlier that day. This one was a potential prophecy. She'd seen multiple ways things *could* happen, and she was free to choose whichever option she preferred.

Her fingers ached to type out her apocalyptic visions and share them with Kizha. Ever since seeing those terrible scenes, she'd been struggling with the disturbing, foreign sensation of holding back tears. She'd even lost control in front of Ellin.

Kizha was Rena's one source of comfort. She knew from what she'd just seen that her friend wouldn't just support her through the tragic knowledge she'd gained. Kizha would *love* her through it. That was something Rena had hardly dared hope for.

Her potential prophecy had made her options clear. She could follow her heart, telling Kizha the whole truth, and the two of them would live the final days of their lives in a haze of love. Sure, they'd support Ellin in her quest to prevent the terrible vision from coming true, but they'd reserve their true commitment for each other, not for a pointless crusade.

Or Rena could keep the knowledge to herself, and Kizha would be the same dependable friend she'd always been, helping from a distance.

Rena wanted to convince herself that she could have the best of both worlds. She and Kizha would spend time together, but they'd also help Ellin. They'd be both passionate and logical.

She knew how pointless such a dream was. Visions didn't lie. After she settled on one of the options, she could only slightly shift the prophesied results. Even a small change required tremendous energy.

I can ignore Ellin, like I always have, while Kizha and I enjoy life for once. Or I can keep my best friend in the dark and use her for her talents.

"Seriously, God?" she murmured. "What kinds of options are those?"

Rena confronted God like this pretty often. She wasn't sure who he was, or even why most people called him *he*. All she knew for certain was that there was a reality beyond the physical—call it spiritual, metaphysical, or magical. Whatever it was, she experienced it every time she had a vision.

The seers of the past had often attributed their powers to God. By following that tradition, Rena felt connected not only to the mysterious deity, but also to the long-dead men and women who had understood what it was like to be blessed—or tortured—by this strange gift. So Rena prayed, especially when her visions left her grieved or uncertain. Sometimes she even thought God answered her.

This time, however, the only person attempting to communicate with her was Kizha, whose ems were still lighting up her flex. The most recent one said,

Hello? Anybody home?

"This doesn't make sense." Rena spoke calmly, like she was bringing an argument to a judge. "It's pointless to try to stop an immutable prophecy." Was she seriously considering giving up her last chance for happiness, all so she could help Ellin on her meaningless quest to defy a vision set in stone?

The problem was, Rena didn't just get visions. She also got

nudges. (Historians called them *premonitions*, but *nudges* felt right to her.) A nudge was a revelation of some sort—undeniable, but without the detail of a prophecy.

The moment she'd written *THE END*, Rena had known, deep in her gut, that Ellin was meant to try to prevent the end of the world, with her big sister's help.

It made no sense.

And it was unquestionably the right way to go.

Rereading Kizha's ems, another nudge hit her. She and Ellin couldn't take the path before them, whatever it was, without Kizha's assistance.

Rena swallowed hard, squeezing her hands into fists so tight, her finger muscles ached.

Then she released her hands and her breath and picked up her flex. She typed,

> Sorry, had another vision. I'm not ready to talk about what I saw, but I'm going to need your technological assistance in the coming days.

Kizha's response popped up a few seconds later, but Rena didn't even have to read it to know what it said.

> *Of course, I'll help you however I can. I hope everything's okay. Are you sure you don't want to talk about it?*

Rena could change the wording of the response she'd typed in the vision, but it wouldn't alter the overall result. She allowed her fingers to type the words she'd seen.

> I wish I could. I'll let you know soon what I need.

They chatted for a while, but Rena was too distracted to keep up much of a conversation. After they said goodbye, she covered her face with her hands and wept.

3

TRETT'S DOOR OPENED. Moisture glistened off his short, brown hair, and he had on a navy blue, short-sleeved undershirt. He'd probably just gotten out of the shower after going for a run. His porch camera must have picked up Ellin's panicked expression, because his brown eyes were wide with concern, and his dimpled smile was absent.

Before he could say a word, Ellin asked, "Are your parents here?" She couldn't bear to be around anyone else right now.

"No, of course not, they're at work." Trett took her hand. "What's wrong?"

With no warning, sobs burst from her chest.

Trett gaped at her, then led her inside. He brought her to the living room, but Ellin shook her head and spoke through her tears. "Back yard." She still needed fresh air.

Trett grabbed a light-brown, long-sleeved shirt and pulled it on as they walked through the rest of the house. When they stepped onto the back patio, Trett's pet caynin loped up to them, his mouth hanging open in what almost looked like a smile. The animal nudged

Trett's thigh with a squat snout, above which two round, maroon-colored compound eyes bulged with excitement, sunlight glinting off their facets. "Not now, Gray," Trett said. The sail-like ears on either side of the animal's face drooped, and he lay down next to Trett's feet.

Trett held his arms out, and Ellin fell into them, crying into his firm shoulder. He held her tightly, rubbing her back. When her tears stopped several minutes later, he murmured in her ear, "Ready to talk?"

Ellin pulled back, sniffling. She patted his shirt, which was wet with her tears. "Sorry about that. Do you have a handkerchief?"

"I'll grab one. Or, actually—" He grinned and pulled off his outer shirt, then sat and offered it to Ellin. "You might as well keep on using this."

Ellin laughed, which felt incredibly inappropriate at such a time but was just what she needed. She wasn't sure if Trett was serious, but she took him at his word and blew her nose on the shirt in her hands.

Still smiling, Trett pointed at his undershirt. "I have another if you need it." His expression sobered as he watched Ellin twist the shirt she was holding. He led her to a bench, and they sat. "Can you tell me what's going on?"

Gray had followed them to the bench, and he nudged Ellin's thigh with his rounded snout. Ellin set Trett's shirt aside and rubbed the mottled, gray-and-black fur between the animal's big ears. His forked tongue darted out of his mouth and licked her forearm. Usually, Gray's antics would have made her laugh, but not today. She murmured, "Down, Gray," and the caynin lay in front of the bench.

Ellin turned to Trett and swallowed, her throat suddenly tight. It was a few seconds before she was ready to speak, and then the words came out as a croak. "The world is ending." She pulled the calendar out of her pocket. "This will tell us when."

Trett's forehead wrinkled as his eyes widened. He stared at Ellin, his mouth opening and closing three times before he finally asked, "What . . . does that mean?"

"Rena had a vision. She said almost everyone is going to die. All over the world." Tears filled Ellin's eyes again.

"Almost . . . everyone?"

Ellin nodded slowly, then repeated everything Rena had told her. Trett wasn't supposed to know about Rena's gift, but Ellin had brought him in on the secret three years earlier, soon after they'd started dating. Since then, she'd shared dozens of Rena's visions with him. It took a lot to phase Trett, but his eyes remained wide and his mouth hung open as Ellin finished describing what her sister had seen.

Ellin held up the calendar. "Rena wrote *THE END* on the day it's supposed to happen. I was going to check the date when she left the room, but"—she let out a sharp sigh and shook her head—"I couldn't do it alone."

That jolted Trett out of his stupor. He took Ellin's hand. "Let's look at it together." His expression shifted into an awkward grimace that was probably supposed to be a comforting smile. Ellin had never seen him so bewildered.

She nodded and opened the calendar. First, she flipped to the current month, Quari. A few reminders were written on the squares. She turned to the next page, which was blank, then the next.

There it was: *THE END*, written on the sixth day of Cygni. A seemingly ordinary Saturday.

Ellin tried to control her breathing as she flipped back through the pages and counted. "Nine-and-a-half weeks."

"Sixty-six days," Trett added, his voice low.

Ellin propped her forehead in one hand, letting her hair fall over her face. Trett rested his warm hand on her shoulder. After several seconds, Ellin lifted her head and locked eyes with him. "I'm going to do whatever I can to stop this from happening."

Trett's gaze didn't budge. "Then I'll do whatever I can to help you."

Ellin took a deep breath through her nose before whispering, "It's immutable."

Trett blinked several times. His shoulders slumped, but his voice was strong. "You can do this. *We* can."

Ellin flashed him a weak smile, then pulled up the left sleeve of her jacket. She peeled her flexscreen off her forearm and firmed it, then found Cygni 6th on her calendar.

She input a command, and the bottom half of the screen's surface lifted into rows of letterkeys. On the proper calendar day, she typed the same words her sister had used: *THE END*. Eyes locked on the flex, she slowly shook her head, frowning at what she'd just typed.

As if he'd read her mind, Trett said, "*THE END*—I don't like that. We're stopping this thing, right?"

"Right."

"Then we can't say *THE END*. You've never accepted failure, Ellin. You're gonna beat the odds like you always have."

Ellin stared at the screen. "Nothing's immutable." She had to believe that, even though it went against everything she knew about prophecy. "Delete all," she said, louder than she'd intended. Her trembling fingers found the letterkeys again, and she typed, *DEADLINE*.

She took a deep breath, released it, and looked up. Her stomach growled, breaking the tension, and she and Trett shared a small smile.

"Do you want a sandwich?" he asked.

Such a strange question when they were considering the end of the world—but she couldn't deny that she was famished. "Maybe it'll help. I can make it. Do you want one too?"

"Stay here; I got it." He stood, then looked down at her, eyebrows lifted in concern. "Are you okay?"

"Yeah."

His look told her he didn't believe her, but he went inside.

Ellin buttoned her jacket. The sun would set soon, and it was getting chillier. She looked around the back yard. Trett's parents spent ridiculous amounts of money to keep this place beautiful, though with their work schedules, they almost never had time to enjoy it.

In the center, a dragon-shaped fountain, breathing water instead of fire, fed a small pond. Trett was the one who'd purchased the dragon. He was obsessed with ancient myths that were thought to have originated on Earth, humanity's home planet.

The fountain always made Ellin shudder. Unlike Anyarian animals, who had compound eyes, this dragon's eyes looked almost human, with irises and elongated pupils.

Most scholars doubted that magical, fire-breathing creatures had ever existed. The stories had all the marks of outlandish myths. Ellin sometimes wondered, however, what real animals on Earth had looked like. Surely there hadn't been beasts walking around with nearly-human eyes. That would've been way too weird.

Behind the pond were all sorts of plants and trees, bright with spring growth. They were all native to Anyari, with the exception of a pear tree in the corner. Ellin stood and walked to it, followed by Gray. White blossoms were scattered among the tree's leaves, and she plucked one. She'd learned from experience that the blossoms smelled terrible, so she kept it away from her nose. She rubbed the soft petals between her fingers, thinking about the humans who'd carried these seeds from Earth to Anyari.

Ancient stories indicated that over six thousand years ago, humanity's home planet had become nearly uninhabitable due to wars and environmental destruction. The people of Earth had sent a colony ship into space. Thousands had begun the journey, but most of them had died at some point of their mysterious, interstellar odyssey. Only a few hundred colonists had settled on Anyari.

There were no written records from Earth; the colonists had lost such treasures on their tragic journey. They'd landed on Anyari with few supplies, but they'd managed to bring several dozen varieties of seeds.

They'd also brought their memories, though most of those had been lost through the years. However, a few traditions had survived the millennia—like religion and those dragon myths Trett loved so much.

"Hey."

Ellin flinched and turned. "I didn't hear you walk up."

Trett pointed at the table in front of the bench where they'd been sitting. "The sandwiches are ready. Gray, don't even think about it!"

The caynin, who'd been sneaking toward the plates, turned and ran across the yard, where he settled in the shade of another tree.

Ellin didn't move toward the food, and neither did Trett. She held out the pear blossom. "I was thinking. Somehow a few hundred colonists survived on Anyari with almost no resources. How do you think they did it?"

"Our history teachers would say they rebuilt civilization through pure determination—and then they did their best to destroy it."

"True." Ellin continued to gaze at the blossom. From war to disease to environmental disasters, the Anyarians' history was one of constant struggle—against themselves and their planet. "Those hard times are mostly over, though," Ellin said. "So many diseases have been eradicated, and we actually take care of our environment now." She turned and walked thoughtfully back to the bench, followed by Trett. Picking up her sandwich, which was stuffed with meat grown in a lab, she said, "We don't even kill animals anymore."

"All that's true, but it's not like humans have turned into a bunch of perfect angels," Trett said.

"I know. I suppose selfish individuals will always exist, but as a society, we've gotten so many things right. Nobody's hungry. There hasn't been a big war in decades."

Trett watched her thoughtfully, ignoring his sandwich. "What are you saying?"

Ellin took a bite and chewed. It was delicious. She swallowed and met Trett's gaze. "I'm saying this doesn't feel like a world on the verge of destruction."

"I agree, but Rena's never wrong. That's why you were crying when you got here. I'll probably do the same once her prophecy really sinks in." Trett shook his head, letting out a confused laugh. "How are you even eating?"

Ellin responded by taking another bite and chewing slowly. An alternate explanation for the prophecy was brewing in her mind. It was a promising possibility—and a terrible one too.

"Ellin?" Trett leaned over and gently tapped her temple. "What's going on in there?"

She ate a couple more bites before putting her sandwich down and saying, "You know, there is one reason seers get their prophecies wrong." Seeing Trett's furrowed brow, she took a deep breath and pressed forward. "What if Rena's losing her mind?"

Trett raised an eyebrow. "You think she's crazy?"

"You know I don't like that term." Ellin had given herself the *crazy* label after losing her parents. It had taken several years and lots of professional help for her to finally disavow the term—for herself or anyone else.

"You're right. I'm sorry. Do you think Rena might be . . . losing touch with reality?"

"It seems a lot more believable than worldwide destruction."

Trett nodded slowly.

"You agree?" Ellin asked.

"I agree it's a possibility. But Rena's never been wrong. We can't ignore what she told you."

"I know. And it's not that I want Rena to lose her mind, it's just . . ." She shook her head.

"It's better than the alternative?"

"Exactly."

Trett bit his lip, then asked, "How old is she?"

"Twenty-six."

"Is that too young for a seer to lose her mind?"

Ellin gave him a helpless shrug. "That's literally the most important question in the world."

4

ELLIN BENT over the beverage maker, squinting to read the screen. Its voice activation features had fizzled out a couple of years earlier, and for the past few months, the screen had been gradually filling up with blank lines. She tried to punch in her coffee order. A tinny voice chided, "Try again, please." She got it right the second time.

"Beverage ready," the machine said less than a minute later. Ellin brought her cup to the kitchen table, took a sip, and savored it. She always drank her coffee with a splash of crem. The thick, white liquid, extruded from the milkplant, was native to Anyari. How had her ancestors on Earth ever tolerated coffee without crem?

Rena entered and sat heavily in a chair opposite Ellin.

"How are you feeling?" Ellin asked.

"Fine."

Ellin knew better. It took a full day, sometimes longer, for her sister to recover from an intense vision. Rena's eyes were bloodshot; she was slouching in her seat; and it looked like she could barely keep her head up and eyes open. Chunks of short, dark hair were sticking up all around her head. She'd never admit to being affected by what she'd seen, though.

Ellin stood. "I'll get you some coffee."

When they were both settled, Rena said, "I'm not working today. I told them I had a headache."

"Good idea." Ellin took a swallow of her coffee and watched her sister, whose sleepy eyes were gazing blankly across the room. Questions multiplied in Ellin's mind. *How are you really feeling this morning? Do you care how this is affecting me? Did you have nightmares too?*

Overnight, Ellin had reviewed all the reasons Rena's prophecy couldn't be true, and she'd become even more convinced her sister was losing touch with reality.

But everything was different in the light of morning. Sitting across from her prescient sister, Ellin's midnight certainty fled. Images of colorless skin and bright blood seeped into her consciousness and settled there. *What if she's right?*

After several silent minutes, Ellin asked, "Any more visions?"

"Nothing apocalyptic, if that's what you mean." Rena didn't even look at her.

Ellin shook her head and took a gulp of coffee. It was nearly lukewarm. *What's wrong with us? She's a seer predicting the end of the world; I'm the one who's supposed to prevent it; and we can't even have a normal conversation.* Every second of silence added oxygen to the embers of Ellin's frustration.

Finally, she pulled her flex off her arm and firmed it. She held it up so Rena could see the screen. "Look!" she said sharply, finally capturing her sister's gaze. "See this countdown? Sixty-five days until the end of the world. You said I'm supposed to try to stop it, but you haven't told me how!"

Rena sat up straight, despite her obvious exhaustion. "Don't you think I'd tell you if I knew? Don't you think I'm begging for more details so we can actually do something about it? I stayed up all night, hoping for a vision, but I don't know any more than I did yesterday."

Ellin felt tears forming. She blinked them away. "What do you expect me to do, then?"

Rena slumped back in her seat. "I don't know. Go to school like usual. I'll just be sleeping today, anyway. Who knows; I might get lucky and wake up with a vision."

Maybe school was a good idea. If the prophecy was true, Ellin couldn't do anything until she had more details. If it was false, she couldn't afford to get behind on her studies.

She grabbed her flexscreen off the table, collapsed it, and laid it on her forearm. It wrapped against her skin, the warmth comforting her. After putting on her jacket, she exited the house.

Trett was just walking up. Ellin closed the door behind her and approached him. "You look as tired as I feel," she said.

He gave her a quick kiss. "Long night?"

"Yeah."

"Me too."

They linked hands and started walking. School was only a few blocks away, and Ellin set a slow pace. As pedestrians, hovs, and solarcars passed them, she updated Trett on the conversation with Rena.

"She wants you to go on with your everyday life, waiting for more information?" Trett asked.

"Yes! This whole thing is just . . . surreal, Trett. When we talked yesterday, she was so insistent that I'm supposed to try to stop this this. But I can't do anything if I don't know anything!"

"Will you even be able to focus on schoolwork today?"

A small laugh cut through Ellin's vexation. "Do I ever have a hard time focusing on schoolwork?"

"Good point."

They walked a little longer, and Ellin said, "One thing I can do is keep a close eye on Rena, looking for anything that seems . . . off."

"Not that she's easy to read."

"I know." Aware of the pedestrians around them, Ellin tilted her chin up to speak softly in Trett's ear. "She's losing her mind. I know she is. I thought about this all night. How is almost everyone supposed to die on one day? Her vision sounded like some sort of plague, but illness doesn't ever move that fast. Isn't it a lot easier to believe that one person is losing touch with reality?"

Trett's voice was gentle and just as quiet as hers. "If you're convinced of that, why are you so upset that she hasn't had any more visions?"

Her stupid, insistent tears returned. "I don't know."

They said goodbye outside the school, and Trett walked toward one of the smaller classroom buildings. Ellin entered the main building, and her shoulders immediately released tension she hadn't known she was carrying. She loved this place; it felt more like home than her house did.

The lobby extended up the entire height of the three-story structure. Sunlight streamed through the high, glass ceiling. The wall to her right was covered in climbing plants, which had just sprouted blue flowers that week. Students sat at tables scattered around the large lobby, while others walked toward the lifts at the back of the room and the wide staircase in the middle.

Mr. Karel, a tall, bearded math teacher, greeted her with a broad smile. Ellin returned the greeting, her own smile genuine and effortless. She always got along with her teachers, but he was one of her favorites.

She stopped in the bathroom, then continued to her public speaking class. It wouldn't start for ten minutes, so she greeted the teacher and relaxed in her seat while other students arrived.

When she'd first started school, Ellin had been more than ready. Ever since she could remember, she'd been aware that her big sister was the most important person in their house. Rena went to school at home and made decisions for the whole family. Five-year-old Ellin didn't know why Rena merited so much attention; she just knew she was sick of it.

School opened Ellin's eyes to a glorious truth: she, too, was special. She'd taught herself to read when she was four, but she didn't know that was abnormal until she saw her classmates struggling to sound out words. She soon discovered reading wasn't the only thing she was good at. Advanced scientific concepts fascinated her, and numbers just made sense. In short, Ellin realized she was smart.

Her parents praised her for excelling, and Ellin soaked up their attention. She tried even harder—reading voraciously, puzzling through math problems for fun, and engaging her teachers in deep conversations that caught them off guard and delighted them. In fact, she usually related better to her instructors than her peers.

After her parents' deaths, Ellin redoubled her efforts at school. Her home life was topsy-turvy, and school was the one thing that still made sense. She relished the absolute truth of facts and formulas and the measurable success of test scores and course grades. When anxiety threatened to take over completely, learning gave Ellin the gift of distraction. She pushed herself to even greater academic heights.

Now here she was, set to graduate at the top of her class in a few months. She'd accepted a full university scholarship and was thoroughly dedicated to her goal of becoming a technisurgeon.

If Rena's prophecy isn't true.

Ellin pushed away the thought and sat up straight as her teacher started the class.

They'd been working on spontaneous speeches all week. The teacher provided a topic, and a student spoke on it for three minutes. Ellin looked around the room. Students tapped their feet, chewed their nails, and wiped sweaty palms on their clothes as they awaited their turns.

Ellin's foot was tapping too, but her nerves were of the excited variety. When her turn came, the teacher told her to speak on water conservation.

Ellin strode to the front of the class. "Historically," she began, "society's water conservation efforts have come in waves." She waited for the light laughter to die down, then continued.

Her classmates smiled at the right places and nodded in agreement. At the end, the other students applauded politely, and the teacher caught Ellin's eye and smiled. Ellin smiled back. The end of the world couldn't have felt farther away.

At lunchtime, Ellin went to the dining hall. She grabbed a nutritional drink and said a quick hello to Trett and a few other friends before heading to the library to drink her lunch and do research for an upcoming history paper.

The library was her favorite room in the school. The lighting was bright but soft; potted plants decorated the walls and floor; and there were plenty of comfortable seats for individuals and groups. A few tall shelves stood in the back, full of valuable paper books printed before everything had gone digital.

Ellin sat at a desk near the bookshelves and took a moment to breathe in the comforting scent of old paper and bindings. She turned on the deskscreen and delved into her research, getting so wrapped up in it that when her flex buzzed to alert her that lunch was over, she didn't notice it for a solid two minutes.

By the end of the day, much of Ellin's morning exhaustion had fled, replaced by the comfortable thrill of expending energy on things she excelled at. As she left her last class, she saw Trett approaching.

He took her hand. "Ready to go?"

She considered the question. At home, she'd just encounter her sister again. Surely if Rena had any further details on the supposed prophecy, she'd em Ellin. Until then, discussions like the one they'd had that morning were pointless.

Spending the evening with Trett was a much more attractive option, but Ellin's history research was calling to her. She'd been halfway through a fascinating article when lunch ended. While she could continue her reading at Trett's house, the library was more comfortable and promised fewer distractions.

She gave Trett an apologetic smile. "Would you be too bummed if I stayed here to study for a while?"

"That's fine." His expression was pleasant, but his lips twitched a little. She knew he was disappointed, though he'd never say it.

Ellin bit her lip, but the ache of guilt in her gut didn't change the facts: the world outside the school doors had given her little but shock, anxiety, and sleeplessness since the day before. She wasn't ready to go back to that.

She squeezed Trett's hand, then let go of it and hurried to the library.

5

SATURDAY, QUARI 6, 6293
-63 DAYS

RENA STOOD in her tiny shower, glaring at the overhead water sprayers. Half of them had been broken for months. She had to perform awkward contortions to rinse off the left side of her body.

That wasn't the primary source of her frustration, though. She bowed her head and stepped forward, placing her palms on the side shower wall and letting hot water spray the back of her head. It ran down her cheeks and forehead, some of it reaching her closed eyes, her nose, and her lips.

"Give me something, please," she whispered.

It had been three days since the prophecy. She'd tried to resume working yesterday but ended up calling in sick again. Her severe fatigue made it impossible to focus on numbers. Now it was Saturday, and she had the whole weekend to obsess over the end of the world.

"You say my sister should try to stop this, and I should help her. I need details."

The prayer didn't seem to do any good. Rena smacked the shower control panel harder than was necessary, and the water stopped flowing. The body dryer turned on, and she held her arms up and rotated in a slow circle. Turning shouldn't have been necessary, but some of the dryer nozzles were broken too.

Rena was still damp when the warm air stopped, but she didn't bother to turn on the dryer again. She stepped out and turned away from the dirty mirror. She didn't need to look at herself to know she had bloodshot eyes, lips pressed into a narrow line, and shoulders slumped in weariness.

When she reached her bed, she lay down with a heavy sigh. *When you're too tired to get dressed, you know it's bad.*

Turning onto her side, she spied her flex on the nightstand. *Kizha.* Rena needed to talk to her. She'd understand.

Except Kizha didn't know about this vision, and she couldn't.

I could talk to Ellin.

Rena almost laughed at the thought. What would Ellin think, after years of distance, if her big sister suddenly bared her tortured soul? Ellin seemed to doubt whether Rena had feelings at all. It was a little late to prove her wrong.

What had Ellin been up to the last couple of nights, anyway? She hadn't gotten home on Thursday or Friday until Rena was already in her room, hours after dinner. *Probably with Trett. Or maybe volunteering.* Ellin was taking an Introduction to Medicine elective, and sometimes she went to a nearby senior recreation center to help in their clinic. Trett often went with her to spend time with the seniors.

At that thought, a wave of *knowing* hit Rena. *We're supposed to volunteer at the rec center together—Ellin, Trett, and me.*

It was the first prophecy of any sort Rena had experienced since Wednesday, and relief washed over her. She had no idea what a rec center had to do with the end of the world, but it was all she had to go on. A strong nudge certainly beat utter silence.

Rena sat up and threw some clothes on, then took her flex to the living room, where she settled on the couch. She looked up the rec center and started reading their volunteer requirements.

Trett arrived at Ellin's house a little after nine in the morning. Rena let him in and gave him a one-word greeting, then turned and walked away.

Trett shrugged. *That's Rena.* He walked down the hall and knocked on Ellin's door.

"What?" Ellin sounded groggy and annoyed.

"Can I come in?"

"Um . . . okay."

He entered and sat on the edge of her bed. Ellin was sitting up, her eyes squeezed into narrow, blinking slits. She was still in her pajamas. "You're cute when you're sleepy," he said.

She scowled. That made Trett smile bigger. He moved closer to kiss her, and she held her hand up. "My breath stinks."

"I don't care." He nudged her hand out of the way and kissed her.

Ellin yawned and rubbed her eyes. "I didn't know you were coming over."

"I emmed you."

She picked up her flex and firmed it, then read the em he'd sent her less than two minutes earlier:

I'm at your house.

She laughed. "You didn't give me much notice."

He shot her a rueful smile. "I was afraid if I gave you any notice, you'd use that time to go to the library." He didn't know what time she'd left the school the last two nights, but he suspected it was late. The librarians there trusted her. In the past, they'd let her stay for hours past closing.

Ellin bit her bottom lip and looked down at her flex again. Her messages from Trett were still open, including the two she'd never answered the night before.

How does she do it? It had been less than three days since she'd wept in his arms, tortured by her sister's vision. The next morning, she'd thrown herself back into her studies. It was like the vision had never happened—or more accurately, like she was determined to forget it. Trett wanted to help her walk through this crisis, if she'd just let him.

Part of him wanted to say all that to her, but she needed him to support her, not accuse her of being in denial. Even if it was true. He settled for, "I've been concerned about you."

Ellin shook her head helplessly. "I'm sorry I didn't get back to you yesterday. I honestly meant to. I was in the middle of something both times you emmed me, and then . . . I lost track of time, I guess. I really am sorry."

I'm used to it. Trett banished the thought and gave her an understanding smile. "How are you, really? Any more information from Rena?"

"Nothing from her, but let me show you some of what I was researching last night. It wasn't all for school."

His eyebrows rose.

Ellin navigated on her flex, then handed it to him. "Read that while I'm getting dressed and brushing my teeth." She smiled, kissed his cheek, and walked into her bathroom.

Trett began scanning the article, which was over a century old. It was all about the last known seer, who'd died shortly before the article was written.

"I marked the most important part," Ellin called through the bathroom door. "Second or third page."

Trett found a paragraph Ellin had marked with a green, hand-drawn arrow. He read it to himself.

As was the case with seers of the past, Tyr's mind disintegrated at the end of his storied life. This is how his wife described it:

"One day, his visions became unreliable. In fact, I don't recall any of them coming true after the first one failed. At first, he seemed fine, other than the continued false prophecies. Eventually, however, he lost all sense of who he was."

Trett continued scanning the article until Ellin returned.

She was wearing sleek, red pants that hugged her curves and a cream-colored shirt that, while oversized, was somehow insanely flattering. She sat next to him on the bed and gestured to the article. "What do you think?"

He gave her a sly grin. "I think you're beautiful. And you just brushed your teeth." He set the flex down, leaned over, and kissed her.

Ellin returned the kiss but broke it off after a few seconds. "The article, Trett," she said with a small laugh. "Come on, focus. What did you think of it?"

He picked up the flex and returned to the passage Ellin had marked. "It's interesting. I've always heard about seers losing their minds, but I never really thought about how it happens."

"Neither have I," Ellin said, "until last night. Apparently, it's like a switch flips. One day, every vision comes true; the next, none of them do. I read other articles, and the pattern was always the same."

"I would have assumed it was gradual."

"Well, it does take years for a seer's mind to completely degenerate. Inaccurate prophecies are just the first symptom of a bigger problem."

Trett nodded. "So I guess if any of your sister's other visions prove false, we'll know that's what we're dealing with."

"Yeah," Ellin said. "I just wish—"

She was interrupted by the bedroom door opening.

"How about knocking?" Ellin snapped at Rena.

Rena ignored the jibe. "Do you two have any plans this morning?"

"We're going to, uh, do something," Ellin turned her head away from her sister to look at Trett with a desperate expression that clearly said, *I don't want to spend the day with my big sister.*

Trett was still focused on the article and the prophecy, and his mind refused to generate any fun activity ideas. "Yeah," he said, "we're . . . hanging out today." He gave Ellin an apologetic shrug.

"Well, I have a plan," Rena said, "and I want you both to join me. You know that senior rec center where you volunteer? I think we should all go help there today. I *feel* like it's something we should do." She gave Ellin a significant look.

Ellin had never told Rena that Trett knew the truth, and they ended up having pointlessly vague conversations when he was around.

Suddenly wide awake and cheerful, Ellin said, "Let's do it. I haven't been there in a few weeks. You'll need to register as a volunteer, Rena."

"Already done." Rena took a step into the room. "I'm glad you can both come. I think it'll be a *very important* way to spend our time." The look she gave her sister was so intense, Trett almost burst out laughing.

The Singing Tree Senior Recreation Center was a gorgeous building made of white granite. The stone, of course, was grown in a vat. Ellin wasn't quite sure how it worked, but no one had quarried real stone in at least a century.

Ellin had been to the rec center plenty of times, but she was still impressed every time she walked in. It was even nicer inside than out. Behind the front desk was a large room where elderly people played games, lounged around wallscreens, and socialized over drinks and snacks. Some people sat in quiet corners, relaxing or reading. Transparent walls at the back and one side of the room revealed exercise equipment, a pool, and a springball court. To the right was the entrance to a state-of-the-art medical clinic. The entire place was busy without being crowded.

Throughout the nation of Vallinger, nearly every city had at least one such facility. The city of Stollton was large enough to have over a dozen. They were all paid for through taxes, and any qualifying resident had unlimited, free access.

Rena, who'd walked straight to the front desk, turned around. "I signed us in. Ellin, they said they already have enough volunteers in the clinic today. We'll all just spend time with the seniors. Talk to them, play games, whatever."

They walked in, and Ellin soon found herself adopted by a group of enthusiastic women playing a complicated card game she'd never heard of. It didn't take long to realize they'd probably only invited her to play because she made them all look like experts.

The women's friendliness made the game fun, despite Ellin's dismal scores. They thanked her for volunteering, commented on her quick grasp of the game's rules, and complimented her blue eyes, which she'd colorized the year before.

After playing for an hour and a half, Ellin took her leave and wandered through the main room. She stepped into the exercise area. Trett's back was to her. He was doing bicep curls alongside a surprisingly spry man whose wrinkled skin marked him as at least a century old.

A smile teased the corners of Ellin's mouth as she watched Trett. He was thin, so most people didn't realize how toned he was under the loose shirts he favored. He'd taken off his long-sleeved shirt, and his undershirt was taut across the muscles on his back as he lifted the weight bar toward his chest.

The other man finished his set and stood. As he stretched his arms, he saw Ellin. He jabbed Trett in the shoulder. "One of us has an admirer, and I don't think it's me."

Trett did one more curl, then stood and turned. He grinned at Ellin. "Ready to go?"

She returned the smile. "Only if you are. I could watch this all day."

Trett laughed and said goodbye to his workout partner. Then he pulled on his loose, green shirt and joined Ellin. The other man sat and started another set.

"Let's see what Rena's up to," Ellin said.

They meandered through the main room until they discovered Rena sitting on a long couch with several seniors, watching a classic comedy episode on the wallscreen. She was actually laughing, not something she often did. Considering how uptight she'd been that week, Ellin was glad to see her finding some release.

Ellin and Trett stood behind the couch and watched the rest of the episode. When it was over, Ellin tapped Rena. "Ready to go?"

Rena got up. Once she was next to Ellin, she said, "This was a good activity for us. Surprisingly . . . uh . . . calm."

Ellin raised her eyebrows. *If nothing happened to justify her premonition to come here, does that mean it was a false prophecy?*

They walked back to the front desk, and Rena signed them out. Just as they turned to exit, a man and woman approached the entrance door carrying a large box. Ellin rushed to hold the door open for them.

"Thanks," the man said. "Wouldn't want to drop this." They set the package down, blocking Rena and Trett's route to the door.

The woman pinched the corner of the black box, and the sides and top melted into a fabric-like substance, which fell to the ground and pooled all around the object. All the shipping and delivery companies used versaboxes these days. The woman slid the flexible material out from under the cargo and folded it. Later someone would form it into another shape for the next delivery.

The item they'd delivered was a squat cylinder made of some material that looked like textured silver. Trett stepped closer. The object came up to his waist. "Is that a Threed?"

"Sure is," the man said.

"Those are expensive, aren't they?" Ellin asked. A Three-Dimensional Projector, or *Threed*, created realistic holographic images. With one Threed plus a good speaker system, the rec center could show well-known plays and concerts, and it would take a sharp eye to realize the actors and musicians weren't in the room.

"Very expensive," the man replied. "Good thing this place has a benefactor." He picked up a small card from the top of the Threed and handed it to Ellin.

"Enjoy," the card said in messy handwriting. The signature was illegible, but a name was printed on the bottom of the card: *ALVUN MERAK*. He was the founder, president, and majority shareholder of the largest technology company in the world. Among other things, they made flexscreens. When Rena had scraped up enough cash to buy the flex wrapped around Ellin's forearm, she'd made Merak even richer.

"The best benefactor any place could hope for," Ellin said. She gave the card to Trett, who read it and smiled before handing it to Rena.

Rena read it. Her eyes grew wide and rolled back into her head, and she dropped to the floor, shaking, her mouth gaping open in a silent scream.

6

THE PROBLEM with visions was that they occasionally looked like seizures.

The problem with seizures was that, thanks to modern medical technology, they rarely happened.

So when Rena had an intense vision in public, it attracted way too much attention.

Thankfully, Ellin had handled such situations for her sister for years. "Everything is fine," she said, raising her voice over the concerned exclamations of the delivery workers, the front desk staff, and at least ten seniors who'd rushed in from the main room. "Please step away; this will pass quickly."

A man at the front desk held a flexscreen and was speaking urgently to someone at the in-house clinic. Ellin pushed her way to the desk, pulling her own flex off her arm. "This isn't an emergency," she said. She pulled up the virtual medical card she kept on her flex and shoved the device in front of the still-panicked man.

The man tried to push her flex away.

"Please read it!" Ellin said.

At last, he stopped talking long enough to read the screen. "Oh," he said, meeting Ellin's eyes. "Pardon me."

She took her flex back and watched him dismiss the clinic worker.

"Thank you," Ellin said. "I'll take her to her doctor as soon as she's calm."

The medical card was an excellent digital forgery, and it always worked. It disclosed a mental illness which caused Rena to experience seizures that didn't physically harm her. While mental healthcare in Vallinger was excellent, everyone knew some illnesses of the mind could only be treated, not cured.

Ellin squeezed back through the crowd and knelt next to Rena, who was now scowling at everyone around her.

"I'm fine!" Rena said. "Let me get up."

A few people resisted until Ellin showed them her flexscreen and assured them she'd take Rena for immediate help. The people clustered around Rena stepped back, allowing Ellin to help her sister to her feet. Moments later, they were on the sidewalk outside, along with Trett.

Rena led the way, walking briskly. She turned her head toward Trett. "Has Ellin told you about my psychological condition?"

"Actually," Ellin said, "I told him about your true condition three years ago. He knows about your gift." She hadn't planned to make such a disclosure, but they had bigger things to deal with than Rena's potential anger.

Rena stopped walking and grabbed Ellin's arm, hard enough to make her flinch. "You what?"

Ellin lifted her chin. "I told him. Because I trust him. Now I'm telling you, because we don't have time to keep playing games where you give me obvious clues about the visions you're having. You can tell us what we need to know, and Trett will help us do whatever needs to be done."

She knew she was overstepping by volunteering Trett, but he smiled and said, "Absolutely. I'm in."

They all started walking again.

"So, you know the truth," Rena said.

"Yeah," Trett said. "It's pretty great, really. A seer."

"Shh—don't say it in public. You also know what happened this week?"

"Yes."

"What did you see in the rec center?" Ellin asked.

"I'm not talking about it here. Let's get home."

When Rena entered the house, she went straight to the sofa, pulling her flexscreen out of her pocket and firming it. Ellin shook her head. Rena's flex was always buggy since she carried it around wadded up like a handkerchief.

After closing the door, Ellin and Trett joined Rena in the living room. Ellin sat next to her on the couch, and Trett situated himself in a chair.

"What did you see?" Ellin asked again.

Rena didn't seem to hear the question. She was frantically typing and scrolling on her flex.

After asking once more with the same result, Ellin leaned over to see what Rena was looking up. Several news stories were open on the flex. Every one of them was about Alvun Merak.

"Was Merak in your vision?" Ellin asked.

Rena looked up, her lips smashed into a pale line. "No, he wasn't in my vision."

Trett kept his tone light and friendly. "Rena, if you tell us what you saw, we can use our own flexes to help you search for whatever you need."

"Fine." Rena tossed her flex next to her on the couch. "When I saw Alvun Merak's name on that card, I had a vision where every person in the rec center was dead." She sounded as dispassionate as usual.

"Just like what you saw the other day?" Trett asked.

"Yes."

"How do you know it has something to do with Merak?" Ellin asked.

Rena stood, crossing to the center of the room and facing them both with her hands on her hips. "I know because *I know*. I can still feel it. Alvun Merak will do something that leads to everyone dying."

"You said before it's not everyone," Ellin said.

Rena barked a laugh. "I've seen three living people in all these visions. The ratio isn't good."

Ellin didn't know how to respond to that. She shifted her attention to Trett, giving him a desperate look.

"Rena, why don't you have a seat again?" Trett suggested.

Rena's jaw tightened, but she followed his advice.

"Let's think this through," Trett said, his low voice soothing. "Hang on." He took his own flexscreen out of his pants pocket. Unlike Rena, he kept it folded neatly in a protective case. After he'd firmed it, he navigated through its menus, and the wallscreen across the room turned on. Several seconds later, a news article about Alvun Merak was on the wallscreen. The title was "Merak Wants Your Money—But He Doesn't Want to Keep It."

Trett replaced his flex in his pocket and walked to the wallscreen. "I read this article last week. Do you know why Merak isn't the richest man in the world?" When neither sister responded, he continued, "It's because he gives so much of his money away. In the past ten years, he's given away more money than any other person has made. That Threed in the rec center was nothing compared to everything else he does."

He held his hand close to the screen and gestured so the article scrolled down. Then he stopped and zoomed in on a photo of the exterior of a hospital. Dozens of smiling staff stood in front. "Five years ago, every nation except Shevatin had virtually eradicated cancer. Now Shevatin's cancer rates are as low as Vallinger's, because Alvun Merak rebuilt their entire medical system. When the project was complete, he gave their government enough money to fund their new system forever on the income from his investment."

"What's your point?" Rena asked.

Ellin turned to her sister. "I think his point is that Alvun Merak might literally be the last person in the world to cause an apocalypse."

Rena grabbed her flexscreen, stood, and walked to Trett. "My turn." She pointed at his chair.

Trett shrugged and returned to his seat.

Rena connected her own flex to the wallscreen, then collapsed her device, crumpled it up, and shoved it back in her pocket. "It doesn't matter if Alvun Merak is the best man who ever lived," she said. "My prophecies aren't wrong. The best we can hope for is to gather information and stop him. I'm sure we all want to enjoy our last two months alive, but we can't. We have to be selfless adults and do whatever we can to stop this."

By the end of her speech, Rena was breathing heavily and blinking hard. She gestured at the wallscreen, pulling up story after story about Merak and discarding them nearly as quickly, ignoring the others in the room.

After watching this for a few minutes, Ellin caught Trett's eye and patted the couch seat next to her. He moved there, and she whispered, "What do you think?"

"She seems so sure," he murmured.

"She does."

"But—" Trett steepled his hands in front of his mouth, then folded and unfolded his fingers. Ellin didn't interrupt. Finally, he said, "She seems . . . off. Manic, maybe."

Ellin nodded. Rena was usually so calm. When she displayed

emotion, it was generally stunted. Now, however, she was motioning wildly at the screen as she reviewed dozens of articles like her life depended on it.

Maybe it did. Maybe all their lives depended on it.

Or maybe a sick part of Rena's mind was lying to her.

As she mulled over that possibility, tears sprang to Ellin's eyes. Watching her sister lose her mind would be the lesser of two nightmares, but that wouldn't make it easy. Ellin and Rena's mom and dad hadn't been on good terms with their own parents and siblings, and Rena was essentially Ellin's only living relative. As fractious as their relationship was, Ellin didn't want her sister to become unrecognizable. "I'm not ready for this," Ellin murmured to Trett.

"For what?"

"To lose my sister. Let's be honest, half the time we don't even like each other—but I don't want her to turn into someone else."

"Still, the alternative—" Trett let the thought hang.

Ellin briefly squeezed her eyes shut. "I know."

Rena's voice, too loud for the small room, interrupted them. "I found it! Come over here, both of you!"

Ellin stood and approached the wallscreen. Trett followed. The screen displayed an article dated the day before from some newsorg Ellin had never heard of. She read the title out loud: " 'Therroan Government Approves Archeological Digging at Cellerin Mountain'."

Rena scrolled and pointed to a sentence several paragraphs down. She read, *"Asked about the location's significance, Alvun Merak said, 'Merak Technologies is honored to fund research into the history of the Cellerin region. This is where human civilization on Anyari began, yet the mountain has never been explored by modern archeologists.' "*

Ellin waited for Rena to say more. When she didn't, Ellin said, "I don't get it."

Rena stepped close enough that Ellin wanted to pull away, but she didn't. "I opened this article and got a strong nudge," Rena said, her breath hot on Ellin's face. "This project has something to do with the coming apocalypse."

Ellin looked at Trett, who was squinting at the screen. "An archeological dig?" he asked.

"Yes," Rena said, "and before you ask, no, I don't know how it's linked. But we have to go there, Ellin. With my gift and your brains, maybe we can stop them." She glanced at Trett. "You'll come too."

Ellin's mouth felt suddenly dry. They didn't even know if Rena's visions could be trusted. This was all happening too fast. She blurted the first thing on her mind. "You want us to quit school?"

Rena stared at her. "School? Seriously?"

Ellin scrambled for a better argument. "Come on, Rena, let's think through this. You know I want to help, but there's no way Alvun Merak will listen to us if we just show up at his dig site on the other side of the world."

"Of course not," Rena said. "Merak probably won't even be there. He's just funding it."

Ellin's mind was racing, but she couldn't seem to form any words.

"You're still thinking about school, aren't you?" Rena asked, a hint of contempt in her voice.

Ellin looked down, blinking away another batch of tears. "It's just that . . . I've worked so hard. You want me to give up everything—" She closed her mouth and completed the thought silently: *when I don't even know if your prophecy is true.*

Rena threw her arms wide, backhanding Trett. She didn't seem to notice, though he rubbed his arm. "You can finish school early. You've got plenty of credits! I know that doesn't quite line up with your perfect goals, and if I could put off the end of the world until after you graduate, I would. But you saw the calendar. We've got two months. If we don't succeed, nearly every student in your school will be dead. Do you want to be responsible for that?"

Now that was taking it too far. Ellin's fearful tears turned angry.

She let go of Trett's hand and finally expressed resentments she'd bottled up for years. "You've always controlled our family—you and your prophecies! Even before Mom and Dad died, we decided what restaurant to go to or where to go on vacation or what flowers to plant, all based on your visions. Isn't it so convenient that when I've worked hard to take control of my own life, you're derailing my plans?"

"That's ridiculous. I didn't make this up, and I'm certainly not threatened by you." Rena's voice had turned flat again, but her forehead was compressed into wrinkles.

Ellin knew that look, though she rarely saw it. She'd hurt her sister. Squeezing her eyes shut, Ellin took a long, deep breath and blew the air out. She opened her eyes, met Rena's gaze, and spoke in the gentlest voice she could muster. "I'm not saying you did it on purpose. It's just . . . well, you know what happens as seers get older."

As soon as she'd said the words, Ellin knew it was a mistake. Rena turned around and reached out a hand toward the wallscreen, gesturing to turn it off. Then she folded her arms and turned back to Ellin. Her nostrils flared, and a hint of pink colored the light brown skin on her cheeks and neck. "You think I'm losing my mind. At twenty-six years old."

Ellin responded with a helpless shrug.

"Let's all sit down."

Trett's voice was a welcome distraction from the tension. Ellin turned and sat in the chair he'd occupied earlier. He and Rena took the couch.

"You think I'm splicing," Rena said.

Ellin stared at her, confused.

Rena rolled her eyes. "That's the scientific term for when a seer loses their mind. You think that's happening to me, don't you?"

Ellin didn't answer, and when she saw that Trett was looking at her expectantly, she turned her gaze to her lap.

He sighed. "Of course we don't want to think that."

"But you also don't want to think the world is about to end."

Trett chuckled awkwardly. "Naturally."

"Tell me, how many books have you read on the history of the seers?" Rena asked. After a pause, she urged, "Both of you, answer me. How many?"

"None," Trett said.

Ellin met her sister's gaze. "One."

Rena's back was perfectly straight, her muscles visibly tense. "I didn't want a degree in accounting."

Ellin cocked her head, blinking. "You didn't?"

"No. I wanted to study the history of seers. Mom and Dad thought it would raise suspicion since it's not a common area of study these days. I listened to them and chose a practical, boring field instead. But ever since I was twelve years old, I've sought out everything I could find on the history of my people. I've read one hundred twenty-three books on the history of seers and over five times that many articles."

"Whoa," was all Ellin could think to respond.

"The youngest seer in recorded history to splice was fifty-four years old."

Ellin leaned forward, her voice earnest. "Rena, if there were any other evidence to support your prophecy, I'd quit school right now and go with you to stop it."

"And since there's not," Rena said, "you'll continue with your merry life and hope my mind doesn't decompose too fast, right?"

Ellin swallowed but didn't answer.

"You're acting like a child who doesn't want to hear the truth." Rena stood.

Ellin didn't say a word as she watched her sister march to her bedroom.

Rena paced in her room, kicking small piles of discarded, dirty clothes, trying unsuccessfully to tamp down her anger.

She thinks I'm insane.

Rena would never forget the day when she was twelve years old, eating a sandwich at the kitchen table, and her mother sat down and explained that seers eventually lost their minds. Every day since then, Rena had dreaded succumbing to such a fate. She'd kept her abilities secret, hoping, as her parents did, that the lack of public pressure would preserve her sanity.

Still . . . she knew how splicing worked. The first sign would be false prophecies.

Since Wednesday, all her visions and premonitions had been related to the apocalypse. How was she supposed to know if they were valid when they were all linked to an event two months away?

Rena sat on her bed and bowed her head, grasping her forehead hard with both hands. She cursed under her breath, and when that didn't give her any relief or clarity, she released her head, reached into her pocket, and pulled her flex out. She firmed it with a harder pinch than was necessary, then pulled up the message thread between her and Kizha. She typed,

I'm ready to tell you the vision.

Her finger hovered over the *Send* icon.

Heat flooded her entire body, along with a nudge so strong, she couldn't ignore it. *If I send this, Kizha will come here. I can't let her do that.*

The only people who were meant to try to save the world were Ellin, Trett, and Rena. The perfect little couple and the person they thought was crazy.

What if I really am losing it, and I'm messing up all our lives for nothing?

"No!" Rena said aloud. She refused to believe she was splicing in her twenties; that would be unprecedented. *My sister's afraid of dying. Probably even more afraid of letting go of her goals. She's in denial. That's all.*

Breathing hard, Rena again moved her finger toward *Send*.

Her whole hand cramped as the premonition intensified. Kizha was meant to help, but only from afar. She couldn't know the truth.

Rena collapsed her flex, tossed it on her desk, and lay in bed, staring at the ceiling. She almost hoped she was splicing. It would be better than dealing with reality.

7

SATURDAY, QUARI 6, 6293

-63 DAYS

Alvun Merak couldn't stop smiling.

He'd spent the last two days celebrating the opening of a new hospital wing. Thanks to a sizable donation from his foundation, cancer patients would be treated with the newest technology in a comfortable, home-like environment. The new treatment eradicated most cancers in three days, twice as fast as older regimens. Merak loved nothing more than funding hope.

His pilot landed the glider on the roof of Merak's estate, situating the vehicle over the lift pod port. A round portion of the glider floor slid to the side, and the lift pod rose up. Merak stepped in and sat in the single seat.

With a whispery *whoosh*, the pod dropped through the roof, depositing him in the corner of the bedroom he shared with his wife, Arisa, on the second floor of their sprawling residence. He stepped out and glanced around the large room. Not seeing Arisa, he walked through the bathroom and her closet. No luck. He reentered the bedroom and strode to the door leading to her study. His quiet knock went unanswered.

Merak frowned. He liked to greet Arisa when he got home from a trip, especially when he was gone overnight. She was usually waiting for him. He'd emmed her on his way in, but she hadn't responded.

Of course. There was one place she didn't take her flex. Merak exited into the hallway, greeted a young man who was repairing a torn lightfilm in the ceiling, and carefully opened the door across from his bedroom.

Arisa sat in a simple chair in the middle of the spacious room, her back to Merak. He entered quietly and lowered himself into a chair at the edge of the room. Arisa had probably heard his steps over the soft, soothing music, but she didn't move.

Despite its lack of windows, the chapel was the brightest room in the house. They'd had lightfilm installed not just in the ceiling but in all the walls and even the door. It provided an all-encompassing, white, comforting light.

Merak watched his wife. Her back was straight, her head bowed. Determined to explore who God was, she was one of the most devoted Rimorians he'd ever met.

Merak respected her dedication, though he'd long ago let go of his own need to believe in an unseen, unknowable power. He knew religion was an important part of human tradition. Anyari's colonists, after all, had arrived on the planet with various spiritual beliefs. Perhaps if he knew more about the specifics of those beliefs, he'd feel qualified to choose one.

That sort of knowledge, however, was unattainable. Some tragedy had struck the colonists, killing most of them and robbing them of their records and whatever technology had gotten them to Anyari. The ones who'd survived had written a few things down, scrawled on cave walls or etched into rock. They'd also kept some history alive through oral tradition. As time passed, however, the stories got more and more muddled.

After several generations, Anyarians had learned to use animal skins to make parchment. They'd written down the religious tales they'd grown up hearing, but the narratives were confusing and contradictory. On top of that, many questioned whether the spiritual history of another planet was still relevant to their new civilization on Anyari.

Through the centuries, countless different faiths developed, many of them based on strange conglomerations of Earth's ancient religious tales. People debated over what was true and even waged wars in the names of their gods.

Then, five thousand years ago, a man named Rimor had developed a new faith. He adopted two common elements of many ancient Earth religions—a belief in one God and the practice of communicating with this God through prayer. Beyond those principles, he didn't claim to know which Earth stories were true and which weren't. The Rimorian religion was built on a simple commitment to explore and pursue the divine. In time, it became the dominant belief system on Anyari.

Through the years, many Rimorian emissaries had claimed to hear from God. They'd recorded their supposed messages, and fifteen hundred years earlier, a council had gathered the ones they considered most important, compiling them into the Sacrex, a book of scripture. Merak had only managed to read the beginning of it.

Arisa had read the book many times. She even claimed to sense God's voice, though she never called herself an emissary. A few official emissaries still existed, though the church never considered adding their revelations into the Sacrex until they died.

Merak didn't think he'd ever return to his mother's simplistic Rimorian beliefs, nor would he adopt Arisa's more nuanced faith. Still, he had to admit that this bright room, filled with quiet, exquisite music, soothed his racing mind.

Just as he was reflecting that he'd had about enough soothing for the day, Arisa's voice rose above the music, ending her otherwise silent prayer with three words: "May it be."

She stood, and Merak followed suit. Arisa faced him. She was wearing a pendant in the shape of a Rimstar, an eight-pointed star with teardrop-shaped loops extending off each point. It was the primary symbol of the Rimorian faith. She appeared calm and at peace, but her eyes were bloodshot, her green irises looking even brighter than usual in contrast.

Twenty years ago, she'd been one of the first people to colorize her eyes. At first, she'd been uncomfortable with the attention she attracted. People were only used to seeing brown eyes, with an occasional hazel pair thrown in the mix. These days, colorization was as inexpensive as a haircut, but Merak had never altered his medium-brown eyes and didn't plan to.

"Why were you crying?" he asked Arisa.

Her smile was warm but tired. "Same as usual. I'm fine now. Welcome home." She wrapped her long arms around his neck and kissed him. "Are you headed into the office today?"

"In a little while. I'll stop at the kids' rooms first."

"It's just you and me at home."

"That's fine. I got them each a little gift."

She smiled again, but her lips trembled a bit.

Merak had refused to install lifts in his house, except the one leading to the roof. He'd told his family countless times, "We have two legs. If we don't use them, they'll get weak."

His own legs, strengthened by long runs and early mornings in the gym, took him down a set of stairs to the first floor and across the home's main hall into the children's wing.

He kept suggesting they rename it the *offspring wing*. Arisa always refused, saying, "It makes it sound like a science lab." He capitulated, but he still thought it was silly. It had been nineteen years since their daughter made them parents. Their son followed two years later. He couldn't consider either of them *children* anymore.

He stopped at his son's suite first, groaning as soon as he entered. Clothes and paper books—his son's favorite luxury—covered the floor, the bed, and the desk. How the boy could live in a place this messy, Merak couldn't guess. He left the gift, a small bag of his son's favorite chewy candy, on the desk. Hopefully he'd find it before it dried out.

His daughter's suite was a different story. Everything was tidy. The pale-green blanket on the bed was perfectly smooth, and her desk was actually clean enough to discern the color: bright yellow, her favorite.

The room looks too juvenile, he thought, not for the first time. He'd talk to the house manager about a remodel. New window coverings and a darker blanket would make the room more fit for a nineteen-year-old. *Nothing but the very best for my girl.*

Merak set the candy on the desk. Then he sat on the bed for a moment, contemplating his upcoming day. When he stood, he turned to smooth the blanket, then stopped himself. *A bedroom needs a little bit of mess.*

SUNDAY, QUARI 7, 6293

-62 DAYS

The next morning, it was still dark when Merak told Arisa goodbye. He was headed on a longer trip this time. Arisa gave him a sleepy kiss and offered to get up and see him off, but he smiled and told her to stay in bed.

Merak took his glider to his personal solarplane. There, he greeted the pilot and settled into one of the comfortable seats.

They took off, and before long, they were flying into the sunrise. The flight was several hours long, and the time change compressed the day significantly. It was already dark in the nation of Therro when they landed. Merak disembarked and walked straight to the research center. Normally it would be closed for the day, but he'd alerted them of his arrival, and most of the windows were lit.

Merak stepped in the lobby. "Misha!" he said to the receptionist. "You don't need to be here at this time of night. Head on out and get a bite to eat."

The young man thanked him and left.

Merak stepped up to the door behind the desk. The flexscreen in his pocket unlocked it. He walked down two hallways, then stopped at the entrance to a large room. In the middle were lab stations with instruments that screamed *state of the art* and *expensive*. More equipment sat along the back wall, most of which Merak couldn't guess the purpose of. Workstations, several of which were occupied, lined the other three walls.

Merak spent a moment watching the researchers, none of whom noticed him standing in the doorway. Fingers and hands flew across letterkeys and deskscreens, dedication and passion clear in the workers' motions. He smiled and said, "Good evening."

Every head snapped up, and cheerful greetings reached his ears.

"How are things going?" he asked.

Several researchers responded, but one voice rose above the others: "You've got to see this, Mr. Merak."

Merak shifted his attention to Efren Rouven, a medical researcher. Despite waiting for dig approval, researchers had been working in Therro for months. They conducted thorough surveys of the dig site, compiled existing records, and analyzed data. Recently, sensors in the area had picked up some unexpected readings, and the lead analyst had suggested Merak bring on several new staff. Rouven was one of those, having just arrived two days before.

Dr. Rouven beckoned Merak to his workstation on the right side of the room. Before Merak even reached him, the researcher began talking. "I've been analyzing readings from the site, and they're very promising." His thick, wavy, black hair trembled as he nodded enthusiastically.

Before Merak could respond, the woman next to Dr. Rouven

stood from her workstation. "Pardon me, Mr. Merak." Her gaze was sharp, and her eyes' orange hue intensified the effect.

Merak racked his brain for her name. She'd started working here the same day as Dr. Rouven. Like him, she was a medical researcher with over two decades of experience. Just before Merak was about to respond with a generic greeting, it hit him. *Dr. Nomi Anson.* "Dr. Anson!" he said, his smooth tone not betraying his brief forgetfulness.

She stepped closer to him, not returning his smile. "I wouldn't call this analysis promising. I'd call it frightening."

8

SUNDAY, QUARI 7, 6293

-62 DAYS

THE MORNING after her argument with Rena, Ellin got dressed and exited her room. Her sister's door was still closed, the light off.

Ellin made hot cereal and sat at the table. She was enjoying it until her mind once again started swirling with questions and possibilities. A twisting, aching sensation entered her gut, forcing her to put her spoon down and push her bowl away.

How quickly will Rena's mind deteriorate? Will she turn into a completely different person? Maybe she'll become unpredictable or violent.

Or maybe it'll give her some empathy.

Ellin wanted to laugh at that last possibility, but she couldn't bring herself to. She hated the thought of waking up to a different sister, even one who'd turned into a kinder shadow of her real self.

Underneath all the questions was the one that Ellin tried to squash down every time it rose into her consciousness. *What if I'm wrong about Rena and she's right about the end of the world?*

Seeking a distraction, Ellin pulled out her flex.

Within minutes, she was lost in research, anxiety forgotten. After an hour, she checked the time: nearly nine. Trett was usually up by now, even on a Sunday. She emmed him, asking if she could come over. When he said yes, she put her food in the refrigerator and walked the three blocks to Trett's house.

He opened the door as she was walking up. "Want to go on a ride?" he asked.

"Sure."

They circled behind his house to the garage where he kept his double hover scooter—*dubhov* for short. It sat next to the family's small glidecraft. Ellin and Rena usually took public transportation wherever their own feet couldn't carry them, but Trett's parents could afford some luxuries.

Trett handed her a helmet ring. She pulled it over her head like a stretchy necklace, then pushed a button. The ring molded to fit her neck, snug but flexible, its warmth as comforting as her flex was on her arm. A thin, firm, breathable membrane shot out of the ring, creating a transparent dome around her head. She took a deep breath, enjoying the scent of ozone the helmet's expansion left behind.

Trett unplugged the dubhov from its charging port and swung his leg over his seat. Ellin got on behind him. The device lifted off the ground noiselessly, and they exited the garage and took to the streets.

"How's your sister this morning?" Trett's voice rang through the small speaker in Ellin's helmet.

"She wasn't up yet when I left. I do have some news, though. I spent an hour this morning reading more about splicing. I know what we need to do next."

"You do?"

"Yeah, but I'd rather tell you over coffee."

"Why didn't you say so? We'll get some at my house." Trett pulled to the right side of the street, like he was about to turn around.

Ellin swatted his arm lightly. "Don't you dare feed me that swill your father drinks."

Trett laughed and kept going. They passed pedestrians, some of whom were walking their caynins. There were plenty of other hovs on the road too, plus a sun-powered solarbus and several solarcars. Overhead, glidecrafts whooshed by, and in the distance, the city's Skytrains sped along their elevated tracks.

Leaves and fronds on all the trees sparkled from the previous night's rain. The spring breeze was light and cool. Ellin released a contented sigh and squeezed Trett's waist tighter. He let go of one of the handlebars and rested his hand on her arm.

A few minutes later, they reached Old World Coffee. It was where they'd gone for their first date and at least half their subsequent outings, and the drinks there were far better than what they'd get at Trett's house. His father had good taste in transportation but scrimped on cheap coffee.

Thanks to distinct genetic differences, biologists could pinpoint which organisms were native to Anyari and which were Original—from Earth. Scientists had created a few hybrids between Anyarian and Original plants, but most species from the two worlds were incompatible.

Humans shouldn't have been able to digest Anyarian food. At a molecular level, it was too different from Earth food. That issue had been solved through human genetic modification. The evidence was in every cell of Ellin's body: her ancestors' very DNA had been engineered, allowing them to utilize Anyarian proteins and nutrients. It was a stunning feat that modern researchers couldn't duplicate. Clearly it had been done before the colonists left Earth, by scientists who'd attained samples of Anyarian plants and animals. Every child born on Anyari benefited from these ancient enhancements.

As much as she appreciated native foods, Ellin owed a special debt of gratitude to her forebears for some of the seeds they'd brought from Earth, like those that grew cacao trees, blueberry bushes, and yes, coffee plants. However, she could've done without the eggplants and carrots.

Inside, Trett ordered tea, and Ellin got her usual—a chocolate cup of coffee. The cup itself was made from chocolate that melted easily on the inside and was resistant to melting on the outside. She added crem, then took a sip of the smooth, chocolatey concoction. *Perfect.* She led Trett outside, where there weren't as many patrons.

They sat, and Trett took her hand and smiled over his cup. "Tell me what you're thinking."

Ellin leaned in close and spoke in a hushed voice. "Remember Rena used that term *splice*? It's a term mostly used by researchers. They call it that because eventually, a seer's mind splices reality and prophecy together." She pulled her hand away, demonstrating by interlocking her fingers.

"That makes sense. How do we know if Rena is splicing?"

Ellin sipped her coffee. "We need to test her." She took a bite from the rim of her chocolate cup. "Let's finish our drinks and go to my house. Our mission today is to provoke a prophecy."

———

Rena's door was still closed when Ellin and Trett got home. They walked through the house, following the checklist in Ellin's mind. She hid Rena's favorite coffee mug and her keys, and Trett moved one of Rena's shoes to the back door, leaving the other shoe by the front entrance. Last, Ellin carefully opened Rena's bedroom door. Rena was still asleep, and Ellin crept past her into the bathroom, where she moved her sister's toothbrush from the countertop to a drawer.

She met Trett back in the living room and settled on the couch next to him.

"Now we wait for her to wake up," Ellin said.

"Any chance she'll think this is a harmless little prank?"

"I wish." Ellin sighed. "She's gonna be pissed, especially if she realizes we're the ones messing with her. It's really not my goal to make her miserable, but from everything I've seen through the years, she's more likely to have a vision if her routines get thrown off. Let's just hope it works."

Trett turned and traced her lips with his finger. "You're brilliant."

She smiled and squelched a surge of desire. *Hold it together, Ellin, we have more important things to focus on.* She gave his finger a peck and pulled her flexscreen off her arm. "Let's see if we can find out anything else about that archeological dig."

They didn't find any information they hadn't seen the day before, so Ellin set her flex to notify her if the term *Cellerin Mountain* appeared in any new stories. Then she worked on her history paper while Trett lay on the couch with his flex, reading a book about ancient human mythology.

Rena still hadn't exited her room when, in mid-afternoon, Ellin's flex buzzed. A newsorg had just posted a video from the Cellerin Project dig site. Ellin played it, keeping the volume low.

On the screen, a young reporter stood in front of a nondescript wall. "I'm in Therro," she said, "where a world-class team of archeologists and researchers has gathered at Cellerin Mountain. This is the first such dig that the Therroan government has ever allowed. We received word a short time ago that preliminary digging has already led to an unexpected discovery.

"Something within the mountain contains a radioactive signature that on-site scientists haven't seen before. They're trying to identify the particular isotope causing the radiation. Precautions are being taken at the dig site to protect workers from the radiation.

"Merak Technologies is funding this entire project. I'm at the Merak facility in Therro now, where Alvun Merak has agreed to speak with us."

The camera panned out, revealing Alvun Merak standing near the reporter. He was tall and fit, with dark hair and kind, brown eyes. His blue, button-down shirt hung perfectly on his frame in a way only expensive, tailored clothes did. He sported a friendly smile as he greeted the reporter.

"I know you've had a long day, Mr. Merak, and I appreciate you joining us."

"It's no problem. This project is all about discovery and education, and we want to keep the public notified of everything we find. Even if that means I miss out on a little beauty sleep—something most people would say I can't afford to lose."

The reporter laughed and asked, "What can you tell us about this new discovery?"

"It's still very early," Merak said, "but the radiation in the area seems similar to the beneficial radiation we use in clinics around the world to heal cuts and perform quick, targeted cancer treatment. We look forward to finding out more about its source and capabilities."

"As do we," the reporter said. She told Merak goodbye and assured her audience she'd be on top of any new information. The video ended.

Ellin and Trett looked at each other, but before either of them could say a word, Rena croaked, " 'Morning."

Ellin looked up. "Good afternoon." Her response earned her a disgusted look from her sleepy sister.

Rena walked into the kitchen. Her voice reached Ellin's and Trett's ears: "Where's my coffee mug?" Dishes clattered, and she added, "First my toothbrush, now this." A couple of minutes later, she walked to her room, holding her coffee, not even looking at Ellin and Trett. She closed her door.

Ellin looked at Trett and sighed. "So much for my plan."

Trett turned on the wallscreen and watched a mindless show while Ellin continued to do schoolwork. Rena stayed in her room. Eventually, Trett left to pick up dinner.

Rena soon appeared. "I'm going for a walk." She got to the front door and muttered, "Where's my other shoe? Why isn't anything where it's supposed to be today?" She strode into the living room, and just as she was passing the couch where Ellin sat, she stopped.

"What?" Ellin asked. Then she realized Rena's pale-brown eyes were glazed over, a sure sign of a vision. Thankfully she stayed on her feet, rather than collapsing quietly as she sometimes did or experiencing a repeat of yesterday's scene at the senior center.

A few seconds passed, and Rena came back to herself and stared at Ellin. "Have you been working at some job you haven't told me about?"

"No, I'm busy with school. You know that."

"Well, I don't know how you'll manage it, but you're getting your own hover scooter very soon. It'll be parked in front of the house. " Her face twitched with a smirk. "It'll be purple." She looked toward the back door, retrieved her shoe, and put it on, adding, "By the way, it's immutable."

As Rena exited, Ellin nearly cried with relief. She probably wouldn't have her own hov until she was a full-fledged technisurgeon at age thirty. It certainly wouldn't be "very soon." Plus, she hated purple. She'd never willingly purchase a purple hov, or a purple anything else for that matter.

It meant her sister was splicing, and while none of them wanted to see that happen, it also meant the world wasn't ending. With Rena's mental deterioration starting so early, maybe it would be a slow process. Perhaps they could even confide in a trustworthy doctor; medical technology had come a long way since the last known seer had spliced.

Ellin tried to focus on her homework, but her mind kept returning to her questions: What would Rena's mental decline look like? What was the best way to broach the topic again? At last, she gave in to her anxious thoughts and collapsed her flex.

Someone rang the doorbell. Ellin looked up at the wallscreen, which showed the porch camera feed in one corner. A man she'd never seen before stood there. He looked straight at the camera, smiled, and waved.

Weirdo. Ellin ignored him, and after ringing the bell one more time and waiting far longer than he should have, he left.

A couple of minutes later, Trett walked in. Ellin jumped up. "I've got news."

Trett was already wearing a huge smile. "Mine first," he said, setting down the food he'd picked up. "Just as I walked up, a man was leaving the house. He said nobody came to the door."

"Yeah, but—"

Trett kept going. "Turns out there was a drawing today at the rec center. Everyone who volunteered there in the last week had a chance to win a hov, provided by Merak. You won!" He grabbed Ellin's hand and tried to pull her to the door.

She planted her feet, trying to breathe past the band of tightness on her chest. "But I didn't answer the door."

He laughed. "Good thing I was out there! I accepted it for you. Come on, let me show you!"

She allowed him to lead her. Just as they got to the door, she moaned, "But I hate purple."

He opened the door and looked back at her, his mouth gaping open. "How'd you know . . . ?"

Ellin let go of his hand and walked past him. It felt like she was trudging through waist-deep oil.

There it was, ugly and glossy and new, a shining, purple confirmation of the coming apocalypse.

She covered her face with her hands and lowered herself to the ground. Immediately, she heard Trett sit next to her.

"What's going on?" he asked, dread filling his words.

Ellin pulled her hands off her face and turned to Trett, refusing to look at the traitorous hover scooter. "Rena's still a seer," she said. "And we have to find a way to stop Alvun Merak."

9

SUNDAY, QUARI 7, 6293

-62 DAYS

RENA SAT ON HER BED, firmed her flex, and pulled up Kizha's most recent em. She typed,

Up for some hacking?

While she waited for a response, she pressed her fingertips to her aching temples. She hadn't yet fully recovered from her PVS after the big vision four days earlier. The prophecies since then had continued to set her back.

The delivery of that purple hov had just added to Rena's stress. When she'd seen it sitting in front of the house, she'd frozen in place, bombarded by conflicting emotions. It erased her fears about her mind deteriorating. It also confirmed the inconceivable, bloody reality of her apocalyptic vision. *It's true. It's all true.*

As she'd eaten dinner with Ellin and Trett, Rena had endured yet another prophecy. It was a premonition, and it had answered a question she'd been obsessed with since yesterday: *How can we get inside Merak Technologies?*

Her flex buzzed, interrupting her recollection. She read Kizha's response.

I'm always up for a little hacking! What do you need?

Gritting her teeth against the urge to tell Kizha everything, Rena kept her message short.

Ellin, Trett, and I need to start internships at Merak Technologies ASAP.

Kizha replied,

I'm calling you.

A few seconds later, Rena accepted a video chat request, and Kizha's face popped up on her screen. Kizha didn't ask why she wanted to intern at Merak Technologies. Instead, her analytical mind attacked the problem of enrolling them into an internship program. She treated it like she was designing a piece of technology, determining what parts she needed and how she could attain them.

Kizha's voice came through her flex speaker. "It looks like they only accept interns who are at least nineteen. Ellin and Trett will have to use the counterfeit IDs we established for them a while back." Her eyes narrowed. "Were you already planning this back then?"

Rena's mouth went dry. Two years ago, when she'd gotten a nudge to get fake IDs for herself, Ellin, and Trett, she'd almost disregarded the ridiculous notion. It had returned, persistent and stronger than ever, until she gave in.

She remembered what she'd told Kizha when she'd asked her to arrange the IDs: "Yes, I'm serious. No, I'm not planning to start a new life of crime." They'd both laughed, and Kizha had promised to help.

How long have all these little prophecies been preparing me for the big one?

"Rena?" Kizha's brow creased over her green eyes.

"I, uh—" Rena licked her lips. "No, I wasn't planning this back then. And we won't just need Ellin's and Trett's fake IDs. We'll need mine too. I don't want to intern under my real name."

Kizha raised an eyebrow, but she still didn't ask any questions.

"Wasn't one of your friends working on social media accounts for those identities?" Rena asked.

"Yeah. She set up a simple AI to create several years of social media history and to post regularly on your accounts. One of my other friends arranged all the government records and the IDs themselves. He even made sure your photos were updated every year. You've all got hover scooter licenses. I'll send you all the info so you can register your flexes under the new identities."

"Wow . . . that's even more than I asked for. Thanks."

Kizha smiled. "You're welcome. It says here that interns get free room and board, but you'll have to fly out there, and you'll need spending money."

"I've been saving what I can." That habit was based on a premonition too. Rena had always saved ten percent of her accountant income. She'd had to dip into the money a few times, but much of it was still there. *All because of a prophecy seven years ago.* She shook her head, trying to bring her focus back to the present. "We have a brand new hov to sell too."

"You got a hov?"

"Ellin won one. Today."

"Well, that's good timing."

Rena nodded, not mentioning what had led them to volunteer at the rec center.

Kizha continued, "The hardest thing will be getting you into Merak's system as interns. Their network is notoriously secure."

"What about that hacker you connected with—the one who specializes in corporate jobs?"

Kizha's eyes widened. "Oh yeah! We were just chatting last week; he's on the lookout for a challenge." She tilted her head, and the corner of her mouth twitched in amusement. "Didn't I connect with him because of another one of your nudges?"

Rena swallowed. She was a little lightheaded. "Yes."

"So your gift has been preparing you for this internship? For at least two years?"

"I guess so." Rena drew in a deep breath. Prophecies that had seemed pointless for years streamed through her mind. How many of them fit into this complex puzzle?

A sense of helplessness swallowed her. She'd always thought God (or whoever controlled her visions) was partnering with her to make the world better. Now it seemed she was merely a tool. The one wielding her had all the power. *I never agreed to this, never wanted it.*

"This thing you're doing," Kizha said softly, "it must be big."

Rena released her breath in a loud sigh. "It is."

Kizha leaned in, her face filling Rena's screen. "Is everything okay?" Her low voice was full of concern and care; her lips were parted as she waited for her answer; her eyes—

"I'm fine," Rena blurted. "I think you'd better reach out to that friend of yours."

Kizha leaned back, nodding slowly. "Okay, I will." She watched Rena with her head tilted, like she expected her to say more.

"Thanks," Rena murmured. She touched her screen and ended the chat.

"We're all starting internships at Merak Technologies," Rena said.

Ellin looked up from the couch where she'd been sleeping. It was late, but Trett was still there, dozing in the chair. After dinner, Rena had instructed them not to go anywhere. Then she'd disappeared in her room for hours.

Trett rubbed his bleary eyes. "Did you say we're all going to be interns for Merak?"

"Yes. Look at this." Ellin was taking up the whole couch, so Rena pushed her sister's legs out of the way, sat in the space she'd made, and held out her flexscreen.

Ellin sat up. On Rena's flex were three digital identification cards. They had pictures of Ellin, Trett, and Rena on them. The first names were correct, but Ellin was no longer Ellin Abrinan. She was Ellin Havier. Rena's new last name was Sheller, and Trett's had changed from Stelios to Coldin.

Ellin's heart started beating uncomfortably quickly. "Trett, you're gonna want to see this," Ellin said. She made room for him, and he joined them on the couch.

"What are we looking at?" Trett asked.

"Fake IDs." Ellin said before turning back to Rena. "Do you have any idea how much trouble we'll be in if we get caught with these?"

Rena zoomed in on hers. "We won't get caught. See, they're perfect; they've even got the digital watermark. That's hard to fake."

"I—" Ellin shook her head. "This is ridiculous. There's no reason for us to change our names or go jetting off to Merak headquarters. We're not characters in some spy film, Rena; we—"

Rena interrupted, "If there was an easier path, we'd be taking it. This is how we have to proceed."

Ellin stood and paced, trying to stave off her panic. "You can go without me! I'll stay at home and research everything happening at that dig site. The moment I find anything suspicious, I'll write letters to Alvun Merak and all his executives. I'll send those same letters to every newsorg on the planet. I'm not leaving town and walking around with a fake ID! It's an arrest waiting to happen!"

"Rena," Trett said in a much calmer tone, "I'm sure you can understand this is all pretty shocking for us. How did you get those IDs so quickly, anyway? You've only been in your room a few hours."

"I've had the IDs for two years." Rena looked at Ellin, whose mouth was gaping. "A nudge," she clarified.

Ellin dropped back onto the couch. "Where did you get them?"

Rena stared at her sister, lips pressed into a thin line, like she was considering what to share. Finally, she said, "I know a hacker. One of her friends got the IDs."

Ellin laughed, because she didn't know what else to do. Since when was Rena, an upright and uptight accountant, connected to society's seedy digital underbelly? "A hacker friend, of course," she said with a harsh laugh. "I suppose you and this hacker have been working on getting us these internships for months too? Without ever mentioning it to me and Trett?"

"No, Ellin, that all started tonight. My friend knows someone who has access to Merak Technology's internal records. He added us to the intern roster."

Ellin turned her disbelieving eyes on Trett. "Help me out here, please."

Trett smiled. It was a look of peaceful diplomacy. "Rena, you have to admit, Ellin's concerns are valid. You want us to use illegal IDs to take on internships we didn't legitimately earn. Why can't we do what Ellin said—work here to gather information and contact as many people as possible? In a company as big as Merak's, the chances of any of us being assigned to the Cellerin Project are miniscule. Plus, corporate internships can be pretty intense. We'll probably have more time to fight this if we stay home."

Rena pursed her lips and closed her eyes. She released her breath noisily before leaning toward Trett and speaking slowly. "When I said we have to do it this way, it's because I got a very strong nudge. Believe me, the last thing I want is to fly to the west coast of Vallinger and sit at some desk in a huge office for weeks on end.

"When that purple hov showed up, you both told me you know I'm not splicing. If you believe my message about the apocalypse, you need to believe this one too. We have to be interns. Our identities must match the facts on our intern applications. Period." She looked at Ellin, and her impatient expression turned the slightest bit gentle. "I hate breaking rules too. I wish we could do this differently."

Ellin's nose tingled and throat tightened as her eyes filled with tears. They had to go; she knew it was true. *Why can't there be another way?* She had a life here, a good life. School had always given her purpose. Maybe it was irrational; certainly it was silly—but the thought of giving up what she'd worked for was torturous. Was it worth it, to save the world? Of course it was. That didn't mean she had to like it.

She held her tears back and spoke in a soft, controlled voice. "Trett can definitely come with us?"

"He has to," Rena replied.

Trett took Ellin's hand. "I wouldn't be anywhere else." He shifted his attention back to Rena. "How will we get there?

All business again, Rena tapped her screen. Three solarplane tickets appeared. "We're leaving in eight days."

"That must have been expensive," Ellin said.

"I've saved up some money." Rena clicked on a marketplace site and showed it to Ellin. "Also, I listed your purple hov for sale."

"Well, thank goodness for small blessings," Ellin said with a little laugh.

Trett asked how they'd manage to convince anyone of their new identities when they had no digital history, and Rena showed them social media sites full of photos they'd never taken and updates they'd never posted. Next, she pulled up a private Merak site for interns only. Their assigned rooms were all adjacent to each other, thanks to the same unnamed hacker who'd gotten them into the program.

Ellin massaged the back of her neck and forced out the words she knew she needed to say. "Okay. I'll go."

Rena's shoulders visibly relaxed.

"Here's the thing," Ellin continued. "If we somehow manage to prevent your prophecy from coming true, we'll need to be ready to return to our normal lives. I'm still planning to be a technisurgeon, even if I have to put it off, and that means I can't stop thinking about university. You mentioned Trett and I could graduate early, but it's too late for us to initiate that process."

"Apparently the power behind my visions had pity on your poor, overachieving soul." Rena's lip quirked in a miniscule smirk. "Six months ago, based on a prophecy, I submitted early graduation applications for you and Trett."

"Six months ago? I was still seventeen. My parents would have had to sign that," Trett said.

"Digital forgery." Rena gave him a guilty little shrug. "About an hour ago, I went back into the system and chose the early exit option for both of you. They'll withdraw you from your classes and issue your diplomas within a week."

Ellin took that in. She might lose her class standing, but she was still graduating with incredibly high marks. Hopefully she could keep her scholarship if they succeeded in stopping Merak.

No, when *we succeed. Because we will.*

At that thought, something shifted in Ellin. Her unfinished history paper, her math assignments, her next speech—they all disappeared from the to-do list she'd etched in her mind, replaced by new objectives:

Stop Alvun Merak.

Save the world.

She'd commit to this like she'd never committed to anything before. If there was a way to destroy the immutability of a prophecy, she'd find it.

Her mouth widened into a grin. *Alvun Merak won't know what hit him.*

10

"I'LL BE BACK in a few minutes," Trett told the glidecraft pilot.

"I have to charge for the time I'm waiting, you know," the woman said.

"That's fine."

He stepped out of the craft onto Ellin's lawn. Just as he was walking up to her front door, it opened. Mr. Karel, Trett and Ellin's math teacher, stepped out. He gave Trett a disgusted glance, then looked away, shaking his head as he walked toward the school.

Ellin was in the entry hallway. Trett stepped in and asked, "What was that all about?"

Her eyes were red and puffy. "I'll tell you in the taxi. We should go."

Trett nodded. "I'll load up while you get Rena." He wheeled Ellin's and Rena's suitcases outside, and the pilot loaded them in the cargo area under the glidecraft.

Two minutes later, they were all settled, Rena next to the pilot and Trett and Ellin in the rear seats. The craft lifted into the air.

"Why was Mr. Karel there?" Trett murmured to Ellin.

"He heard I'm not coming back. He got an administrator to teach his classes so he could come talk me out of it."

Trett put his arm around her shoulders and pulled her close. "I'm sorry." He kissed her hair.

"He was here for two hours. I had to repeatedly lie to my favorite teacher about where we're going. Do you have any idea how hard that was?" She was clearly holding back tears.

Trett, too, hated having to lie to his friends and family. No one could know where they really were, lest someone blow their cover. They'd told everyone that they'd gotten jobs surveying uninhabited land in the far north and would be out of communication range. "If it helps at all," he said, "I think Mr. Karel blamed me for you leaving. He gave me the dirtiest look I've ever seen."

Ellin groaned. "When he heard we were leaving together, he thought it must've been your idea. As if I'd never choose to graduate early unless my boyfriend had some emotional hold on me. I thought he trusted me more than that."

"He knows you as someone who practically lives at school. You have to admit, leaving like this is out of character for you."

"I know." She sighed. "How did it go with your parents?"

"It was fine. I don't know why I waited until this morning to tell them I was leaving. I guess I was afraid they'd be upset."

Ellin turned her head and met his gaze. "Maybe you hoped they'd care enough to try to stop you?"

He sighed. "Yeah. I guess so. I shouldn't be surprised that they were fine with it. 'Surveying with scientists in a frigid wilderness? Sounds like a good opportunity. You'll get college credit for it? Even better.'"

"I'm sorry, Trett. Was it weird saying goodbye?"

He blinked away tears. His parents had always been distant, but saying goodbye for what might be the last time had been awful. He'd had to pretend to be cheerful, since as far as his parents knew, he'd only be gone a couple of months. *Hopefully that's true.*

He realized he hadn't answered Ellin's question. "Yeah." His voice was soft. "Saying goodbye was weird."

She placed a hand on his cheek and kissed him, then relaxed against him again.

Before long, they were at the airport, standing in front of a massive, sleek solarplane. The afternoon sun glinted on the red Sonic Air logo. The name was an artifact from the early days of faster-than-sound air travel. These days, all passenger planes were both sonic and solar, powered by the sun's rays.

Once they were in the air, Trett yawned. "I think I'll grab a quick nap."

"Okay." Ellin barely looked up from her flex. She'd pulled it out as soon as they were seated, and she was scouring news sites for more information on their new employer.

Trett closed his eyes and didn't wake until the plane was descending two hours later. In that time, they'd traveled nearly four thousand clommets across the nation of Vallinger, from the east coast to the west. He turned to Ellin and took the hand she wasn't holding her flex with. "We're about to land."

She spared him a quick smile, then pulled her hand away. "Almost done reading this article."

A few minutes later, they stepped off the plane into dry, hot air. It felt more like summer than spring. Why any company would have its headquarters in the desert was beyond Trett's comprehension.

As soon as they stepped onto the ground, a glidecraft pilot approached. "I'll take you to the Merak Technology campus."

"We have luggage," Rena said.

"Someone else is retrieving it and will deliver it to your rooms."

Trett exchanged an impressed smile with Ellin, and they all followed the pilot to her craft.

A few minutes into the flight, she pointed. "There's the campus."

Trett looked out the window. He knew Merak's headquarters

were outside the city of Amler, so he'd assumed there would be a few buildings surrounded by open land. Instead, he saw what appeared to be a small town with hundreds of buildings of all sizes. "Which buildings are part of the campus?"

The pilot laughed. "All of them." She circled the area, showing them features of the campus: a compact solar array that provided all its power, plus countless research buildings, offices, and manufacturing plants. "Most of our employees live here with their families," she said, pointing out an extensive housing section and a school.

She directed their attention to several buildings in one corner devoted to interns—dorms; a dining hall; classrooms; a small store where they could buy snacks, toiletries, and Merak-branded souvenirs; and a recreation building that included a pool, sport courts, exercise equipment, a Threed theatre, a coffee shop, and a restaurant. Then she pointed in the distance, where long-term employees had their own on-site shopping and recreation options.

They landed near the intern area, and their pilot gave them instructions on accessing schedules and maps on their flexes. Then she took them to their rooms.

When the pilot left, Trett walked into Ellin's room. "We've got a few minutes before dinner. Want to explore?"

She tapped her flex a few more times, then collapsed it and wrapped it on her arm. "Sure."

After telling Rena they'd meet her at dinner, they walked out of the dorm, holding hands. Smooth, ecophalt pathways ran through the campus, bordered by native desert landscaping. Trett admired the trees, with their wispy, brown fronds that swayed in the breeze. Underneath were countless varieties of squat plants with waxy stems and leaves. *Not bad for a desert.*

He shifted his attention to Ellin. "It's nice getting some time alone."

She smiled, but her expression looked strained. "I spent the whole flight reading up on Merak Technologies. It's such a huge company. I can't think how we're going to stop them from digging in Therro."

Trett saw the tension in her shoulders and felt it in her hand, which grasped his too tightly. They stopped next to a nondescript classroom building. He leaned against the wall and opened his arms, and she walked into them and returned his hug. Then he tilted her chin up and gave her a gentle kiss.

"I know what's supposed to happen in fifty-four days," he said. He kissed her again. "Right now, though, this feels good. Being here with you."

She returned his kisses, but afterward her smile was still forced. "It does feel good," she said, "but someone's watching us."

Trett looked around, not seeing anyone.

Ellin pulled away from his grip and turned, pointing at a fence about a dozen steps away from them. Trett had noticed the fence from the air. It surrounded the whole property and, he now noticed, was nearly twice his height. The top half was comprised of closely spaced black metal bars with ornamental spikes on top. The bottom half was made of the same metal, but it was curled into beautiful, decorative shapes.

"See it?" Ellin asked, pointing at a tiny camera perched in the fence.

"Oh," Trett said. "I suppose a place this big has a good security system."

"Of course," Ellin said. She turned back toward him and stepped close, speaking in a quiet voice, like she wanted to be sure anyone monitoring the area didn't pick up her words. "It just feels weird, you know? They make this place so fancy, where you've got everything you need. You can even live here. Then they surround it with this fence that's too tall to climb. It's like they don't ever want you to leave."

Trett tried to laugh off the discomfort her words elicited. "Come on, Ellin. It's a company, not a prison. I'm sure the fence is there to keep strangers out, not keep employees in."

"I'm not saying they'd actually prevent anyone from leaving. It just gives me a weird feeling, you know? It's like they want to both intimidate us and welcome us." She stepped away from him. "Anyway, we should get to dinner."

"I guess we should." Trett took her hand again.

They walked back toward the street. The sun was low in the sky, and the shadow of the fence loomed over them.

***

TUESDAY, QUARI 16, 6293
-53 DAYS

Ellin had troubled dreams, though she couldn't remember any details when she got up. Once she was ready, she knocked on Trett's door. He was dressed and ready. Rena met them in the hall, and they all walked to breakfast. It was delicious.

After eating, they went to a classroom for their initial orientation. Within minutes, there were twenty interns in the room. Every desk was full, leaving Ellin wondering if they'd taken three other people's spots at the last minute. That felt wrong, but with the survival of humanity at stake, she supposed some deception was justified.

Now that they were here, her goals were clear. She'd be the best intern they'd ever seen. She'd be confident, responsible, and trustworthy, earning the right to work in whatever department she chose. Within four weeks, she'd be at Cellerin Mountain in Therro, trying to stop the dig.

From the front of the room, a voice greeted them. "Good morning."

Ellin shifted her attention to the speaker, an attractive, middle-aged woman.

"Welcome to Merak Technologies. My name is Tereza, and I'll be guiding you through your initial intern training. You're joining nearly sixty other interns who entered the program before you. Together, you comprise some of the most intelligent, driven young adults in Vallinger."

The lights in the room dimmed, and a huge wallscreen behind Tereza lit up. As she told the interns the history of Alvun Merak and Merak Technologies, images and video played on the screen. It was slick, well-rehearsed, and, Ellin hated to admit, inspiring.

Alvun Merak's mother had raised him, struggling to provide for him. She didn't have a university degree, nor did either of her parents. Merak, however, had earned two degrees in four years, three fewer years than most people took. While he was in school, he'd started his first business, a technical support firm that, within months, was granted a contract to repair and maintain most of the deskscreens and wallscreens on the university campus.

During his university career, he'd also started his first charity. It connected struggling students to volunteer tutors. He was still on the board of directors of that organization, which now operated in over a hundred cities around the world.

Merak's big break was when he'd invented Flexen, a substance that used nanotouch technology in an astounding variety of ways. He'd found investors and developed the first modern flexscreen. He even sold Flexen to other flexscreen manufacturers, but Merak models were still the best and most popular worldwide.

As Merak's company had grown, so had his generosity. The Merak Foundation was the largest charity in the world and was always ranked in the top five in ethics and efficacy.

The presentation didn't address Merak's personal benevolence. Ellin knew from articles she'd read over the past week that Alvun Merak tried to keep his donations a secret when the money came from his own pockets, rather than from his foundation. Despite his efforts, word often got out, and experts estimated that Alvun Merak gave away between eighty and ninety-five percent of his impressive income.

Ellin tried to tamp down her growing admiration of Merak. *This is the man who will destroy the world.*

"And now," Tereza said, "Mr. Merak himself."

The screen filled with an image of Alvun Merak. He was in the nicest glidecraft Ellin had ever seen. His mouth widened into a kind, genuine smile.

"I'm thrilled to meet you all," Merak said. "I know you're wondering if this video is pre-recorded. I'll assure the young man in the green sweater in the second row, I'm talking to you live."

He waited for the excited laughter to die down before telling them how honored he was to meet them and how much he appreciated them choosing to intern at Merak Technologies. Then he bid them goodbye.

The rest of the session was filled with logistical details of their training and the possibilities for their future with Merak. Tereza was clearly capable, organized, and personable. Ellin was sure she could meet and exceed the internship expectations, just as she'd always done in school.

When they wrapped up, Ellin turned to Rena and Trett. "I'm going to go meet Tereza," she said.

Trett grinned. "Of course you are. I'm surprised you didn't sit in the front row too."

"The two of you ate breakfast so slow, there weren't any good seats left." Ellin gave him a playful scowl before walking to the front of the room.

Tereza was still at the lectern, tapping on her flex. Naturally, it was the latest Merak model.

"I'm sorry to interrupt," Ellin said.

Tereza looked up and gave her a warm smile. She held out her hand. "I'm Tereza."

Ellin returned the handshake. "I'm Ellin."

"I caught your eye a few times during my presentation. You certainly looked inspired by Mr. Merak's story."

"He seems like an incredible man."

Tereza's smile grew even wider. "You have no idea."

"I've been reading about the archeological work the company is funding in Therro," Ellin said.

"Oh yes, we're all excited about that."

"It's fascinating!" Ellin tried to school her face into just the right expression—eager willingness without desperation. It was tough, considering how important this conversation was. "I'd love to work out there so I could see it in person."

Tereza's expression shifted just a smidge. She was still smiling, but professional politeness replaced her friendliness. "I'll tell you one of the most important things you need to learn as an intern. We all find our greatest fulfillment as a part of Merak Technologies when we prioritize not what's best for ourselves, but what's best for Merak."

Merak the man or Merak the company? Ellin didn't dare ask the question out loud. Instead, she relaxed her face into an even wider smile. "Of course. How inspiring."

Tereza regained her warmth from seconds before. "Inspiring is an apt word for it. For everything Alvun Merak does."

Ellin engaged her in conversation for several more minutes. She focused more on Therro than anything but brought up several other Merak projects as well. Tereza's eyes lit up as Ellin proved her understanding of the company's work in various fields.

Eventually, Ellin realized there were others waiting to talk to Tereza. She said goodbye and walked back to Trett and Rena. When they were outside, she murmured, "Tereza isn't Merak's employee. She's his disciple. A true believer. I don't think we'll get anywhere in this place unless we convince everyone we're just as loyal as she is."

11

Alvun Merak couldn't sleep.

Truth be told, he hadn't slept well since—well, he couldn't think of a time in his life when he'd slept well, for any number of reasons. Messing up his internal clock by traveling halfway around the world certainly didn't help.

He got out of bed and put on lightweight shorts, a shirt, and running shoes. Then he left his private cottage and walked through the compound. Using the flashlight on his flex, he navigated past silent buildings where loyal Merak employees worked during the day. The only ones awake now were the night guards, three of whom waved as he passed them. With all the confidential work being done here, Merak didn't hesitate to spend money on excellent security.

Even at night, there was an energy about this place, a sense that they were doing something big. The radiation they'd found would change the world for the better; everyone here expected it. Or most of them, anyway. The overly cautious of the bunch would come around soon.

He arrived at the small glidecraft he kept behind his office. Once inside, he retrieved a black device about the size of his palm. After several seconds, every hair on his body suddenly felt like it was standing at attention. His skin still looked normal; the strange sensation was just the effect of activated antiradiation technology.

Two minutes later, he was in the air. It took only minutes to travel to the dig site. He landed the glidecraft and disembarked. Then he removed his flex from its protective case and firmed it. Once he'd set it to glow just brightly enough to light his path, he collapsed it and let it wrap around his forearm. He took off at a run.

Merak loved running at Cellerin Mountain. He'd been doing it ever since he'd started visiting here, years before they knew whether the government would allow them to dig. He'd always been certain he could convince them. It had required countless meetings, plenty of ass kissing, and a few creative incentives offered to the right people.

And it had all been worth it.

Merak ran to the edge of the huge mountain, where archeologists had barely begun their careful work. They called it a *dig*, but that was a misnomer. The archeologists and their crew were simply moving rocks.

According to data from their sensors, there was a small cave at the edge of the mountain. Its entrance was covered by a massive pile of loose stones that archeologists said had been there since humanity's early days on Anyari. After so many thousands of years, the stones now blended in with the mountain itself. The pile extended nearly thirty mets from the edge of the mountain. At its tallest, it was over four mets high, twice as tall as Merak.

Researchers guessed the radiation source was in the hidden cave, and workers had started moving stones to access it. The Therroan government insisted they work by hand when possible to protect the grounds. So far, environmental inspectors seemed happy with the cautious nature of the work.

Merak slowed to a walk. He didn't need the gentle light of his flex, as large floodlights illuminated the dig site. Running his hand along some of the ancient stones hiding his prize—the world's prize—he considered the new hospital wing he'd just funded. What new technology could he bring there within the next few years, thanks to the discoveries being made right here?

He turned away from the stones and kept running. A few seconds later, he passed the night guard and waved. The guard returned his greeting; he'd likely picked up the signal from Merak's flex as soon as the glidecraft arrived.

Picking up his pace, Merak exited the dig site and continued running along a narrow road at the mountain's perimeter. Here in the southern hemisphere, the autumn air felt great in his lungs. It beat the weather back home on the other side of the equator—spring in the desert felt too much like summer.

The original Anyarian colonists had landed somewhere near this mountain. A few museums even had metallic relics that had likely come from the colonists' landing craft, but nature and ancient looters had reclaimed most of the treasures left behind by Anyari's first residents. It didn't help that the Therroan government had never approved much archeological research. No one knew what historical treasures might still be awaiting discovery.

Merak's long strides took him over loose stones and past scrubby bushes. The road turned around a rock outcropping, and an old, green building came in sight. He jogged up to it and stopped, breathing hard.

The building had been a gift shop and café, but it wasn't close enough to any trailheads to do much business. Its owners had cut their losses two decades earlier, abandoning the place. Merak was surprised the government had ever approved it in the first place. Perhaps the owners had offered their own *incentives* to select officials.

Merak Technologies had purchased the building a couple of years earlier, getting a bargain price with very little negotiation. Merak knew that once the dig really got going, tourists would be curious. If this little shop reopened, it would be even easier for people to visit and get in the way of the archeologists' research. With Merak as the owner, the place would stay shuttered.

Of course, that was before they'd found radiation at the site. Besides the scientific potential of such a discovery, it had the convenient side effect of keeping people away. Tourists didn't carry antirads.

Merak held his flex up to the electronic lock on the building's back door. He'd been running for less than a clommet and had planned to go much farther, but his lack of sleep had led to heavy limbs. It was time for a break. He stepped inside and turned on the light.

There weren't any chairs in the building, so Merak sat on the floor, leaning back against the large door of a walk-in freezer. He pulled his flex off his arm and firmed it.

Seeing an em from his son, Merak smiled and sent a reply. Gil immediately responded, and Merak chatted with him for a few minutes. Then he sent Arisa a quick goodnight em, though it was still early afternoon back home.

Next to his ems was his mailbox, full of In-Depth Messages —*IDMs*, used for longer communications. Only a select group could em Merak, but anyone could IDM him. Despite digital filters and an assistant who further sifted through the messages, Merak received more IDMs than he could ever reply to. Several dozen awaited his attention. He sighed and began scanning the subjects and senders.

One stood out. It was from Tereza, the head of Merak Technologies' intern program. The subject line read, *List: new class.*

Merak smiled. Tereza had a knack for picking out the brightest and most motivated interns. When she sent him lists, he kept the names and descriptions in the back of his mind and often personally assigned a few of them to important projects. Some of Tereza's recommended interns from years past now held high positions at Merak Technologies and the Merak Foundation.

The new intern class seemed promising. Tereza hadn't had a chance to meet most of them in person but had read their histories in detail. One young man, Tereza claimed, was more skilled than many of Merak's software engineers. A woman who was a few years older than the other interns had a great head for numbers.

Then a name halfway down the list caught Merak's eye: *Ellin Havier.*

His mouth curved up in a half-smile. His daughter's name was Ellin. It was an old-fashioned name, not one he heard often these days. He read Tereza's description:

Only 19 yrs old, but clearly brilliant & driven. Talked to me after orientation. Very familiar with/excited about our current work. Already requested assignment to Therro.

Tereza had described plenty of interns through the years as *brilliant and driven.* However, most didn't manage to impress her with their knowledge of the company on day one. He didn't know if Ellin's passion was genuine or exaggerated for Tereza's sake, but it really didn't matter. Anyone motivated enough to research Merak Technologies in detail and to establish an early relationship with an executive was someone worth keeping an eye on.

It didn't hurt that her name was Ellin, and she was the same age as *his* Ellin. *Such a similar personality too,* Merak thought. Even before she'd started school, his daughter had been motivated by a desire to achieve. He chuckled, remembering how she'd demanded, in that lisping voice of hers, that her daddy buy her more blocks. She didn't even like playing with blocks all that much, but Gil had built a tower taller than himself, and she'd been determined to build a bigger one.

Merak shook his head, his smile remaining. He didn't buy into Arisa's spiritualism, but something like this made him wonder if some things were meant to be. He'd have to meet this new Ellin when he got back to Amler.

Standing, Merak discovered enthusiasm had replaced his drowsiness. He left the building, locked it, and set off running at a faster pace than before.

12

Ellin finished breakfast (including a chocolate cup of coffee that was even better than the fare back home) and set off for her new assignment. Day two at Merak Technologies had begun.

The previous day, the new interns had been told what departments they'd work in. Thanks to Rena's mysterious hacker friends, she, Trett, and Ellin were all placed in areas where they might gather information on the dig in Therro.

Rena would work in Accounting, where she probably had more expertise than most of the employees. Everything cost money; if there was anything illegal going on at the dig, surely she could find it.

Trett was placed in Merak's office, though with the number of workers there, he might have trouble getting close to the man himself. It didn't help that Merak was in Therro, and nobody knew when he'd return.

Ellin had been assigned to the best source of information she could imagine: the Press Office. It was a few minutes' walk from the dining hall, giving her time to think and hopefully work out a few of her new-job jitters.

She was fairly buzzing with alert focus. Until recently, she'd thought this sensation was reserved for her scholastic and career aspirations. It seemed her single-mindedness had merely shifted direction, perhaps even strengthened. *I think what I loved about school was that it gave me big goals to focus on. Maybe that's all I've ever needed: a big goal. Saving the world is as big as it gets.*

She wondered, as she often did, what her parents would think if they could witness her determination to fight for the lives of everyone on Anyari. Her father's voice filled her mind: *Ellin, you can do anything you set your mind to.* The memory brought a little lump to her throat, and she swallowed it down as she arrived at the Press Office building.

When she stepped inside, she blinked several times, trying to match her expectations to the reality before her. When she'd heard "Press Office," she'd pictured perhaps a dozen people working on press releases. She'd thought that once she arrived at the correct building, she'd have to figure out what room to navigate to.

It turned out the entire, seven-story building was the Press Office. Ellin approached a wallscreen with an interactive map and stared at it. One floor was dedicated to video studios, another to video editing. Writers occupied the second floor. There were floors for text editors, administrative offices, and research. The third floor was unlabeled.

"Are you Ellin?"

The polite voice caused Ellin to stop perusing the map. She turned to face a man who was probably in his early thirties. "That's me." She held out her hand.

He shook it. "I'm Jovan. I'm sorry I wasn't here to meet you when you arrived. I'll be overseeing your internship here. Care to start with a tour?"

"That sounds great."

The map had been impressive, but it hadn't begun to convey just how much was happening here. Like she'd expected, the Press Office sent out press releases so reporters could write stories. However, the department also hosted a dedicated team of writers who composed everything from short articles to in-depth features, all written for specific newsorgs. Graphics and video experts inserted interactive elements. According to Jovan, the newsorgs often preferred Merak-generated content over anything their reporters would have had time to write.

Another team produced documentaries on Merak Technologies' technical innovations and the Merak Foundation's charitable work. Some of the latter productions were optimized for Threeds. Three-dimensional pictures were thought to make viewers feel more connected, leading some of them to volunteer their time and money.

It was the most modern place Ellin had ever stepped foot in. Several times, Jovan pointed out technology that Merak had developed but hadn't made available for sale yet. The facility catered to its employees' comfort too. A small coffee stand sat on one side of the lobby, serving free, gourmet drinks and snacks. Even the lifts and bathrooms were beautiful and comfortable.

At last, Jovan said, "That's about it. The questionnaire you filled out last week made it clear you're a skilled writer, so today we'd like you to work on an article about the Foundation's vaccine distribution program. One of our writers will sit next to you and train you."

"That sounds great. What about the third floor? We skipped it."

"We always skip it. It's the one boring area in an exciting building." Jovan smiled widely and led her back to the lift.

They entered the second-floor writing room, which took up the entire level. There, Jovan introduced her to her trainer. The woman showed Ellin to a workstation, then sent a list of facts to the deskscreen there. "Read the facts, and write whatever story seems appropriate," she instructed before returning to her own work.

Ellin picked up the earcaps waiting at her station, hoping they'd been sanitized since the last person used them. When she held them to her ears, they molded to fit, blocking out most of the sound in the room. She selected a fast-paced instrumental playlist from her deskscreen, and the music filled her ears.

When she was halfway through with the article, the coffee she'd brought caught up with her. She headed for the bathroom, which was right next to the lift.

A sudden desire, stronger even than her urge to use the bathroom, hit Ellin. *I've got to see what's on the third floor.* She looked both directions. Seeing no one, she pushed the call button. The door to one of the lifts opened. Inside, she pushed the glowing "3" on the wallscreen.

ENTER YOUR SECURITY CODE, the screen instructed.

Ellin sighed and pushed the appropriate icon to open the lift doors. She went to the bathroom and returned to her workstation.

At lunch, Ellin, Rena, and Trett sat at a small table in the corner, ignoring their fellow interns.

"They've got me analyzing expenditures from the campus food service department," Rena said. "I hope the two of you are having more luck than I am."

"You remember how you said Tereza wasn't just an employee, she's a disciple?" Trett asked.

Ellin's mouth was full of a surprisingly delicious salad, so she just nodded and said, "Mmm hmm."

"Well, if you think she's bad, you should meet the people in Merak's office. If he told them to swallow poison, they'd have a contest to see who could do it the fastest."

"I wonder how he holds such sway over them," Rena said.

"You know, I honestly think he's a good man," Trett replied. "Obviously he's good at earning money, but he's a great leader too. He's earned the respect of the people who work with him. I don't think he's faking his desire to help others."

Ellin put down her fork. "If he's that good of a man, maybe we can reason with him."

Shaking her head, Rena said, "No chance. He's rich. That means he's good at making decisions and sticking with them. Nothing you say will convince him to give up what might be the archeological dig of a lifetime. Besides, how are we ever going to meet him?"

Ellin shoved a huge wad of lettuce in her mouth to prevent herself from snapping at her know-it-all sister. She took a couple of deep breaths through her nose as she chewed. After swallowing, she gave Rena a bright smile that hopefully didn't look too fake. "We'll meet him—or at least I will—because I'm going to stand out as the top intern here. They asked me to write one article this morning. I wrote two and started on a third. My trainer couldn't believe it."

Rena wouldn't be swayed. "Be realistic, Ellin. There may be only eighty interns, but a hundred thousand other people work for Merak. Trying really hard won't get you very far here."

"You know—" Trett began.

Ellin cut him off. "First of all, Rena, don't talk to me like I'm a child." When Rena opened her mouth to argue, Ellin barreled on, giving up on her pretense of diplomacy. "Second, *trying really hard,* as you put it, has always worked for me in the past. It'll work here too."

Rena spared a short eyeroll for her sister before turning her attention to her food. She picked up a piece of artisan bread that was dotted with at least six different types of seeds. Her face twisted in disgust. Ellin knew that look; Rena had always preferred simple fare. Suddenly, Rena dropped the bread, and her eyes glazed over.

"Oh great," Ellin said, glancing around to see if anyone was watching.

The vision only lasted a few seconds. Then Rena looked straight at Ellin, her eyes clear again. "Why do you want to see the third floor?"

Ellin's eyes widened, but she recovered quickly. "I was just going to tell you both about that." She explained the mystery of the floor she hadn't been allowed to visit.

"I just saw you entering a code in the lift and walking right into that department," Rena said. "No one was there."

"Maybe it was nighttime?" Trett suggested.

"Yeah, the building was pretty dark." Rena stood, the look on her face intense. "I'm going to my room; I've got half an hour before I need to be back in Accounting." She sped off, leaving a half-full tray of food behind.

"What do you think she's up to?" Trett asked.

"No idea, and I've learned not to ask when she gets like this."

Trett's face broke into that heart-stopping grin. "It's kind of nice to get a few minutes alone." He leaned over, giving her a kiss.

Ellin smiled, then stood. "Actually, I need to go back to my room too. I'm out of the loop on the progress in Therro, and all they want me to focus on in the Press Office is vaccine stories. If I leave now, I can catch up on the news."

Trett was still smiling. "Don't you think your mind will be more clear if you take a few breaks?"

He was right; she was usually more productive in the afternoon if she took a true break at lunch. She sighed and sat. "Okay, I'll stay here."

"I'm glad." He took a bite.

Ellin watched him. His shoulders were relaxed, and when his eyes met hers, he swallowed and gave her a sweet grin before taking another bite.

How is he so calm? We're trying to stop the apocalypse, and he looks like he doesn't have a care in the world. Despite her resolution to enjoy the rest of lunch, her mind wandered to the story she was working on, the news she might be missing, and the countdown on her flex. Her salad forgotten, she brought her hand to her mouth and chewed on a dry cuticle while Trett ate his lunch in silence.

THURSDAY, QUARI 18, 6293
-51 DAYS

It was the middle of the night when Ellin woke to knocking at her door. She staggered out of bed. "Who is it?"

"It's me," Rena's voice called.

Ellin opened the door. "You could have emmed me. Your notifications always come through, day or night."

"I didn't think of that." Rena touched a panel on the wall, turning on the overhead light. Ellin groaned, covering her eyes.

"I have a security code for you," Rena said.

"A what?" Ellin found her desk chair and sat.

"A security code. For the third floor of the press building."

"What time is it?"

"Almost two. I told you, in my vision, you visited the building at night."

Squinting at her sister, whose level of alertness was probably illegal at this time of night, Ellin said, "I'm not breaking into a building! I'll never gain respect at this place if I do something like that, and they'll never send me to Therro if they don't respect me."

Rena raised an eyebrow. "I could try to convince you it's not really breaking in when you have a code. Or you could save us some time and just go, because you know you're going to do it eventually. I saw two potential realities. You do this, we find out something important. You don't, and we're stuck here with no useful information at all."

Ellin groaned. "Where'd you get the code—oh, your hacker friend, right?"

Rena nodded. She was blinking fast, Ellin noticed, and her gaze had dropped as soon as she'd heard the word *hacker*. What was she hiding? Too tired to dwell on her sister's oddities, Ellin pushed the question away. "You want me to go tonight?"

"We're on a timeline."

"I don't want to do this!" Ellin knew her voice was as shrill as a ten-year-old's, but she didn't care. She was helpless against her sister's perfect prophecies. She'd never dreamed of breaking and entering, but apparently she had to forget that for the night.

Rena's only response was two raised eyebrows.

Ellin sighed. "Let me see the code."

Rena handed over her flexscreen. The security code was six digits long, and Ellin repeated it to herself several times, even typing it into an imaginary keypad in front of her. "I've got it."

"Better be sure."

"I am sure. But how do you know I'll be safe? Just because I have a code doesn't mean I won't get caught by security. I'm sure there are cameras."

"There are. Maybe nobody's monitoring them. You'll be fine." Rena walked to the door. "Get dressed and go. Find out whatever you can while you're there; you might not get another chance."

"You promise I'm not going to get eaten alive by a guard caynin? Or arrested and given a life sentence?"

"Ellin, you've seen the technology at this place. Their guards don't need animals to help them. Anyway, you know you'd never get a life sentence for trespassing."

"When the world's ending in fifty-one days, most sentences are life sentences."

Rena's face turned somber. "True." She drew in a deep breath and let it out in a shaky huff. Then she lifted her chin and met Ellin's eyes. "You'll be fine. You won't be arrested. Now go."

"I'm bringing Trett with me."

"I know," Rena said. "He's already getting dressed."

She left, and Ellin gave the closed door a dirty look. Of course Rena knew.

Fifteen minutes later, Ellin and Trett were at the Press Office building. The security code got them in the front door. Ellin took deep, slow breaths, trying to slow her rushing heart and calm the acidic guilt in her stomach. She wasn't sure whether she despised herself or Rena more at that moment. She shook her head hard as she led Trett to the lift.

"Hey," he said, grabbing her hand before she could push the button.

Ellin turned to him.

Trett smiled. "It's gonna be all right."

She released a long sigh, looking longingly back at the front door. "I hate this."

"You know, some people get a thrill out of breaking the rules."

Ellin turned back to Trett. He was giving her that look she'd always loved, one of mingled adoration and hunger. His barely-parted lips conveyed a clear message: *Kiss me.*

So she did. Within moments, she was sandwiched between the lift door and Trett, her hands tangled in his hair, all attempts at controlling her breathing and heart rate forgotten.

Since they'd started planning their trip, they'd had to focus night and day on packing, quitting school, and getting their cover story straight. They'd been acting like partners in a business sense, not a romantic one.

That wasn't really a new phenomenon. Back home, Ellin and Trett had shared plenty of quick, sweet kisses, but she'd always had a hard time releasing her inhibitions around him. It was one of the drawbacks to being a driven person, she supposed. Her intense focus on the future made it impossible to live in the present. She didn't like it, but she didn't know how to change it.

Tonight, though, she'd careened off her well-worn path, the one where she met goals by following rules. She was standing in a dim building she'd accessed illegally in the middle of the night. The absurdity of the situation drove home the sudden uncertainty of her life.

So for the first time in months, Ellin let go of her need to know what would happen next. She let herself go in Trett's arms, drinking him up, convinced there was nothing better than the feel of his mouth on hers. Every part of her skin felt charged with electricity, assuring her that, even without school, she had everything to live for.

The crazy thing was, Trett was right. Surely making out in the lobby of the Press Office in the middle of the night was forbidden. And that filled her with a befuddling, feverish wildness.

Then an entirely unwanted thought invaded Ellin's mind. She pulled her mouth off Trett's. His lips moved to her neck.

"Trett?"

"What is it?" he murmured.

"Do you think Rena saw this in her prophecy too?"

Trett lifted his head and laughed, the warm sound echoing in the empty space. "Probably." His fingertip traced the hollow of her neck, then the folds of her ear. "Does it matter?"

"I guess not." But thoughts of Rena had reminded Ellin why they were here. At this crucial moment, making out with Trett seemed both silly and selfish. She reached up and enfolded his hand in hers, pulling it off her ear. With a quick, deep breath, she tried to tame the heat still racing through her. "That kiss was . . . well, I spent all day writing, but I can't come up with words to describe it." She laughed softly, then sobered, holding his gaze. "Trett, right now, we can't afford to do anything but keep our heads down and figure out a way to fight Merak."

Trett gave her a tentative smile. "We were keeping our heads down. So to speak."

She rolled her eyes. "You know what I mean."

Trett stepped away from her. He shoved his hands in his pockets and pressed his lips together. The muscles in his jaw tightened.

She stood up straighter. "Wait, are you pissed because I stopped kissing you?"

Trett's eyes widened, and he pulled his hands from his pockets, holding them up defensively. "No, Ellin—no, don't ever think that. I told you from the beginning, the second you say stop, I'll stop. You told me the same."

"What is it, then?"

He shrugged. "It's fine. Maybe you're right. But listen, Ellin, I can hardly wrap my mind around the end of the world. I don't *want* to think about it all the time."

"Do we really have a choice?"

Trett sighed and looked off to the side. Then he turned back to her but didn't meet her eyes. "I guess we should go up."

Ellin watched his muscles turn rigid as he shuttered his emotions. Her chest ached in response. She wanted to assure him this wasn't personal; she was just trying to be rational and responsible. Now wasn't the time for a heart-to-heart talk, though. They had to get out of this place before they got caught. She pushed the button to open the lift.

Once inside, she pushed "3" and entered her code. Nervous again, she fumbled, getting the last number wrong. Her second try was successful, and the lift rose.

It opened onto one large room. It was the size of the Writing Department, but there were only eight workstations. Ellin led Trett out of the lift and into the room. Most of the ceiling was dark, but dim lighting in all four corners gave the room a ghostly glow.

They sat at a workstation. Just like Ellin's deskscreen on the floor below, the one in front of her was labeled with the department name and device number: *Screening Department 4*. "Apparently we're in the Screening Department, whatever that is," she said, waving her hand over the screen to wake it up. Another security code prompt popped up. She tried the code Rena had given her. It worked.

The screen looked mostly like the one she'd used earlier that day, but an unfamiliar icon sat in the center. It read *TBS*. Ellin clicked it. A neat table filled the screen.

"To Be Screened," she read, her voice a whisper. Underneath the heading was a list of news stories. Many of the titles included the word "Merak." In the second and third columns were publisher names and dates. The earliest date was Cygni 20th. Ellin glanced at the current date in the corner of the screen, confirming that it was the 18th of Cygni.

"Why are all the dates in the future?" Trett asked.

"I have no idea." Ellin clicked on one, and it opened. It was a short article on Merak Technologies' recent flexscreen software update. She opened another article that detailed a new charity venture, then a third that described a recent stockholder meeting.

"These are all normal articles, just like the ones we read when we were preparing to come here," Ellin said.

"Still, those dates . . ." Trett's voice trailed off.

Ellin closed the TBS list and examined the screen. All the icons appeared innocuous. She clicked the one for messages. Ems popped up on the left side of the screen, IDMs on the right. She pulled up the first IDM.

Trett read the subject line aloud. *"Tomorrow's article on Merak."* He continued with the short message. *"Perfect. We appreciate your help on this. My best to your family. -Ev."*

Ellin navigated to the oldest message in the thread. It was from the same man who'd sent the most recent one. She read it silently.

Hi, Sheller,

Hope you and your family are well. I reviewed the most recent story Kellum plans to release on Merak's ventures into solar power.

Mostly it looks great, but it discloses a little more of our proposed timeline than Mr. Merak is comfortable with. It's too early to know if it's reasonable, and we wouldn't want to raise shareholder expectations only to disappoint them in the future.

I trust you can help us with this. My thanks in advance.

Let's talk soon,
Evling Rainer

Ellin read the entire IDM again, out loud this time. "I think this is Evling Rainer's workstation," she said.

Trett nodded. "And this guy Sheller works for Kellum International." Kellum was one of the largest newsorgs.

Ellin scrolled down and scanned the rest of the message thread. In it, Sheller agreed to adjust the news story according to Merak's preferences. Ellin looked at Trett, who was reading the screen, shaking his head.

Many other messages were similar, with Evling Rainer requesting changes, large and small, to news stories from a large variety of newsorgs and even from the very writing department where Ellin worked. Sometimes he even requested that a story be cancelled altogether. The message recipients always agreed.

Over half the IDMs were positive. Rainer thanked his contacts for stories that were well-written and, in so many words, gave them permission to publish. In one of these, the newsorg representative's response caught Ellin's eye. It read,

No problem, my friend. Enjoying the new boat. We drink to you every time we sail!

They looked further back in the messages, seeking similar words of gratitude, and had no problem finding them. One woman appreciated the fine wine that had shown up on her doorstep. Another loved her cottage on the sea. A well-known newsorg editor thanked Rainer outright for the monetary gift that had just posted in his account.

"You're seeing the same thing I am, right?" Trett asked.

Ellin nodded. "Merak Technologies is controlling the press."

$$13$$

WHY AM I HERE?

Trett stood in line in the dining hall, surrounded by busy interns, waiting to order from the varied dinner menu. Two weeks in, this was one of many routines he'd settled into. *I guess I'm just biding my time until the end of the world.*

Merak was still in Therro, so Trett's position in the man's office seemed pointless. He'd never expected to personally bring Merak down, anyway. Trett's main goal on this quest was to support Ellin— and it was impossible to do that when she was constantly busy in the Press Office.

"Hey."

Trett turned toward the voice. Ellin was behind him, grinning.

"Hi! You're not staying late in the Press Office?"

"Not tonight. Let's grab our food and go to my room. I'll em Rena and tell her to meet us too."

Before long, all three of them were entering Ellin's room. She closed the door, dropped her food on her desk, and greeted them with a wide smile. "Jovan, my boss, called me into his office today. He loves what I've been writing, and he wants me to work on an important article." She grinned, bouncing on the balls of her feet.

"An article on what?" Rena asked. "Spit it out."

Ellin shot her a brief glare, but then her smile returned. "It's an in-depth feature on the most recent scientific findings in Therro."

Trett's mouth broadened into a smile. "That's great!"

"A feature on Therro," Rena said. "That's a step in the right direction."

Ellin nodded. "I've started looking through all the information they sent me, and it's overwhelming. Way more than we've been reading in the media." She pulled her flex off her arm and sat at her desk. "I've gotta get some more work done tonight."

⁕

FRIDAY, CYON 1, 6293

-36 DAYS

"Ellin?"

Ellin looked up. From across the dinner table, Trett was staring at her, one eyebrow raised.

Jovan had forced her to leave at 5:30 since it was Friday night. She'd used her flex throughout dinner, trying to reach a good stopping point on her research. "How long have you been trying to get my attention?" she asked with a strained smile.

"I said your name three times."

Ellin set her flex down and rubbed both her eyes. "I'm so sorry, Trett. I've been reading the same paragraph over and over. My brain is mush after all the research this week, and I'm not even close to ready to write my article." She reached out, and he put his hand in hers. "I don't want to ignore you, you know. It's just"—she shook her head helplessly—"every day counts. Every *minute* counts."

His expression softened. "I know, but you said it yourself, your brain is mush. Come outside with me. Rena's already there. I have a surprise for you."

They put their dishes in the cleaning chute and exited, then walked around to the back of the building. Rena was waiting there next to two hovs, one single and one double.

Ellin gave Trett a questioning look.

"The Lanterns are streaming a live show tonight at the Threed theater in the city," he said. "I got tickets and asked Rena to rent the hovs."

Ellin and Trett didn't always have the same taste in music, but The Lanterns were the one band they both loved. They'd never had a chance to see them live, but they caught streaming shows as often as they could.

"That sounds amazing," Ellin said. And it did. Nothing would be better than letting music wash over her while she danced or cuddled with Trett in a quiet corner. The problem was, every time she looked at her flex, she saw the countdown. They had thirty-six days left. Free time was a luxury they couldn't afford. She pressed her lips together and hesitantly met Trett's gaze. "I can't," she said quietly.

Trett turned to look toward the border of Merak's complex. The tall, metal fence was visible in the distance. "You know," he said, "you're allowed to leave this place. Give your mind some time to recharge."

A helpless sigh left her mouth. "I wish I could. Really, I do, Trett; you have no idea."

"Ellin." Impatience was thick in Rena's voice. "You're not trying to graduate number one in your class anymore. Take a night off."

Ellin was short on sleep and had skipped more meals than she cared to count that week. If there was ever a time she could have used some empathy from her sister, this was it. "One night off, great idea," she snapped. "Can you call whoever's scheduling the apocalypse and ask them to postpone it a day or two for me?"

Rena's expression turned intense. "Is what you're researching that important?"

"I think it might be."

"Then we'll stay here and help you."

In the silence that followed, Trett released a long breath. "I have a better idea. Rena, you haven't had any visions in the last week or so. Could it be you're too adapted to your new routine?"

"It's possible."

"Why don't you go to the show just to shake up your schedule? Maybe it'll lead to a vision or two. I'll stay here and help Ellin."

Rena arched an eyebrow. "Will you really get any research done?"

Trett chuckled. "Ellin's focus is immutable."

Ellin shrugged, giving him a regretful smile.

"Are you still listening?" Ellin waved her hand in front of Trett's face. They were sitting next to each other on her bed.

He blinked. "Yes, I just—I didn't realize we were enrolling in a crash course in university-level chemistry."

She set aside her flex, which she'd been reading aloud from. "Do you see why my research is taking so long? All this information was written by experts who can't write in a way normal people understand. It's infuriating!"

Trett raised his eyebrows. "You're loving this, aren't you?"

"Is it that obvious?" She laughed.

Trett leaned over and ran his thumb across her smiling lips. "Maybe it wouldn't be obvious to anyone else, but I know you. Now take me through the last minute or two of what you were telling me."

She flashed him a grateful smile and picked up her flex. "Actually, I came across a video I think will help us both understand it better." She found the video and tapped the screen to play it.

"In the past," the video's baritone narrator began, "radiation therapy nearly always came with unfortunate side effects." Photos faded in and out: blistered skin, a woman holding her stomach, and a man who was clearly exhausted.

"He looks like me," Trett said, and they both laughed.

"A century ago, researchers discovered how to eliminate these side effects," the narrator continued. "We entered the modern era of beneficial radiation." He described how this radiation was used not only to fight cancer, but also to destroy illness-causing microbes and to heal cuts and burns.

When the video was over, Trett and Ellin went back to their research, sharing interesting findings with each other. By midnight, they had a better grasp on the science behind beneficial radiation. Neither of them could keep their eyes open, so Trett left for his room, and Ellin fell into bed.

The next morning, she knocked on his door before the sun rose.

He opened the door and rubbed his eyes. "Really, Ellin?"

She smiled brightly, entered the room, and turned on his wallscreen. "Today," she said, "we get to analyze data from the Cellerin Project."

He went back to his bed and lay down. "Yippee."

———

SUNDAY, CYON 3, 6293

-34 DAYS

"This coffee sucks," Rena said.

Ellin glanced at her sister. "That's because it's mine from yesterday."

Rena frowned into the cup. "Oh."

I should be laughing at that, Ellin thought. After researching all weekend, with limited sleep and short bathroom and meal breaks, none of them were in the mood for humor.

Over the last two days, the immense responsibility to stop Rena's prophecy had filled Ellin with an anxiety so dense, she felt she'd physically burst. She'd taken a couple of walks with Trett, but the warm, desert air hadn't helped a bit. Desperately, she searched for information that would convince the world of the dangers of the Cellerin Project.

It was Sunday night, and they were in Rena's room, which still smelled like the sandwiches they'd picked up from the dining hall for dinner. They'd all become snippy with each other, even good-natured Trett.

Ellin scanned the screen of her flex, then examined it more closely. Her eyes widened. "Guys—I've got something." Trett and Rena sat up straight as Ellin sent the pictures from her flex to the wallscreen.

"What are we looking at?" Trett asked.

Ellin gestured to the screen. "These graphs represent particles emitted by three different radioactive isotopes. See this first one? It's the same radiation they probably used last time one of us went to a clinic to get a cut or burn healed. Next, we've got radiation from whatever's inside that cave at the Cellerin site. The last one is from an isotope a scientist generated sixty years ago."

She stared at Trett and Rena, awaiting a response.

"The second one—that's from the Cellerin Project?" Rena asked.

"Yes."

"It kind of looks like the third one."

"Exactly; they're very similar!" Ellin felt a tingle of excitement rejuvenating her sluggish body. "Let me show you something else." She pulled up an obituary of a friendly-looking man.

"Who's that?" Trett asked.

"He's the scientist who discovered that last isotope. He died two days after his discovery. In fact, worldwide scientific agencies have advised against anyone trying to recreate his work. The radiation from that isotope is too dangerous."

After a minute or two of silence, Trett said, "Tell me we're looking at this wrong."

Ellin ran a hand through her greasy hair. "We're seeing it right. The radiation at the dig site is similar to beneficial radiation, just like Merak's been saying—but it's far more similar to the radiation that killed that scientist."

TUESDAY, CYON 5, 6293

-32 DAYS

Trett crawled into bed on Tuesday night. He checked his flex one more time, just in case he'd missed a message from Ellin. *Nope.*

Considering the quality of information they'd gathered, Ellin had hoped to write the article quickly. Apparently it had been harder than she'd expected—two days had passed, and she'd barely left the office. She ate meals at her desk, only responding to about half of the *How's it going?* ems he and Rena sent.

Just as he was dozing off, his flex dinged.

It was an em from Ellin to both Trett and Rena.

DONE! See you in a few.

Trett got up and turned his light on. There was a knock at his door, and Rena came in. She had dark circles under her eyes. He was sure he did too.

Ellin soon joined them. "That was way harder than I expected."

She explained that newsorgs wouldn't publish an in-depth explanation of radioactive chemistry. She'd had to write something simple enough for the average person to read and frightening enough to spur them to action.

Trett listened, but half his attention was on *her*. Not her words, but her raised eyebrows and enthusiastic gestures. Her blue eyes were far brighter than anyone's should be at this time of night.

He felt his mouth turn up in a slight smile. *She loves this.*

The next thought came on its heels. *When's the last time she looked at me that way?*

He chided himself for the thought. The world was ending, and he was concerned about whether Ellin was excited to see him? He shook off the pointless musings and returned his focus to her.

"This was so much more fun to write than those short articles they had me working on before," Ellin said. "I worked with another department to create an interactive illustration. It's a simplified version of those three graphs I showed you Sunday. I included plenty of opinions from people who want the dig to continue, but anyone who really reads it is going to think twice."

"Did you proofread it?" Rena asked.

Ellin flashed her sister a rueful smile. "Seven times. Then I sent it to my boss."

"Good," Rena said curtly. "Because I don't know if you've checked the date lately, but it's Cyon 5th, and we only have thirty-two days left. I'm going to bed." She exited the room without another word.

Trett watched Ellin, who was still grinning even after her sister's pessimistic departure. He wanted to celebrate with her, but he couldn't generate the same excitement she clearly felt. *We traveled across the country together, and our rooms are next to each other, but I feel farther from her than ever. Does she feel it too? Does it bother her that we haven't had a real conversation in weeks?* Their late-night argument in the Press Office still weighed on him. They needed to talk—but it wasn't the right time. Ellin had earned this moment of triumph.

"Hey." He smiled at Ellin and held his arms out. "I'm proud of you."

She returned the hug, then kissed him. "Thanks."

For that moment, everything felt right again.

14

TUESDAY, CYON 5, 6293

-32 DAYS

RENA WOKE WITH A GASP.

She never had prophetic dreams, though she'd read about past seers experiencing such a phenomenon. Instead, she woke when it was time for a vision, like the prophecy was knocking on the door of her sleeping brain, demanding she forsake her rest and give it attention.

She sighed and closed her eyes again, waiting. The vision flooded in.

Alvun Merak's unmistakable face, classically handsome with intense brown eyes, filled her mind. With the indefinable certainty that sometimes came with visions, Rena knew this one was immutable.

Her perspective zoomed out until she could see Merak's tall, fit form. He strode down a hallway in a place she somehow knew was his house. It was, of course, a lovely home, modern and luxurious. Through a window at the end of the hallway, she saw the night sky.

Merak walked into a room and placed his hand on the light panel. Soft brightness illuminated a large bedroom. The walls were a buttery-cream color, and both the blanket on the bed and the curtains were dark green. A yellow desk sat along one wall. Everything was tasteful and homey. Merak looked around and smiled, then turned the light off and returned to the hall.

The vision ended.

Rena huffed and looked up at the ceiling. *You woke me up for that?* The vision didn't seem to have any relevance to the problem at hand, and she certainly didn't need to take any action based on what she'd seen.

Even short, innocuous visions left Rena in a mild post-vision state, rendering her both exhausted and stimulated. She needed more sleep, but knew she'd have to wait for it. So she sat up and grabbed her flex off the floor where she'd dropped it the night before.

She, Ellin, and Trett had kept their commitment not to contact friends and family, but Kizha was an exception. It was vital to have a way to reach her when they needed technological detective work, so Kizha had set up an ultra-secure chat portal. Rena used it with Ellin and Trett too, so their chats wouldn't be detectable by any Merak monitoring. Maybe they were being too cautious, but Kizha insisted a little paranoia was healthy.

It was well past midnight where Kizha lived, but she didn't have a regular sleep schedule. Rena wasn't surprised that her friend's icon showed her as available. She sent a quick message.

Still up?

The response was almost instantaneous.

Yes. How's it going?

Rena stared at Kizha's icon—her curly, black hair, big smile, and bright-green eyes. She'd always liked those eyes.

In her mind, Rena drafted the response she wished she could send. *Everything's good, except that the world is ending in a month. We're trying to get the word out, but let's be honest, I know how this ends. I want to meet you and touch you, to actually live for a change, but for some reason, I have to help Ellin and Trett do whatever they can to stop the inevitable. Now I'm losing sleep so I can have pointless visions of Alvun Merak walking around his house. I guess that's about it; how are you?*

She shook her head and laughed softly. Shoving aside the words she wanted to type, she settled on,

I'm fine. And you?

I'm good, just getting sleepy.

I bet. I'll let you go. Talk tomorrow?

Sure.

Rena collapsed her flex and dropped it on the floor, then fell back onto her pillow.

Kizha had never pressured her to explain all the recent hacking requests, and despite frequent urges to tell her everything, Rena had stayed silent. The problem was, her whole life was now centered around her apocalyptic vision. With that topic off the table, it seemed there was nothing to talk about.

Kizha seemed different lately. She was still friendly, and she clearly loved the extra hacking projects. During video chats, however, Rena saw the questions behind her friend's smiles.

An image invaded Rena's mind, of Ellin and Trett making out in the Press Office lobby. Rena wasn't one to whine, but she indulged in a short, mental tantrum consisting of three unspoken words: *This isn't fair.*

After tossing and turning for half an hour, Rena sat back up. The vision of Merak in his house wouldn't leave her mind. Perhaps it was more than informational. *You want me to act on this, God? Is that why I'm awake?* Despite the brief prayer, her confusion persisted, as did her unwelcome state of alertness.

She emmed Kizha again.

I know you're trying to sleep. No need to respond tonight. I'd really like more information on Alvun Merak. History, family, whatever you can dig up that's not readily available.

After she sent the message, sleep came easily.

WEDNESDAY, CYON 6, 6293
-31 DAYS

The next day, frequent visions pummeled Rena. None of them were long, but they were frighteningly vivid. They were all snippets of the day of the apocalypse.

Every single one was a shrouded prophecy, the one variety of vision she truly hated. There was one difference between immutable and shrouded prophecies. After a shrouded prophecy, she couldn't tell anyone what she'd seen. If she tried to verbalize it, her breath caught in her throat. Any attempt to write it resulted in stiff, cramped hands. She'd even tried to act out a shrouded prophecy once. All her limbs had locked up, and she'd fallen on her face, breaking her nose and chipping a tooth. She was convinced shrouded prophecies were cruel pranks, played on seers by God or fate or whatever mysterious power governed their gifts.

Some of Rena's visions involved images of people dying—falling, turning stark white, bleeding out—all horrid reminders that no matter what Ellin and Trett did, there was no hope of saving the world.

Rena wasn't in any of the visions, but that didn't surprise her. She never saw herself in immutable or shrouded prophecies, and her research told her that was typical. She supposed seers would lose their minds earlier in life if they spent their time trying to change their own unalterable futures.

By the end of the second day of prophecies, Rena's PVS symptoms were overwhelming, only subsiding during visions. Several coworkers commented on her dazed expression, and she left work early. This was why she preferred working from home.

Wanting to avoid fellow interns in the dining hall, she brought her dinner to her room. She finished eating, then emmed her trainer in Accounting to let him know she wouldn't be there the next day.

That night, Rena finally got the sleep her body was craving. It was mid-morning when she woke, her mind informing her it had a prophecy for her. She released a loud groan, sat up, and waited.

During a vision, Rena had little control over her body's movements. Her internal reactions, on the other hand, were often fierce. As this vision progressed, her consciousness cringed, gasped, and sighed. Near the end, her lips twitched, trying to smile.

When the final scene ended, her mouth settled into a true grin.

Now that was a prophecy. Thank goodness this one wasn't shrouded. She'd need to talk to Ellin about it soon. *Maybe we're actually getting somewhere.*

FRIDAY, CYON 8, 6293

-29 DAYS

Not wanting to be annoying or too obvious, at first Ellin didn't ask Jovan for feedback on her article. Instead, she threw her energy into her new assignments. By lunchtime on Friday, however, she couldn't wait any longer.

She put down the sandwich she was eating at her desk and emmed Jovan.

Did my article look okay? Any idea when it will go live?

Hours later, Ellin was preparing to leave when her flex vibrated. She pulled it off her arm, firmed it, and read,

Sorry, your article's on hold.

In her three weeks on the job, Ellin had learned enough to know that *on hold* meant *rejected by the Screening Department.* Her article wasn't delayed; someone had thrown it in a digital rubbish bin.

Ellin's jaw and shoulders tensed. She drew in a breath and then let it out slowly, attempting to release her taut muscles. She wanted to stomp into Jovan's office, lean over his desk, and demand, "Do you have any idea how hard I worked on that article?" Of course, that would be stupid.

Not as stupid as being more pissed about his disrespect than about him foiling our plan to stop the end of the world. She almost laughed at herself. *Priorities, Ellin.*

An image of the expensive metal fence came into Ellin's mind, and she pictured a paper printout of her article, impaled on its spikes. What would people think if they knew a handful of Press Office employees were determining what the world watched and read about Merak Technologies?

Ellin glanced at the time on her deskscreen. She was late for dinner. Again. She grabbed her things and left.

The small dining hall was crowded, and she, Trett, and Rena had to share a table with three other interns. Ellin ate silently and quickly, mulling over her defeat. When Trett and Rena finished eating, she practically dragged them to her room, where she gave them the bad news.

Trett looked nearly as disappointed as Ellin felt, but Rena was sporting an odd smile.

"What is it, Rena?" Ellin asked.

"I had a vision. You need to go back to the Screening Department tonight. Your goal is to log into the system and send your article to a prominent newsorg. You know they'll publish it if it comes straight from that department."

Ellin was still staring at Rena. "Why do you look so . . . gleeful?"

"I'm not gleeful. It's . . . don't worry about it. It was a potential prophecy, and if you don't go back there, you'll be sitting in this room the day before the apocalypse, no closer to stopping it than you are now."

"I want to know what you saw!"

"Just go. You'll be fine. This is important." She wouldn't meet Ellin's eyes.

"There's something you're not telling me."

Rena pressed her lips together.

Ellin was used to Rena keeping some prophetic details to herself. Foreknowledge could change a person's reactions. Other times, Rena was incapable of sharing what she saw. Ellin understood it, but she didn't have to like it. She moved to her bed and sat on it. "Fine. But if Trett and I are going to be up in the middle of the night again, we'd better get some sleep."

"Trett's not going this time."

Ellin huffed. "I'm going to bed."

Despite her pronouncement, Ellin couldn't get to sleep until her normal bedtime, leaving her exhausted and cranky when she rose in the middle of the night. Trett was waiting outside her room with hot coffee. She gave him the best kiss they'd shared since their joint trip to the Press Office.

"That was . . . nice," Trett said when she pulled away.

"You brought me coffee at two in the morning. You're the nice one."

He looked at her thoughtfully. "Ellin," he began. He swallowed, then smiled. "You'll do great. Wish I could go with you."

Ellin got the feeling he'd been planning to say something else, but all he did was watch her drink her coffee. She gave him one more quick kiss, then left.

The security code still worked at the front door and the lift. *So far, so good.*

She sat before the same deskscreen she'd used before and entered the code. This time, an error message popped up. She retyped the code. No luck. She tried a second workstation, then a third, with the same results. Breaths coming faster, she entered the code on every workstation in the room—twice. It simply didn't work.

Ellin threw her hands up. *What kind of game is Rena playing?* She stomped back to the lift and took it to the lobby. As the doors opened, she released the frustrated groan she'd been suppressing. "That was pointless!"

From the darkness of the lobby outside the lift, a man's voice emerged. "Pointless, huh?"

Ellin froze. Nerves flooded her neck, arms, and hands with an electric tingle, and her muddled brain considered dashing past the man. Or should she close the lift doors, ascend one floor, and take the stairs down? Maybe she could even hide in a bathroom until morning.

The man in the lobby made her decision for her. His hand reached out of the darkness, grasping the edge of the lift door and preventing it from closing. Then the body connected to the hand stepped into view.

Ellin found herself staring at the friendly, smiling face of Alvun Merak.

15

SATURDAY, CYON 9, 6293

-28 DAYS

"Care to step out, and we'll chat?" Alvun Merak sounded like he was about to laugh.

Not seeing any other options, Ellin exited the lift. "I'd rather go back to my room, if that's okay."

Now he did laugh. "Not yet."

The lift doors closed, leaving them in near-darkness.

"Let's head to those chairs." Merak pointed to a corner of the lobby, lit by a dim emergency light.

Ellin followed him. Once they were seated, he held out his hand. "I'm Alvun Merak."

She shook his hand but didn't introduce herself.

"And you," he said, "are Ellin Havier."

She nodded. "How do you know my name?"

"Our security team saw you sneak in a few weeks ago." Merak pointed at the ceiling. "The cameras are too small to see, but they provide a high-resolution image. It didn't take long to identify you and Trett."

"Oh." Ellin scanned the lobby, hesitant to meet the eyes of the man who'd just caught her trespassing in one of his buildings. Her gaze fell on the lift, and an image flashed into her mind—her and Trett kissing, her hands tangled in his hair. "Oh—!" she said again, cursing the heat in her cheeks. "Did you—watch the videos?"

Merak laughed again. "It's okay, I was young once too."

Ellin forced herself to look at him. "Why didn't you send us home?"

"Our security team knows not to confront interns who break a few rules." Merak leaned back in his seat, his arms folded, the picture of relaxation. "We don't want you to do anything harmful, of course. We send interns home if they get into fights or vandalize property. However, the most successful corporation in the world needs employees with curiosity and determination. My goal is to convince you to focus such admirable character traits on improving Merak Technologies, rather than whatever your original motive was."

"That makes sense, I guess, but . . ." Ellin let out her breath in a *whoosh*. "Actually, no, it doesn't make sense."

"You may wonder why I'm the one confronting you in the middle of the night, rather than one of our excellent security staff."

"Yes. Yes, I was wondering that."

"I always keep apprised of what the current class of interns is doing. When talent comes our way, I want to put it to good use quickly before we lose that person to our competitors." Merak unfolded his arms and leaned forward, propping his elbows on his knees. "You've set yourself apart with your work in the Press Office. Over the last several weeks, you've made it to the top of Tereza's shortlist of the most promising interns."

Ellin's eyes widened. After the initial training session, she'd hardly seen Tereza. Apparently the head of the intern department was still keeping close tabs on them.

Merak continued, "When I realized the talented journalist I'd heard about was the same person they'd caught sneaking into the Screening Department, I asked to be notified if you were caught in any other clandestine activities." He chuckled. "I flew back in town last night—perfect timing, wouldn't you agree? I got the call from Security and jumped in my glidecraft to meet you here."

"How—great."

His expression, which had remained lighthearted until then, turned serious. "Ellin, why did you break into a Screening Department workstation?"

Break in. She immediately felt the same band that always tightened around her chest when she got in trouble—not that it happened often. She swallowed. Telling the truth had never steered her wrong before. She'd stick with that tactic as long as she could. "My boss wouldn't tell me what was on that floor. I was curious."

"How did you get a security code?"

"I, uh—I'm friends with an intern who has friends who are hackers." She immediately regretted the words. *Okay, maybe telling the truth isn't always the best plan.*

Oddly enough, Merak was smiling. "Too bad your friend's not the hacker; we can always use more of those." His cheerful expression disappeared, and his gaze, suddenly flinty, met hers. "Tell your friend we'll be watching network traffic from all the interns much more closely from here on out."

"Okay."

"Good." Cheerful Merak was back. "I want to hear about you. You're highly intelligent but not averse to breaking a few rules. It's an intriguing combination."

Ellin wanted to laugh. If only Merak knew how much she hated breaking rules. "What do you want to know?"

"Tell me about your life."

"Only if you'll tell me about yours too." She didn't know where that demand had come from.

Merak's eyebrows rose, and his mouth dropped open. He recovered his smile quickly. "Fair enough. You go first."

She told him the truth about her parents' deaths and about being raised by her sister. His mouth dropped as she spoke, and then he looked off to the side, wiping one eye. Ellin swallowed back her own emotion and pushed on, describing her scholastic achievements. However, she told him she'd graduated a year before, a story that lined up with her age on her fake ID.

When she finished, Ellin looked up at Merak. He was studying her, his brow furrowed.

"What?" she asked.

"Well, first—I don't know what to say about you losing your parents, except that I'm genuinely sorry."

All she could do was nod in response.

Merak cleared his throat, and his mouth broke into a gentle smile. "Second, I'm just trying to figure you out. The nerd who spent all her time studying comes to Merak Technologies and breaks into a building."

"I guess it was time to live a little." She laughed, hoping it didn't sound as forced as it felt. "Your turn. What's your story?"

"You saw the video and heard Tereza's presentation. You know my story."

"I know the version of your story you want interns to hear."

"True." His smirk told her he appreciated her pushing him. "You know I grew up with a single mother. What that video didn't disclose is who my father was. Mind you, this is something we've kept out of the media." He looked toward the lift. "Third floor, you know."

Ellin nodded, though his nonchalance about the Screening Department made her a little queasy.

Merak continued, "My father was a member of Vallinger's legislature. Don't try to identify him; you won't succeed. He was a rich, powerful, terrible man.

"My mother was one of his aides. When she became pregnant in an encounter I'm convinced was rape, the illustrious legislator fired her and paid her just enough each month to keep her alive." Merak paused, locking his gaze on Ellin's. All his lightheartedness had fled. "He used his influence to ensure my mother never got a decent job, and he prevented her from receiving public assistance. Between her meager wages cleaning hotel rooms and his tiny contribution, she barely managed to care for me.

"In the meantime, my father used his power as a legislator to line his own pockets and systematically abuse his staffers. He also attempted to roll back environmental regulations and put a halt to many public assistance programs. Thankfully, his efforts in those areas were ineffective. But he had a fantastic smile and a wonderful speaking voice, so the public reelected him over and over. Until . . ." Merak stopped talking and pressed his lips into a tight, closed-mouth smile.

"Until?" she asked.

"Until I had enough power to get him out of office." He leaned back, folding his arms. Several seconds later, he cleared his throat. "You okay, Ellin?"

She realized she'd been staring at him, trying to decipher him the same way she'd analyzed all the Cellerin Project research. She released another awkward chuckle. "Sorry. So . . . is that why you do so much charity work? To utilize your influence better than your dad did?"

"Yes." He uncrossed his arms, leaning forward again. "I want to prove to the world that it's possible to gain great power and use it in truly good ways."

"But—" Ellin sighed. "The Screening Department. It doesn't seem ethical."

Something flashed in Merak's eyes, but it disappeared almost immediately behind a mask of control. His voice was steady and friendly when he answered her. "It's not my goal to offend you, Ellin, but I think a fifty-three-year-old man who's spent his adult life making the world a better place knows more about ethics than a nineteen-year-old barely out of school."

She lifted her chin. "I'm not sure what age has to do with it."

That flash in his eyes again. It was sharp and dark, and it fled just as quickly as it had before.

"Do you know why we kill or modify newsorg stories?" Merak didn't give her a chance to respond, continuing, "My corporation and my foundation have both made our society healthier and happier. In the last twenty years, the average lifespan has increased from ninety-five to one hundred and six years old. Much of that is due to research supported by Merak Technologies and outright funded by the Merak Foundation. We've also inspired half a billion people to volunteer their time to help others."

He reached out. Ellin stiffened, thinking he was going to touch her shoulder, but he withdrew his hand before making contact. The intensity in his eyes didn't wane. "Ellin, we influence the media when we know the information they're about to release will harm this world instead of helping it. That's the only reason we ever step in."

Ellin couldn't keep herself from asking the question at the front of her mind. "Why would it have hurt the world to know about the dangerous radiation at the dig site in Therro?"

Merak stood from his seat and walked a few steps away, then turned back toward her. "Because the radiation isn't dangerous!" His voice had tripled in volume, and his hands gestured emphatically. "It will make our world a healthier place with medical advancements you can't even imagine. And we haven't announced this publicly yet, but I also have scientists researching how to convert it into a safe, immensely powerful source of energy. It's beneficial radiation, Ellin! I'm well aware that a few conspiratorial kooks want to get their names into news stories, but the world doesn't need to hear such nonsense!"

Merak had stepped closer to Ellin as he spoke, and now he stood over her. She combatted her twinge of intimidation by standing to face him. She squared her shoulders and lifted her chin, meeting his gaze. "I take it you read my article."

"I did. It was an extraordinarily well-written pile of rubbish."

Her mouth dropped open. *My research is sound!* she wanted to say. But how was she to convince the leader of the most successful company in the world that she understood the science of his pet project better than he did?

Ellin had been so convinced that if she worked hard, she'd stand out, and she'd earn enough respect to have clout. Then people would listen to her, and they'd cancel the dig. She'd succeeded her entire life through determination and by following the rules. Why wasn't it working now, when the stakes were higher than they'd ever been?

Merak inhaled deeply, released his breath, and, to Ellin's surprise, smiled warmly again. "Why don't we sit back down?" When they'd done so, he continued, "I apologize for my frustration, Ellin. I recognize you don't have access to all the available information. I'd like to share something with you."

He stood up just long enough to pull a folded flexscreen out of his back pocket. It was thinner than any Ellin had seen before, and when he firmed it, she leaned over to get a closer look. The screen resolution was incredibly sharp.

"Newest model, still in testing." Merak's eyes sparkled as he held his index finger over his lips. "Top secret, of course."

"Of course."

"M-Flex, open the interactive Tona sent me yesterday," Merak instructed the device. Then he handed the flex to Ellin. "Look at that and tell me if it changes your mind about the dig."

When Ellin tapped on the icon that had popped up, a three-dimensional diagram of an atom seemed to rise out of the screen. "Whoa!" she said.

With a delighted grin, Merak said, "This model uses small-scale Threed technology. Now, before you complain about the diagram, I know atoms don't really look like that. This is an oversimplification that any member of the public can understand. Play around with it; you'll get the hang of it."

He was right; the interface was remarkably intuitive. Ellin manipulated the atom diagram, looking at it from all sides. As she did so, a friendly, intelligent voice explained that it represented the beneficial radioactive isotope scientists expected to find at the Cellerin

Mountain dig site. Then the interactive took her through a presentation on the capacity this little atom had to change their world. The whole thing was slick and accessible, something the public would go wild over.

"We have a two-dimensional version of this for articles, as well as a non-interactive video version," Merak said. He quieted until Ellin met his gaze. "Do you see why we declined your article?"

"Yes."

She did see, but not in the way Merak meant. She was still confident in the research she'd done. Yet if she didn't know about the prophecy, she might have seen things differently. Merak honestly didn't know that the scientists advising caution were right—that they would, in fact, be horrified to know how accurate they were.

This pretty, three-dimensional interactive didn't convince her that the Cellerin Project's work was safe. It did, however, show her who Merak was. He wasn't just rich enough to pour money into technological research and charitable work. He was rich enough to purchase truth, or at least a counterfeit good enough to fool the world and himself.

"You look thoughtful," Merak said.

She handed the flexscreen back to him. "This is incredible," she said with perfect honesty.

Merak's smile told her he'd interpreted her words in the way most beneficial to him, just as she'd known he would. "I knew you'd be on my side—on the side of Merak Technologies and the side of the world —once we had a chance to talk. And I'm glad, because I want to bring you to Cellerin Mountain. I want you to be my press representative there."

Her mouth dropped open. "I haven't even been interning for a month."

"I know. I also know you've got what it takes. You'll have this whole Press Office behind you." He grinned. "Plus, if I transport you to the other side of the world, another company is less likely to recruit you."

"Okay, um—" She stopped, gathering her wits, not wanting to sound like the eager teenager she was. Merak was a businessman. Surely he admired tough negotiators. "I'm honored. I want to bring Trett with me. I'll be happier if he's around, and he's at least as smart as I am."

Merak responded, "Well—"

Ellin cut him off. "My friend Rena needs to come too. She's amazing with numbers; I know you could use someone like that in Therro."

Merak nodded slowly. "Rena's on Tereza's shortlist of effective interns, not too far below you. You're right, we could use some help on the accounting end of things in Therro. I'd be happy for her to come along."

"And Trett?"

He looked thoughtful. "Normally I'd say no. I don't want you to be distracted, but I get the feeling that's not a problem for you. Am I right, Ellin?"

She allowed herself a short laugh. "You could say that."

"Good." Merak sat up straight, all business. "I'm flying to Therro in two days. You and your friends can hitch a ride with me. My staff will em you the details." He stood. "I'll walk you out."

Ellin blinked twice. So this was how the owner of a massive company got things done. She might have trouble keeping up with him. She rose and followed Merak to the front door.

As Ellin walked toward the dorm, her eyes were pulled inexorably toward the tall fence, but it was lost in the blackness. She wrestled with an uncomfortable twist in her gut. Something told her that despite Merak's seeming openness and her own dissembling, he knew her far better than she knew him.

16

MONDAY, CYON 11, 6293

-26 DAYS

It was still the middle of the night when Ellin, Trett, and Rena arrived at Merak Technologies' private airport. Alvun Merak stood next to a solarplane, waiting for them.

Despite the hour, Merak greeted them with a cheerful "Good morning!" After introducing himself to Trett and Rena, he gestured to the plane. "Shall we go?" He pressed something on his flexscreen, and a section of the plane's side collapsed and reformed itself into a set of stairs descending to the runway.

Ellin's eyebrows lifted. "Nice."

Merak smiled. "Come on in."

The plane's interior was set up like a living room, though it was more tastefully luxurious than any home Ellin had ever visited. Merak sat on one end of a sofa and invited the rest of them to settle themselves wherever they felt comfortable. When they were all belted in, the plane took off.

Merak leaned forward, propping his elbows on his knees. With a wide smile, he asked, "What do the three of you know about Therro?"

"It's the birthplace of Anyarian civilization," Trett said.

Merak nodded. "I'm sure you can see why we were so excited to get this dig approved. We know there must be unfathomable archeological treasures, particularly around the mountain." He pulled out his flexscreen, firmed it, and said, "I'm sending each of you some information on the area and on the Cellerin Project. It'll keep you busy on the flight. I know you probably want to sleep, but with the time change, you'll be better off tonight if you don't."

By the time Ellin pulled her flexscreen off her arm and firmed it, a notification was waiting for her, informing her of the items Merak had shared. She glanced at Rena, whose screen showed the same files. Trett was already scrolling through his.

Somehow, Merak had access to all their flexscreens. Ellin pushed away the disturbing thought, then pulled up a video. She was about to play it when she realized she didn't have any earcaps. She didn't want to use the device's speakers in this relatively small space.

Rena didn't have any such qualms. She started a video, and the sound blared through her flex's speakers.

"Oh, I almost forgot," Merak said. He handed each of them a pair of brand-new, high-end earcaps. "My gift to you."

Ellin thanked him, placed the caps on her ears, and settled into her seat, starting up a documentary on the history of the Cellerin Mountain area. The video focused on cave dwellers who'd lived in the sides of the mountain thousands of years before. Some experts believed most of the dwellings hadn't even been discovered yet. No wonder Merak was so excited to dig there.

The Cellerin Mountain region of Therro was a welcome relief after the desert they'd been living in. There were green trees and grasses, and the temperature was mild. It was raining, but Merak had tossed a pop-up rainblock in the air above them as soon as they'd disembarked. The thin membrane hovered over him and his three guests as they walked from the tiny, private airport toward a group of buildings surrounded by open land.

Two caynins loped up to Merak, forked tongues lolling out of their mouths. He petted them both and said, "We have several guard caynins on the property. There's too much valuable information here not to protect it. Since you're with me, they know you're trustworthy. They'll take your scents back to the rest of the pack."

Merak pointed to several buildings. "I think you'll find our accommodations quite comfortable. The building on the right serves as lodging for many of those working on this project."

"Is it a hotel?" Rena asked.

"No, it's private. We purchased this land five years ago. That's how long it took us to get approval to dig." Merak pointed again. "The building next to it is where we're headed. It's the research center. It'll be an hour or so before they close for the day, and I'd like to introduce you to some of the scientists."

Ellin looked to her left, where Cellerin Mountain rose far into the sky. Unlike most large mountains on Anyari, it was freestanding, not part of a range. Ellin felt tiny in its shadow. It was an inspiring sight, and she could see why people trained for months or years to climb to the top.

She yawned. Despite her lack of sleep, her mind was whirring amid all the newness. She'd never dreamed she'd travel halfway around the world like this, at least not at such a young age. Even the reason behind it didn't stifle her excitement.

They arrived at the research center, and Merak held the door open. Ellin entered first.

The receptionist at the front desk looked up, his gaze sharp and wary. "May I help you?"

"Uh—" Ellin looked behind her, relieved to see Merak coming in.

"Oh, Mr. Merak!" The receptionist stood. "Welcome."

Merak's face lit with his signature smile. "Thanks, Misha. I brought three of our most promising interns with me. All right if I take them on a tour?"

"Of course!" The receptionist touched his deskscreen, and the door behind him clicked.

Merak opened the door. "Appreciate it, Misha." He led them through the halls to a large room full of research equipment and workstations. "This is our lab. We have scientists here that specialize in so many areas, I can't keep track of them all. Pardon me, Aline?"

A woman at one of the workstations turned, brows raised in response.

"What's your specialty again?" Merak asked.

"Weather alteration," she responded.

"Oh, right!" Merak looked at Ellin, Rena, and Trett. "Ever heard of that?" When they all shook their heads, he laughed. "That's because it's a field in its infancy. Mark my words: in the next decade, we'll see massive changes in how we respond to weather—and how it responds to us."

"The Cellerin Project will help with that?" Ellin asked.

"We hope so. I brought several of my foundation's top researchers here, including Aline. It's an incredible brain trust, all in one place."

"That it is," Aline said. "Can I get back to work?"

"Of course." Merak looked at Ellin and lifted an eyebrow, his eyes twinkling. "She's nearly as determined as you are."

He led them to a workstation on the right side of the room. The man sitting there stood and faced them.

"Welcome, Mr. Merak," the man said, holding out his hand.

"Efren, good to see you." Merak shook his hand. "Ellin, Rena, and Trett, this is Dr. Rouven, a medical researcher. We were lucky enough to lure him away from his position at a prestigious university. He's been behind some remarkable advances in public health. Dr. Rouven, do you mind showing these interns your latest research? Ellin here is our new, full-time Cellerin Project press representative. Don't hold back on the details; she'll want them all." Merak grinned at Ellin, and she couldn't help but smile back.

"Of course," Dr. Rouven said. "Grab some chairs and gather around."

Ellin took off her jacket and draped it on the back of a swivel chair, then rolled the chair close enough to see Dr. Rouven's deskscreen. Trett and Rena did the same.

"I have business to attend to, but I'll send someone to take you to your rooms at the end of the work day," Merak said. He pivoted and left the room.

Using high-quality interactives, Dr. Rouven explained the technology that allowed them to tame harmful radiation, making it beneficial without compromising its efficacy. He was an enthusiastic teacher who explained advanced concepts with simple clarity.

"This is the same technology we use throughout the world in hospitals and clinics," Dr. Rouven said. "We have every reason to believe the new isotope hiding in Cellerin Mountain will be even more effective than the ones we're currently using. The radioactivity here is stronger, but our technology can handle it."

Rena had started squirming half an hour in, but Ellin was captivated, and she thought Trett was too. "Have you tested it yet?" Ellin asked.

"We've scanned the radiation emanating from the dig site," Dr. Rouven said, "but the medical devices will only work once we get our hands on the source of the radiation. We haven't been able to recreate the isotope in the lab. In fact, we haven't even identified it with any level of certainty. When we dig far enough to harvest the radioactive substance, we'll begin the first phases of testing. It'll be some time before we do any human trials; Mr. Merak always insists that we follow the highest safety standards."

He continued to talk, becoming even more animated as he shared statistics of how many lives the new radiation might save.

When a young man entered to show them to their rooms, Ellin looked at the clock, unable to believe an hour had passed. She smiled at Dr. Rouven and thanked him.

As they followed Merak's employee out of the building, Ellin caught Rena watching her with raised eyebrows, reproach written all over her face. Ellin looked away, but she took the warning to heart. As good as Dr. Rouven's intentions might be, the man was wrong, to a terrifying extent.

Ellin's room was well appointed and comfortable. A workstation waited for her with a top-of-the-line deskscreen. The screen was glowing, and there was a message on it:

> I don't expect you to work in your room, but I'm guessing you will anyway. This'll make it easier.

> -Alvun Merak

Ellin shook her head. *Is he kind, or is he manipulating me into working nonstop?* Either way, she wasn't complaining. It was a really nice deskscreen.

She walked to the bed and sat. It was insanely comfortable, and she lay down and closed her eyes. *Just for a minute or two.*

The next thing she knew, the flexscreen on her arm vibrated, waking her.

Blinking, Ellin pulled her flex off her arm, firmed it, and found twenty messages from Rena, all sent within the past three minutes, each one reading,

DINNER TIME!

Ellin sent a terse response assuring Rena she'd be ready soon.

As she got up, Ellin heard something crinkle in the pocket of her light jacket. She reached in and pulled out a slip of paper, folded in fourths.

Paper? She rarely used paper and had no idea how this piece had ended up in her pocket. She unfolded it and found a note.

I know what Dr. Rouven told you, and I think you should hear the other side.

Meet me at the walking path behind the dining hall after dinner. You can bring your friends if you feel more comfortable. Don't talk to them about this note. You never know who's listening.

Tear this up and drop it in the dining hall compost bin.

The note wasn't signed.

Ellin tore the paper into tiny pieces and put them in her pocket. In the hallway, she met Rena and Trett. They walked to the dining hall behind their new lodgings, passing two Merak security guards along the way. As instructed, Ellin dropped the note in the compost bin as she entered.

The food was even better than what they'd eaten at Merak headquarters. Afterward, Ellin suggested a walk.

"I think that's a very, very good idea," Rena said, giving her sister and Trett a significant look.

Ellin stifled a laugh, and they exited the back of the building.

It was getting dark, but solar-powered lights lit the walking path. They walked for several minutes before encountering a man and a woman.

"Hi, Ellin," the woman said. She was tall and appeared to be in her forties. She had very curly hair, a warm smile, and orange eyes that reflected the dim light. Ellin felt somehow that she'd met her before, though she knew that was unlikely.

"Trett and Rena, right?" the woman continued. "I'm Nomi. I was in the research room today."

"Oh," Ellin said. She hadn't noticed the woman and tried to keep her confusion off her face.

Nomi smiled. "It's okay, I didn't expect you to see me. I've learned to keep my head down around this place." She gestured to the man, who appeared to be in his late twenties. He couldn't have looked more different from Nomi. He was short, with stick-straight hair. "This is Dr. Septimus. You can call him Sep. We both appreciate you meeting us."

"Meeting you?" Trett asked.

Ellin told him and Rena about the note, adding, "I wasn't sure when it was safe to say anything."

"The two of us have been meeting on this path for weeks," Nomi said. "We don't think it's monitored. And the security guards never seem to come back here."

"What did you want to tell us?" Rena asked.

"Let's walk." Nomi led the way and began her explanation. "As I said, I'm Nomi, but around camp, they call me Dr. Anson. I work in the same field as Dr. Rouven: medical radiation research."

"What about you, Sep?" Trett asked.

The question seemed to startle Sep. "Oh—uh, I research ancient civilizations." He flashed them a shy smile.

"As I said in my note," Nomi continued, "now that Dr. Rouven has given you his take on our research, you need to hear the other side of things."

She spent a few minutes explaining her concerns about the safety of the dig-site radiation. "Dr. Rouven is convinced we can modify our current technology to make this radiation safe. I don't think we have enough information to determine that."

"Has anyone involved with the Cellerin Project had any health issues?" Trett asked.

"No, but the safety standards here are top-notch. Our sensors detected the radiation on the first day of the dig. Since then, every person in the vicinity of the project wears an antirad. It completely neutralizes the radiation in a field around the wearer."

"What do Merak and Rouven think about your concerns?" Ellin asked.

"Rouven disagrees with me, and Merak listens to Rouven. In fact, a few weeks ago, I was convinced I was about to be fired. I've played the ideal employee since then. I marvel over Dr. Rouven's research and claim to agree with it. Then I do my real research in secret, on a second flex that I only use in the city. I'm pretty sure Merak isn't monitoring me off campus."

"Wait." Ellin stopped walking, and the rest of the group followed suit. "This sounds very . . . clandestine, for lack of a better term. Why do you trust us?"

Nomi gave her a small, closed-mouth smile. "Before you came, Merak messaged your article—the one that never got printed—to Dr. Rouven and me. He instructed us both to do all we could to convince you of the truth. I suppose you could say I'm just following instructions."

"I want to tell the world what I've found in my research," Ellin said, "but they'll never print anything I write that questions their official stance."

"I know. Still, I'm glad to know there are people here who *want* to get the word out. Perhaps by working together, we can find a way."

"I still don't understand why Sep is here," Rena said.

Ellin swung her gaze toward her sister. *Blunt as ever.*

Sep just nodded. "Well, uh, since we're all stopped here, I guess I should . . . show you what I've found?" He looked to Nomi for confirmation, and when she nodded, he pulled a flexscreen case out of his pocket.

Once he'd unfolded the screen and firmed it, he said, "I have, well, a secret flex. Just like Nomi. It's not connected to the network right now; I'll only show you things I've saved on the device."

"I have a secret flex too," Rena said.

Ellin swiveled her head to gape at Rena and saw that Trett had done the same.

Rena returned their stares. "What did you think I was doing in the city the day before we left, getting my nails done? You said Merak was keeping us under tighter surveillance. I was afraid his people would hack our encryption."

Ellin shook her head and shifted her attention back to Sep. "I'd love to see what you found."

Sep clicked something on his flex, and his mouth broadened into a smile. "Did you know that where we're standing isn't just the birthplace of Anyarian civilization, it's also the birthplace of Anyarian poetry?" While his voice was still soft, his words now flowed smoothly. "In the early centuries after the colonists arrived, they had no way to write things down, beyond some paintings in caves and a few engravings on tablets. They focused on surviving, not rediscovering the art of papermaking. However, they developed a rich oral history which they preserved through rhyming, epic poetry. Later, their descendants wrote much of it down.

"Of course," he continued, "language has evolved significantly since the colonists came. I've studied various dialects spoken by early Anyarians in order to evaluate other scholars' translations and determine which are most accurate. Let me read you a passage:

"The air is warm
The grass is long
Come listen, child
To an ancient song—"

"Sep?" Nomi interrupted, giving him a warm smile. "We don't have all night."

"Oh. Sorry. I'll try to make a long song short." He winked, which made Trett laugh, before continuing, "Among the oldest of the preserved poems is a tale of the tragedy that befell the colonists as they journeyed to Anyari. Some sort of stone penetrated their ship, disabling it and killing most of the colonists."

"Pardon me." Trett raised a hand, getting Sep's attention. When Sep nodded, Trett continued, "I'm sorry to interrupt. I know this is your field, but . . . we've all heard stories about a space rock disabling the colony ship and killing most of the passengers. I always thought it was just one of many hypotheses."

Ellin nodded in agreement. "Our science teacher last year said the plague hypothesis is far more reasonable, because an interstellar vessel would've been very well shielded. Even Anyarian spacecrafts have decent shields, and they've never exited the solar system."

Sep nodded, eyes sparkling in the dim light. "Good questions—very good! Most scientists agree with you, because they see no way that a *space rock*, as Trett called it, could stop a group of humans capable of traveling through the stars.

"Yet historians and scientists tend to differ on this point. You see, we only find plague tales in later writings. The earliest writings talk about a stone. While the colony ship would surely have effectively shielded against *ordinary space rock*, the early writings describe something quite *extraordinary*." He began to navigate through his flex again, then froze and looked up at everyone. "This may take a while."

"We can sit on some benches around the next bend," Nomi said.

"That's right! I'll find the next passage while we walk."

Sep accompanied Nomi down the path, fingers flying across his flex as he walked. Ellin, Trett, and Rena exchanged shrugs and followed.

They sat on the benches, and Ellin saw movement in her peripheral vision. When she looked that direction, she saw a knee-high reptid creature sitting on its hind legs, the nearby lantern reflecting off the basket-weave texture of its shiny, bright-blue skin. Its compound eyes were reflective silver, and Ellin would swear they were fixed on her. "Is—is that thing safe?" she murmured.

Nomi laughed. At the sound, the animal fled. "It's a shimshim," Nomi said. "Native to Therro. They're plant eaters, perfectly safe—though if you're eating a salad outside, one of them might leap on your lap to share it with you."

"I'll remember not to have any salad picnics," Ellin said.

Sep cleared his throat and brought their attention back to the ancient writings. He read them passages about two stones: the one that had supposedly caused such destruction to the colony ship, and another that was special to the colonists. The terms used to describe both stones were often identical, leading Sep to believe they were one and the same.

"Listen to this!" he exclaimed.

"The stone did shine
With vivid light
Brightening
The darkest night.

"As seasons passed
Its heat did grow
Melting winter's
Ice and snow."

Sep looked up. "You see? The colonists' stone became luminescent, then hot. Other poems tell us that eventually, those who handled it developed burns. Several grew sick and died."

"That sounds . . . radioactive," Ellin said.

"Precisely! One poem describes the deaths with quite gruesome language. Let me find it . . . Ah, here it is.

"Skin turned white
As winter snow.
From mouths and eyes
Red blood did flow."

Ellin's and Trett's heads both swiveled to stare at Rena, but she kept her gaze on Sep, her expression blank.

Nomi leaned forward. "You see why Sep's research is vital?"

Nobody answered. Ellin was still reeling from the poem. She scrambled for something to say, finally settling on, "Why wouldn't they get rid of this stone as soon as it started hurting them?"

"They did eventually, in a way," Sep said. "We aren't entirely sure why they waited so long. My favorite hypothesis is based on a passage describing a young boy who stood close to the stone." He found it quickly and read,

"The lad went home
Where he did see
With inner eyes
What was to be."

Sep looked up. "Did you catch that? He saw *what was to be.* Some historians believe this stone brought the gift of prophecy to Anyari. Perhaps it gave foresight to a few people, and the colonists didn't want to destroy it, lest that eradicate the seers' powers."

"Hold on, hold on." Rena held up both hands. "I've read a few books about seers."

Ellin coughed at her sister's straight-faced usage of *a few*.

Rena ignored Ellin. "For all we know, Earth had seers too. I've read stories about a stone that created the first seers, but most scholars consider those tales purely mythological."

Sep shrugged. "It's merely one possibility. What's important is that the colonists seem to have hidden the stone rather than destroying it. Perhaps they hoped to protect the seers' gifts. Perhaps they had another reason. Whatever the colonists' rationale, dozens of ancient epics refer to a dangerous stone being hidden in a large mountain, almost certainly Cellerin Mountain. Here's my favorite."

He found the reference and read aloud,

"We placed the stone
Within a cell
Past countless rocks
We hid it well."

Sep leaned closer to Rena. "Does that remind you of anything?"

Rena's bland expression didn't change.

Ellin wet her lips. "Can I see that, Sep?"

He handed her his flex.

"I've read more on the Cellerin Project than Trett or Rena," Ellin said. "The object emanating radiation is in a cave. That could be what the *cell* is referring to in your poem, right?" Seeing Sep's excited nod, she continued, "And here, where it says *past countless rocks*—I remember seeing that the cave is covered by a massive mound of loose stones."

"Precisely," Sep said.

Ellin handed the flex back. "Even if this radioactive isotope has a long half-life, it has to be weaker now than it was then. It's been thousands of years. Wouldn't we expect the radiation to be manageable, especially with our modern technology?"

"That's why I call this stone *extraordinary*," Sep said. "The stories are clear: the stone became more dangerous as time went on. It was always a warm, luminescent stone, but the light and heat grew more intense as time passed. By the time the colonists hid it, it was so hot, they had to wrap it in animal skin before handling it."

"That's not how radiation works," Trett said. "I'm not an expert, but I've gotten some pretty good tutoring in the subject lately." He grinned at Ellin. "Radiation gets weaker, not stronger, unless something like sunlight causes a reaction to make more of the isotope."

"I'll address that," Nomi said. "You're right; radiation loses strength as time goes on. I would've written off the old poetry as a silly myth if it weren't for the readings my colleagues have been taking at the dig site. The radioactivity of whatever's in that cave increases daily."

"How do Dr. Rouven and the others explain that?" Trett asked.

"They're falling over themselves trying to figure it out," Nomi said. "Perhaps it's faulty software; perhaps it's because we're moving stones out of the way; perhaps the measuring equipment is creating microfissures in the stone, allowing more radiation to escape.

"The thing is, none of their hypotheses make sense. The on-site researchers aren't even touching the area close to the cave yet. They're taking measurements from a small vent in the base of the pile of stones, using noninvasive sensors. The numbers are sound. Yet they're unwilling to consider there may be some artifact that doesn't fit our current scientific knowledge."

Ellin's mind had been spinning as Sep and Nomi spoke, and she found her mouth was suddenly dry. She swallowed and asked, "How old do you think these poems are, Sep?"

"They were first written approximately three hundred years after the colonists arrived on Anyari. Furthermore, we have reason to believe they were all transcribed from older oral tradition. You see—"

Ellin held up her hand, quieting him. "That's helpful, Sep, and I'm sorry to interrupt. I want to make sure I have this right. Six thousand years ago, when colonists arrived on Anyari, some weirdly radioactive stone was killing people. And it's been getting stronger every day since then?"

Nomi locked eyes with Ellin. "Precisely—if we're correct, and I believe we are. I hope to gather enough evidence to stop the dig. Our second step will be neutralizing the isotope. I'm already researching the best ways to do so, preferably from a distance so we don't have to resume excavations."

Everyone was silent.

Ellin took Trett's hand. She swallowed hard. "I think I can speak for all of us. Our goals are the same as yours, and we'll do whatever we can to stop this dig."

Nomi and Sep both smiled, and then Nomi stood and shocked Ellin by giving her a tight hug. She did the same to Trett and Rena.

They began walking back. Trett and Rena asked the researchers questions, but Ellin was silent. Something about Nomi was still niggling at her. She still seemed familiar.

Nomi looked back, then slowed to match Ellin's pace. "You okay?" she asked.

In that question, Ellin realized what her subconscious had recognized the minute she'd met this woman: Nomi reminded her of her mother. Ellin's mom would always ask "You okay?" with a gentle smile similar to Nomi's. And Ellin got the feeling not many people could match Nomi's intelligence, but her mother could have.

Ellin's mother hadn't been perfect. Her overprotectiveness toward Rena had harmed the whole family. She'd been brave, though, a woman who fiercely fought for what she believed was right. Maybe Ellin was projecting too much onto this woman she'd just met, but she thought Nomi would do whatever it took to stop Merak.

A certain lightness filled Ellin's heart, even as a familiar ache gripped it. "I'm okay."

17

FRIDAY, CYON 15, 6293

-22 DAYS

"I THOUGHT I was the only one who worked this late."

Startled, Ellin spun around in her chair. "Mr. Merak!"

Ellin was working in the same large room they'd visited upon their arrival four days ago, and now Merak was standing in the doorway. He smiled at Ellin and entered. The only other person in the room was Nomi. Merak greeted her as he walked by her workstation.

When he reached Ellin, Merak pulled up a chair. "How do you like working in here with all the scientists? We can get you a quieter space if you'd prefer."

Ellin shook her head. "Oh no, this is great. I hear them discussing their research, and it helps me understand the project." She also liked working close to Nomi, being reminded that someone else disapproved of the dig.

"And your friends?" Merak asked. "Are they enjoying their work here?"

"Rena loves the accounting office, and Trett's doing okay." She didn't mention that Rena was more competent than every other employee in her department or that Trett, who was on a team that ordered supplies for their small community, hated being "waist-deep in sheets and shampoo."

"Excellent," Merak said. "What were you working on just now?"

She swallowed. *No need to be nervous; you've talked to him before. He's just one of the most powerful men in the world.* "I've written a few stories on the dig, but this morning, the Press Office asked me to work on a follow-up to an article I wrote back at head-quarters. I just finished it."

He nodded encouragingly. "What's the topic?"

"Your foundation's efforts to make cancer treatment more affordable."

"Can I read what you've got so far?"

He wants me to sit and watch while he reads what I wrote? Heart beating wildly, Ellin rolled her chair to the side so Merak could sit in front of her screen. She watched his face as he read. *He's smiling. That's got to be a good sign. Wait, the smile's gone. He just raised his eyebrows. What does that mean? He hates it. I knew he would hate it!*

When Merak finished, he turned toward Ellin, folded his arms, and leaned back against his seat, his brown eyes fixed on her. She was about to blurt out something about still needing to proofread it when he spoke. "You're very talented."

She gaped, then felt herself smile, even as her face grew warm.

Merak returned the smile. "The article needs one more thing, though." He turned back to her workstation and began typing.

Ellin barely resisted the urge to lean over and read what he was writing.

He stopped typing, a thoughtful expression on his face, then resumed. At last, he said, "There you go." He rolled his chair to the side.

Ellin returned to her workstation, found the paragraph he'd added, and started reading it out loud. "*In a recent interview, Alvun Merak said . . .*" She turned to Merak. "So I interviewed you, did I?"

He chuckled. "Lucky you; I don't usually grant interviews to interns." He pointed at the screen. "I gave you a good quote."

Ellin scanned the quote, which was full of the type of hope that would make readers open their hearts and maybe even their bank accounts. "You're right, this is just what the article needed. Thank you."

Merak's face broke into a warm smile as he stood. "Don't work too late. The dining hall will close soon." He gave her shoulder a squeeze, then left.

Ellin began proofreading, but she was only on the third paragraph when Nomi walked over and sat in the same chair Merak had just vacated. "Seems he's taken a liking to you," Nomi said with a smile.

"I'm not sure why."

"Probably because, as an unpaid intern, you work harder than most of his salaried employees."

Ellin laughed. "That could be it."

Nomi leaned forward. "You know, Ellin, if you continue building up trust with Alvun Merak, he might actually listen to your concerns about the dig. He wrote me off almost as soon as I got here. He sees me as a pessimist, and there's no place for such people in his company. But you—you might get somewhere with him."

"I tried talking to him back at the headquarters—"

"I know." Nomi placed her hand on Ellin's. "Just because he didn't listen to you then doesn't mean he won't now. You're impressing him, and for good reason. You're doing a great job here." She let go of Ellin's hand and stood. "Hang on, my flex is buzzing." She pulled it out of her pocket and firmed it. "Oh, thank goodness, it's my wife. Our schedules haven't synced up all week, until now. I'm going to chat with her in my room."

"I'm sure you miss her," Ellin said.

"I'm sure you miss your family too." Nomi waved and left.

Ellin turned back to her screen, but it was blurry. She tried to blink her tears away, but they kept coming.

What's wrong with me? I guess I'm just tired.

She knew it wasn't that, though. Her eyes drifted to the doorway Nomi had just walked through. For the last four days, Nomi had continued to remind Ellin of her mother every time they interacted.

Then there was Merak. The way he'd given her that proud look and said, "You're very talented"—it was exactly the sort of thing Ellin's dad used to say.

Ellin's chest ached with longing, and her tears turned to sobs. She gave in to the emotion, burying her face in her hands.

She relived the weeks after the Skytrain crash, allowing herself to picture the awful images that had flashed on wallscreens everywhere. Twisted metal. Smoking train cars. Helpless emergency workers.

When she'd had enough of those nightmarish memories, she imagined what it would be like to still have two overprotective, proud parents, to be able to pull out her flex right now and have a video chat with them. To see their faces and hear their voices.

When the tears had run their course, Ellin pulled out a handkerchief and blew her nose. *How pitiful am I, losing my grip on my emotions, all because two friendly adults remind me of my parents? Why am I grieving right now, anyway?*

She was pretty sure she knew the answer to that last question. She was grieving because she was lonely. *I see Trett every day, but I'm lonelier than I've ever been.*

Ellin thought about Nomi's reaction to the message from her wife. Nomi had lit up, thrilled to connect with the person she loved.

Why don't I react that way when Trett ems me?

There were plenty of reasons. *I'm driven, that's all. Or I'm just not that sentimental. Really, who can blame me for being extra focused when we're trying to save the world?*

All her explanations felt like excuses. The truth was, she'd always been like this, and she had no idea why. Ellin took a deep breath and allowed painful thoughts to enter her consciousness, ones she'd been suppressing for weeks now:

Maybe I don't have what it takes to be in a relationship.

Maybe something is truly broken between Trett and me.

Maybe it's me who's broken.

She looked at the clock. Dinner was over. Trett had probably grabbed some food for her. She pulled her flex off her arm and checked her ems. Sure enough, Trett had tried to contact her.

The first em read,

Hey, you coming to dinner?

Half an hour later, he'd written,

I got you a sandwich.

Five minutes ago, the last em had arrived.

Going for a run. I'll be back in my room in half an hour or so.

Ellin propped her elbows on the workstation and pressed her forehead into the heels of her hands, unwilling to submit again to her tears. She took a few deep breaths, then shut down her deskscreen and emmed Trett.

On my way to my room. Thanks for the sandwich; I'll pick it up it when you get back.

She read the message over, then swallowed and added,

Sorry I missed your ems. Sorry I missed dinner. Again.

18

WEDNESDAY, CYON 20, 6293

-17 DAYS

"Tea and chocolate-spiced coffee?"

Trett smiled as he looked up at the server who'd approached the table. "I guess we're here too often if you already know our orders." He confirmed the drink he wanted, as did Ellin.

Ellin's flexscreen buzzed, and she glanced at it. "Rena says she's on her way."

The three interns had been in Therro for nine days. Nearly every night after dinner, they checked out hovs (provided by Merak) and drove into the nearby city of Krenner, which was only ten clommets from their temporary home. In the little coffee shop, they discussed strategies without too much fear of being monitored or overheard by Merak's people. Nomi and Sep often joined them.

Trett watched Ellin. Her head was bent over her flex, and frown lines compressed her forehead. Several days earlier, something had shifted in her demeanor toward him. The distance he'd been sensing

146

between them had yawned into a massive valley, and he had no idea why.

We've got to talk, he told himself. *I've gone over this conversation enough times in my mind; why am I waiting?* He opened his mouth, then shut it. *Not now. She's too distracted. Let's see what happens in seventeen days.*

Then he thought about what would happen if they failed in their quest. Did he really want to spend the last two-and-a-half weeks of his life observing his girlfriend's misery, unable to help because he was afraid of having a hard conversation?

The server brought their drinks. Ellin stopped the work she was doing on her flexscreen and reached out for her coffee. Trett grabbed her hand before it reached her mug.

Ellin looked at him across the table, her eyebrows raised.

"Let's talk," Trett said quietly.

"Right now?" With her free hand, she gestured to her flexscreen. "I'm in the middle of something."

In contrast to her annoyed tone, her expression was vulnerable. Scared. Trett tamped down his first instinct, which was to back off. This was too important. "I think we can both spare five minutes. Right?"

"I guess so. Should Rena be here for this?"

"Definitely not." Trett gave her a half-smile, but he knew it looked forced. He took a deep breath and rushed forward. "Are you happy? With us?"

"Us?"

"Us. You and me."

"We've been a little busy to think about *us* lately, haven't we?"

"I know we've been busy, Ellin." Her hand was tense under his, so he pulled his away. "In fact, I wasn't going to talk to you until this is all over, assuming things end well. But I—" He stopped, and all the words he'd planned fled. He took a deep breath. "I've been thinking. This thing we're doing, trying to save the world . . . it's like a test. I want to know—I *need* to know—if we can make it through together."

"What are you talking about? We're doing our best to make it through. And"—Ellin pointed at him, then at herself—"we're together."

"We're not together, not really!" Trett's voice was quiet but intense. "We're basically coworkers. We're barely even acting like friends."

Ellin leaned across the table. She had tears in her eyes, and her quiet voice was shrill, bordering on panicked. "I'm working nonstop to be sure we actually have the chance to be friends for more than seventeen more days. I just need you to be patient. As soon as we stop Merak, we'll go back to how we were before."

"I don't think you get it, Ellin." His limbs ached with the desire to get up out of his chair, pull her close, and bring the awful conversation to a halt. But he owed it to them both to be honest for once. His eyes filled with tears, and he forced the words out through a tight throat. "I don't want to go back to how we were before. It was the same back home as it is here. I love how driven you are, Ellin. I do! You know my parents, though. They're basically roommates who hardly ever see each other. I've always wanted more than that for myself—and for you. Back home, I kept telling myself that you just needed to graduate, or meet your career goals, and you'd finally be able to relax enough to enjoy our relationship. Now, I . . . I'm afraid that's never going to happen. Please tell me I'm wrong."

Ellin's chin trembled. "Are you saying you want me to give up my goals for you?"

"No!" Trett's response was immediate and passionate. He started to reach out, but Ellin withdrew, pressing against her chair. He pulled his hand back to his lap and closed his eyes for a moment, trying to find the right words. When he opened his eyes, Ellin was wiping her nose with a napkin. "I don't want you to give up your goals," Trett said. "They're part of you, and I care about you, all of you. What I want is for us to help each other fulfill our dreams. And I want to pursue each other with as much passion as we pursue our goals. If we don't, I'm not sure what the point is."

Tears ran down both Ellin's cheeks. "We might not even be alive in seventeen days, Trett. We have to stay the course."

"We might not be alive tomorrow."

She swallowed.

Trett continued, "We're not guaranteed anything. Ever. All I'm asking is that we make the most of every day, no matter how many we have left. Let's fight Merak with all we have—but let's fight for us too."

Ellin wiped away a tear that was making its way down her cheek. "I don't know how to do that."

"We can figure it out together."

"I—" A sob interrupted Ellin's attempt to talk.

Trett watched as she took several shuddering breaths. He didn't reach out to her, certain she wouldn't react to it well, but holding back caused him physical pain. Other people in the café glanced at them, then looked away.

After a couple of minutes, Ellin tried again. "Last week, I realized there's something . . . something wrong with me." She stopped, drawing in a deep breath and blowing it out slowly. "I want to treat you the way you treat me," she continued, "and I honestly don't know how. I don't want to be so focused on the things I'm doing that I can't even remember to read your ems or meet you at dinner, but . . . *I don't know how to stop that.* I've tried so hard. I can't get it right, Trett. I can't." Another sob escaped, and she covered her mouth.

"We can figure it out—" Trett began.

Ellin shook her head hard and took her hands away from her mouth. Her sobs suddenly halted, though her cheeks were still wet, and pain filled her eyes. "I've tried to figure it out for three years. I can't ask you to keep waiting for me."

"I'm willing—"

"No, Trett." Her voice was soft. "If we stop this thing in seventeen days—and we will—you deserve someone who will treat you as well as you treat her."

Trett stared at her, suddenly very aware of his own breathing. "What are you saying?" he whispered.

Just then, Rena walked up. Ellin gave her sister a look that would wither a houseplant.

Rena looked between them. "Looks like I'm interrupting something."

Ellin said, "It's okay, we—" She looked at Trett. Her brows knitted in grief, and she pressed her lips tightly together. She didn't take her eyes off him as she said softly, "We were just breaking up, Rena."

"Ellin—" Trett said.

She reached out and took his hand. "I'm sorry. For everything."

Rena sat. "Weird timing for a breakup."

Trett and Ellin were silent.

Ellin's flex was on the table in front of her, and her eyes were pointed downward, but she wasn't focused on the article on the screen. She wanted desperately to flee the awkwardness of this stupid café and lock herself in her room, but she forced herself to wait. Nomi and Sep should be arriving any minute, and she had an update for them.

I just broke up with Trett.

The thought brought another lump into her throat. She'd considered bringing up their relationship at least ten times in the past few days, but she'd never had the courage to do it. Why had Trett, the chronic avoider of tough conversations, chosen that moment to initiate a discussion?

Whatever his reasons, she'd known she couldn't give him any false promises about how she'd be a better girlfriend for the next seventeen days and beyond. It had taken a lot for him to confront her. He deserved the truth.

The truth is, I can do advanced math and write impressive news articles, but cultivating a healthy relationship is beyond me.

She wondered how he was taking it, so she risked a glance up. He was watching her, misery written across his face. Ellin blinked several times as she looked down again, shame melding with her grief.

A few minutes later, Nomi and Sep walked in. Sep sat across from Rena, and Nomi pulled up a chair next to Ellin.

"Didn't think I'd make it tonight; I was stuck analyzing some data with Rouven," Nomi said. "I convinced him I had cramps and needed to head home." She smiled at them all, then seemed to pick up on the atmosphere at the table. Her expression turned serious, and she turned to Ellin. "You okay?"

Ellin nodded. Nomi didn't look convinced.

Rena leaned toward Nomi, her expression intense. "Anything new on your end?"

Nomi didn't answer immediately. Her eyes were still on Ellin. When Ellin didn't volunteer any more information, Nomi addressed the whole table. "Unfortunately, I do have an update." Before she could say more, the server arrived.

"Nothing today, thank you," Sep said softly when the server offered to take their order.

Nomi continued, "The workers have been moving the stones blocking the cave, but they weren't permitted to uncover the cave itself, pending some ecological studies and a government approval. Today, that approval came through."

That pulled Ellin out of her introspective silence. "I can't believe I didn't hear about this!"

"The news came in after you left." Nomi sighed and looked between Ellin, Rena, and Trett. "This isn't good. It means they'll pick up the pace, and they'll probably reach the cave in two or three weeks. Please tell me the three of you are making some progress."

For the last week, Ellin, Rena, and Trett had been working on a project in this little coffee shop. Rena had reached out to her hacker friend, seeking message records of publishing executives around the world. As information came in, she shared it with Ellin and Trett, who'd both purchased cheap, used flexscreens to use on public networks in the city of Krenner.

All three of them had spent hours searching IDMs and ems from various executives, looking for anything negative indicating someone in the press might stand up to Merak. When they found keywords like "Merak," "Therro," and "Cellerin," they dug deeper.

Grateful to have something to focus on besides Trett, Ellin spoke up. "We did find something useful. I have to say, though, it makes me feel dirty, looking through people's personal messages."

Rena rolled her eyes, but Nomi gave Ellin an understanding smile. "You're doing the right thing, even if it doesn't feel like it."

"I hope you're right. Anyway, we've found plenty of communications about the Cellerin Project. Most of the execs are obviously in Merak's pocket, but I did see something promising yesterday. It's between the owner of Rayson Media and his wife."

She pulled up a message thread on the buggy old flex she'd been using and breathed a sigh of relief when the system didn't crash. "The messages on the right are the owner's, and the ones on the left are his wife's," she said. "Apparently they're going through a divorce."

When she set her flex on the table, Nomi and Sep leaned over to read it.

My attorney says you have to give me one of the glidecrafts.

I'm sure she does.
I bet I know which one you want.

Just give me the newest one and I'll walk away.
With the other things we agreed on, of course.

Forget about it.
I'm giving that one back to Merak.
I'm done playing his games.

Then give me the one you bought two years ago.

Not a chance.

When Nomi and Sep looked up, Ellin said, "Just before this, the owner was emming with one of his employees about a story the Screening Department asked them to change. The owner seemed angry in that conversation too."

Suddenly, Sep sat up straight. He was staring at Rena. "Are you okay?"

Ellin looked up and saw that Rena's head had dropped to the table. "Damn it," she said under her breath.

"Rena's fine," Trett said. "She has a psychological condition that causes mild seizures. She'll come out of it soon." He gave them an awkward smile.

Ellin took a deep breath. "She doesn't have a psychological condition."

Trett turned to her. "Are you sure we should—"

She cut him off. "We have to tell them."

"Tell who what?" It was Rena, who'd already snapped out of her vision.

Ellin held her sister's gaze. "We have to tell Nomi and Sep that you're a seer."

Rena's expression remained neutral. "That's not funny, Ellin." She turned to Nomi and Sep. "I have a psychological condition. It's nothing to worry about."

"No! You don't!" Ellin realized how loud she was when her tablemates looked warily around the café. She shifted to a harsh whisper. "Rena is a seer, and if we're going to work together to stop Merak, Nomi and Sep should be aware of that."

As soon as she said it, Ellin braced herself. Sharing Rena's secret with Trett had been one thing; telling two new acquaintances was something else entirely. She was crossing a boundary her sister had always trusted her to respect, and she knew there would be fallout.

Rena stared at Ellin, the rapid rise and fall of her chest the only testament to her fury. Her gaze shifted to Nomi and Sep. "I agree, you should know everything. First of all, Ellin and Trett broke up. Hopefully that won't affect their judgment from here on out, but if they're distracted, that's why."

Ellin blinked, alternating between equal desires to cry and to scream. A hand took hers. It was Nomi, who was watching her with deep compassion. Ellin released her breath and resolved not to let Rena get under her skin.

"Second," Rena continued, "yes. I'm a seer." She proceeded to tell them in gruesome detail about her end-of-the-world visions. Even as their faces betrayed more and more horror, she remained emotionless, her voice monotone.

Rena finished, and the table was quiet for several seconds before Sep asked, "When?"

Her expression still unchanged, Rena replied, "Seventeen days."

"Oh no." Nomi slumped in her seat. Sep sat next to her, frozen and wide-eyed.

"Rena," Trett began, his voice hesitant, "what did you see just now?"

"If Nomi and Sep reach out to the owner of Rayson Media to tell him what they've learned, he'll publish it."

"Why should they do it?" Ellin asked. "I'm the press representative."

"I don't know why," Rena said. "I saw two options. They submit the information, and it gets published. They don't, and we're stuck with more pointless brainstorming. You really want to try a third option we know nothing about?"

"Well, then." Nomi sat up straight, clearly trying to compose herself after the news she'd heard. "I guess Sep and I had better get busy." She swallowed. "Ellin, please send me the Rayson exec's contact information." She pulled out her flex, but before she firmed it, she froze and asked in a hushed voice, "What are the chances of us actually stopping this . . . what Rena saw?"

Rena's head dropped for a few seconds, and Ellin thought she might actually be emotional. When she met Nomi's gaze, however, her face and voice were calm. "Slim to none."

"Understood." Nomi's voice caught on the word.

"We're still going to try," Trett said. "With everything we've got."

The two researchers both had wide, stunned eyes. In unison, they nodded.

"Nomi, Sep," Trett said, "I know this is a lot to take in."

"That's an understatement." Sep's voice was strained. He coughed, then said, "I presume the three of you have had time to adjust to this . . . this reality. With so few days left, Nomi and I don't have that privilege." He sat up straight and spoke with a boldness Ellin wouldn't thought him capable of. "All we can do is fight."

"Yes, we'll fight," Nomi whispered, but there were tears in her eyes.

Ellin looked at her sister again. Rena's face was as impassive as ever. *Just once, I want to see her show a little bit of compassion and grief like a normal human.*

"I'm going to check the news," Rena said, pulling out her flex. "Ellin, send that contact to Nomi."

Ellin returned her gaze to her flex, but she couldn't focus. She sipped her coffee. The spices and chocolate tasted bland, and the drink felt like a jagged stone in her stomach.

19

Rena stood next to her bed, gulping in air like she'd barely avoided drowning. "Oh, God." It was the most eloquent prayer she could come up with after the visions she'd just seen.

Her room was dark, so she brushed one finger against the panel on the wall. The lightfilm in the ceiling glowed at its lowest level.

I'm soaked. The visions had left her sweating like she'd just finished a race. She pulled off every bit of her clothing and stepped toward her small dresser to grab something else to wear.

Walking, it turned out, was a terrible idea. She was swaying on her feet. Hyperventilating. Lightheaded. She stumbled to her bed and sat, head between her knees, trying to control her desperate intake of air.

It was Saturday, and she'd planned to sleep in. Instead, she'd woken and had immediately been greeted with visions of the day of the apocalypse. This time, some of the faces she'd seen were familiar: Kizha, Ellin, and Trett. She knew their fates now. The three people she was closest to in this world. The visions, however, were shrouded. The information, torturously heavy and sharp, was hers alone to carry.

"What about me?" she pleaded as her breathing slowed. She knew she'd never see her own future, though she'd never desired it more.

On the floor about a met away from where her head rested between her knees, Rena's flex vibrated. She sat up slowly. She was no longer lightheaded. Her breathing was more or less under control. She picked up her flex, firmed it, and felt a harsh laugh exit her throat.

Kizha had emmed her. How was Rena supposed to talk to her now? She still didn't dare tell her friend about the original apocalyptic vision, lest Kizha come join them and distract them from their plans. And she couldn't share her newest vision with Kizha even if she wanted to.

She read the message.

I finally found some info! Check your IDMs.

The flex Rena held was the one Merak knew about, and though she and Kizha still used the secure chat portal, these days they didn't talk about anything confidential on it. When Kizha told her to check her IDMs, she meant the ones on Rena's secret flex.

Rena didn't dare do that on Merak property, where someone might hack into her flex. She sent Kizha a quick response, then stood and walked to her dresser. It was empty; she'd meant to do laundry that morning. *Dirty clothes, then.* There were plenty in piles on the floor. Once dressed, she emmed Ellin and Trett.

I'm going into the city.

Rena used her flex to check out a hov and helmet. She picked up the vehicle and drove into Krenner. A few solarcars passed her, but the streets were almost deserted. Dawn wouldn't arrive for another hour yet.

Thankfully, the café they frequented was open all night. Rena sat at a table in the corner, ordered coffee, and firmed her secret flex. She opened her IDMs, tapped on the message from Kizha, and read it.

Hi! I hope you're doing okay.

I found some info on our friend. Sorry it took so long; it wasn't easy to dig up.

He's been married since he was 21. I found an old article on his wife, Arisa. She doesn't seem to like the spotlight, but this piece was complimentary, so I guess the Screening Department never took it down. She's on the board of his Foundation and has been since the beginning. She plays a large role in determining where they spend their money, but she stays in the background and lets him take the credit. She's also a devout Rimorian, which is interesting, as I can't find anything indicating he shares her religious beliefs.

I hadn't seen any mention of them having children, but I knew he was probably the type to protect his kids from media exposure. So on a whim, I found a way into the public records. I had to get past a few password requirements, but I finally found birth records. They have a daughter who's 19, and get this—her name's Ellin. Strange, right? They also have a 17-year-old son named Gillar.

I don't know if any of this helps, but I enjoyed the challenge. I'll keep digging.

Let's video chat soon. I miss seeing you.

Kizha

Rena's coffee arrived, and she took it from the server without comment, bringing it to her lips and taking a big gulp. It burned her throat, but she barely noticed.

She went back to the paragraph about Merak's kids. She wasn't surprised that Merak had children. That bedroom she'd seen him visiting probably belonged to one of his kids.

But . . . *Ellin?* It wasn't a common name these days. In fact, it hadn't been the name their parents had planned on—until nine-year-old Rena had met her brand new sister, looked at her parents, and said, "You need to name her Ellin."

They'd laughed. "We're naming her Leela, in memory of my grandmother," her father said.

"No." Rena remembered being both somber and self-assured, even at that age. "I got a nudge. You need to name her Ellin."

And they did.

Rena had never understood why she'd had that premonition. She still didn't.

Get this—her name's Ellin. Crazy, right?

Rena sipped her coffee.

Ellin and Trett sat in the dining hall, silently eating breakfast. On weekends, the food was even better than on weekdays. Ellin's hand pie was so stuffed with vegetables, it looked like a miniature mountain. She dug in, savoring the first few bites.

Looking up, she found Trett watching her. He immediately broke eye contact, returning his attention to his food. Ellin squeezed her eyes shut and swallowed. She took another bite, but her hunger had fled. *How can I miss him this much when it's only been three days? When he's sitting right in front of me?*

Nomi and Sep arrived and sat at a neighboring table. In a voice just loud enough for Ellin and Trett to hear, Nomi said, "Hand pies are good, but I like oatmeal even more." She glanced over, caught Ellin's eye, and turned her attention back to her food.

Oatmeal was their code word for *Let's meet at the coffee shop in the city as soon as possible.* It seemed silly to Ellin, like something from a bad spy movie, but it worked. In a building owned by Merak, they couldn't be too careful.

Ellin and Trett had already checked out hovs so they could join Rena in Krenner. They finished eating and set off down the road.

Most of their past hov trips had been enjoyable. Ellin had let herself relax, chatting and laughing through the helmet microphone. This time, she and Trett didn't link their mics to each other's speakers. Trett let Ellin take the lead, and she kept looking back, wondering what he was thinking as he floated behind her.

Her stomach, constantly twisted in knots these days, released a little of its tension when she got to the coffee shop and saw Rena. She didn't love spending time with her sister, but being around Trett was slightly less awkward when Rena was there.

"I have new information," Rena said after Ellin and Trett ordered. "I'll read it to you. It's from my friend." Keeping her voice low, she shared several facts she'd learned about Merak's family.

Ellin shook her head. "When he told me his life story, I'm surprised he didn't mention he has a daughter with the same name as me."

"Technically you have the same name as her," Rena said.

Ellin raised an eyebrow.

"She was born before you," Rena said, her gaze oddly intense.

"Right." Ellin shrugged. "I didn't get a chance to check the news this morning. I'd better do that." She pulled up the news interface on her flex.

"I'm surprised Nomi and Sep aren't here yet," Trett said.

Ellin looked up. "Me too." Nomi's salary enabled her to keep up a glidecraft rental, and that got her around faster than a hov. She always brought Sep with her.

Ellin searched for news stories using the word *Cellerin*. Scanning the results, she gasped. "You've both got to see this." She tapped the screen and shared a story to Rena's and Trett's flexes.

The story was on the homepage of Rayson Media's primary publication, *The Vallinger Report*. The headline read,

Caution is Warranted at Cellerin Mountain, Researchers Say

Trett's eyes widened. "They published it!"

"They did indeed," Rena said.

For several minutes, the table was quiet as they all read the feature. The server brought Ellin's and Trett's drinks, but Ellin ignored hers.

"Do you think Merak will know Nomi and Sep were behind this?" Trett asked.

"I hope not," Ellin said. "The story only quotes researchers who aren't here in Therro. It never mentions on-site sources."

They continued to discuss the article, which included much of the evidence Nomi and Sep had gathered. It was the most natural, normal conversation they'd had in three days.

After half an hour, Ellin said, "I wonder what's taking them so long."

"I'm sure they just got a late start," Trett said.

Ellin nodded, then looked back at her flex. She pulled up one news publication after another. "Nobody else has picked up the story, at least not that I can find."

"Are you really surprised?" Rena asked.

Trett tilted his flex toward her. "Look, though—it's all over social media."

"Are you talking about the accident?"

All three of them looked up. Their server was standing at their table.

"What accident?" Trett asked.

"Oh, you said something was all over social media, so I thought that's what you were talking about. A glidecraft crashed a couple of clommets outside Krenner. Nobody could've survived. Everyone local is talking about it."

Dread sprouted in Ellin's stomach, and she wondered if this was what Rena's premonitions felt like. "Do they know who was in the craft?"

"No, it was a rental, and the agency won't give up that information unless a court requires them to." She flashed a bright smile. "Anyone want a refill?"

<hr>

They couldn't get their hovs close to the crash site. It was cordoned off with energy tape that would deliver a slight shock if touched. The glidecraft was smoking, black char marks on its body.

There were enough unburned surfaces to discern the vehicle's original finish—a glittery, royal blue. More than once, Ellin had heard Nomi gush over the color, saying she hoped someday she could buy a craft just like the one she'd rented.

"We should go," Rena said.

"I just want to see if we can get closer," Ellin protested.

Rena jerked her chin to the right, and Ellin and Trett looked in that direction. There was another glidecraft hovering nearby. It was stark white, marked only with the name of a rental agency.

"Our boss is in there," Rena said. Seeing Ellin's questioning expression, she tapped the side of her helmet. "Trust me on this. Let's go."

Ellin couldn't help but look at the white craft as they drove by. A rented glidecraft—for a man who had a far more comfortable private craft.

A man who had every reason to get rid of two rogue researchers.

20

As soon as they got back to camp and returned their hovs, Trett pulled his flex out of his pocket. He read it and groaned.

"What?" Rena asked.

"They need me to come into work today."

"On a weekend? Why?"

"Doesn't say." He turned toward the supply warehouse, not even looking at Ellin as he walked off.

Ellin turned to Rena, wishing she knew for once what her sister was thinking. "Pretty terrible what happened to Nomi and Sep, right?" she heard herself say.

Rena turned to Ellin, her expression unreadable. "Of course it's terrible. But nearly everyone is about to die; I'm not sure it matters that it happened to them fourteen days early."

Ellin gaped at her sister, then shook her head. "I'm gonna take a nap."

She returned to her room and lay down, but she couldn't sleep. So she slipped her shoes back on and walked the paths behind the dining hall.

It wasn't long before her flex vibrated. It was an em from Trett, sent to her and Rena on their normal channel, not the encrypted one. He'd clearly written it with the assumption that someone else might be monitoring their communications.

Dr. Anson and Dr. Septimus died in a glidecraft crash this morning. I'm helping prepare for their memorial. The service is in two days.

Ellin collapsed her flex and slapped it back on her arm. It stung, and she was glad.

She'd known it was Nomi and Sep in that craft, but reading Trett's confirmation made it that much more real. Had Merak been behind it? If so, how had he known what Nomi and Sep were working on? Did he know her secrets too?

Ellin spun around, suddenly convinced someone was watching her. The path was empty.

Then, with no warning, she was crying. She sat on the crushed gravel path and wiped her palms harshly across her wet cheeks. "This is stupid," she sobbed. She didn't even know why she was weeping for people she hardly knew.

Except underneath it all, she did know why. Images of Nomi, Sep, and Trett entered her mind. In the last three days, she'd lost them all, in one way or another.

After she took several deep gulps of air, her breathing steadied again. She pulled her flex off her forearm and firmed it. If someone was monitoring her flex usage, they might have seen Trett's message. They'd probably expect Ellin to look for more information. She clicked the news icon and navigated to local stories.

The crash was there, but the article was short. No one knew what had caused the craft to go down, and so far, no one had leaked the victims' names to the press. Or perhaps they had, and the Screening Department had squashed the story.

Ellin absentmindedly scanned through news articles, returning to world news when she didn't see anything interesting in the local section. Her eyes widened at the headlines she found:

Merak Technologies on the Verge of Medical Advancement in Therro

Archeological Update: Breakthroughs at the Birthplace of Civilization

Unlimited Lifespans? Merak Researchers Are Optimistic

She'd written every one of these stories. When they hadn't been immediately printed, she'd figured they didn't meet standards.

Now it was clear: it wasn't that the stories weren't good enough. They were too good. The Press Office had held them back, reserving them to combat any negative media that made it past the Screening Department. More would doubtless be published in the coming hours.

Scanning one of the articles, she saw a video at the end, something that hadn't been in her original draft. She clicked on it and watched Dr. Rouven explain beneficial radiation in a warm, intelligent voice, using words anyone could understand. He was followed by an animated Therroan historian discounting "conspiracy theories" about a "magical space rock."

Ellin was convinced that anyone who read the article in *The Vallinger Report* would disregard its dire warnings once they watched the video and read the accompanying article.

She pulled up the other two articles she'd written. They included the same video. Nomi and Sep's story had been out for mere hours, and it was already buried in an avalanche of optimistic crap written by Ellin herself.

Are their deaths totally purposeless? Ellin closed her eyes and thought back on conversations she'd had with Nomi. A name popped into her head, the person from home Nomi had missed the most: *Lorella . . . but what's her last name?*

She clicked the search icon on her flex, pulled up the letterkeys, and typed, "Nomi Anson Lorella".

The first result was a profile of Nomi. It was several years old, but it included the information Ellin had been looking for:

> Dr. Anson has been married for eight years to Dr. Lorella Shover,
> a professor of art at Inger College.

One more search, and Ellin had Dr. Shover's contact information. She drafted a quick IDM expressing her condolences, finishing it with the all-too-inadequate sentence,

> I didn't know your wife well, but I do know she was brave, intelli-
> gent, and kind. I am committed to honoring her by following in
> her footsteps.

She scheduled it to send in two days, just in case Nomi's wife hadn't gotten the news yet. Then Ellin collapsed her flex, placed it on her arm, and walked back toward camp.

"I want to help with the memorial service."

The receptionist at the small executive office building raised her eyebrows. "Have you been invited to help?"

"No, but I worked with Nomi—uh, Dr. Anson—in the research room. I want to do something."

The door behind the receptionist clicked open, and Alvun Merak stepped out. His mouth broke into a wide smile. "Ellin, what are you doing here on a weekend? You should be out enjoying city life. Or at least taking a nap. You've been working hard lately!"

"Thank you, Mr. Merak. I worked in the same room as Dr. Anson, and I'd like to help with her memorial."

His eyebrows rose. "I'm surprised you've already heard about that."

"My boyf—uh—my friend Trett was pulled in to help."

"Of course. I'm headed to the supply warehouse now. Walk with me, and we'll see if there's something you can do."

"Thank you."

They walked to the warehouse, but Merak stopped short of the door. Ellin halted too.

"Did you get to know Dr. Anson well in your time here?" he asked.

"We haven't been here long, but I liked her a lot."

Merak nodded. "So did I." He blinked, and his eyes shone with unshed tears.

Ellin schooled her face, not allowing her shock to show. Merak had been at the scene of the accident in an unmarked glidecraft. Just that fact had nearly convinced her he was responsible for the crash. Yet here he was, clearly emotional as he talked about it.

"Did you know her well?" Ellin asked, more to break the silence than anything. "And Dr. Septimus?"

Merak gave her a sad smile. "Our little camp is like a family. I know every person who works here. I'd had plenty of meetings with both of them, discussing their findings. I can't tell you how troubled I am to know they're gone. I even took a glider out there to see the accident when I heard about it. Not sure why I put myself through that, but . . ." He shrugged.

Ellin swallowed. "You—you did?"

Merak nodded. "Not my own glider; I didn't want to attract the press. I want to respect the families and keep this out of the media if we can. I had to see for myself though." He blinked again and swallowed, and this time, a single tear escaped his eye. He caught it with a finger before it could roll down his cheek.

"I'm sorry," Ellin said, her own eyes filling with tears.

"Thank you, but I'm the one who should be sorry. I didn't mean to upset you. Let's go in, shall we?"

Inside, a manager gave Ellin a few options of where she could help. Before she could respond, Merak said, "I don't know why I didn't think of this before. Ellin, why don't you research Dr. Anson and Dr. Septimus and write their eulogies? We'll distribute them on the camp network."

"That sounds great."

He told her she could use a workstation in the warehouse office, or she could return to her room. She saw Trett counting chairs. There was something comforting about watching him work. She chose the deskscreen in the office.

Nomi and Sep were both well known in their fields, and there was more information about them on the network than Ellin would ever need. She set to work prioritizing the most important facts and digging up anecdotes that reflected the two researchers' personalities.

As she worked, Ellin kept an eye on the warehouse through the glass wall that separated it from the office. She'd assumed Merak would check up on things and head back to his office. Instead, he stayed. He carried supplies, gave feedback where requested, and helped Trett stack chairs on carts.

The more she watched, the more Ellin was convinced of one thing: while Alvun Merak had taken some actions that were unethical, such as controlling the press, he was a good person. She tried to picture him ordering a hit on his employees, but such an image didn't match with the man who'd cried with her on the porch and was now pitching in to help with the memorial.

When they'd met in the lobby of the Press Office weeks earlier, Alvun Merak hadn't been ready to hear the truth. That was before he'd personally witnessed her work ethic. Now, he clearly respected her, even trusted her enough to be vulnerable with her.

Ellin had to try again. She'd approach him and insist he listen to reason. With their deadline only two weeks away, what could she lose?

She couldn't tell Rena. Her sister would insist they wait until some prophecy came along to guide them. For once, Ellin wanted to act boldly and live with the consequences.

Her eyes roamed over the warehouse, and she caught Trett watching her. He looked away, and that simple action shot tightness into her chest. *I can't tell him either. He might want to come, and I can't handle that right now.* She'd approach Merak alone.

Maybe all their strategies were too complicated. Saving the world might be as simple as initiating a conversation.

Late that afternoon, Ellin saw Merak standing at the front door of the warehouse, waving goodbye to the workers. She leapt up, opened the door behind her workstation, and slipped outside.

It didn't take long for her to run around the building, but Merak's brisk steps had already carried him halfway to the executive office building.

Ellin kept running and called, "Mr. Merak!"

He turned.

She caught up with him and smiled through her panting breaths. "I was hoping we could have a chat."

"Sure. Walk with me?"

"Thanks."

She matched her strides to his, their feet creating a soothing cadence on the crushed gravel. Ellin couldn't think where to start the conversation.

Merak said, "I'm sorry you and Trett broke up."

Ellin's head swiveled to face him.

He explained, "You almost referred to him as your boyfriend earlier, and then you corrected yourself. Plus, you never once talked to each other in the warehouse."

"You're very observant." She looked away from him, not sure what else to say.

"I care about the people who work for me." His voice held a smile. "You're smart and driven. You'll find someone who appreciates that."

"Thanks." Ellin took a deep breath. "Actually, I'm concerned I won't have a chance to find someone who appreciates me."

He laughed. "You'll have plenty of chances, Ellin."

It was a clichéd answer, but a kind one too. Once again, Ellin could picture her father responding in the same way. How many conversations like this had she missed out on in the last eight years? After a few seconds steeping in the comfort of Merak's words, she chided herself, *Get back on track.*

She took a deep breath. "Mr. Merak, may I be honest with you?"

"Always."

"I'm concerned for the health of everyone at this camp. Even more for those at the dig site." Ellin wasn't about to tell him she was frightened for the rest of the world; he'd think she was crazy. "I've been looking at all the research, and the radiation levels are rising as we get closer to uncovering whatever is hidden in that mountain. What if it's dangerous? You said yourself, there's an incredible brain trust here. Right now, we're all at risk."

Ellin stopped talking, waiting for his response. She dared to glance his way and found him watching her thoughtfully.

He didn't speak until they'd nearly reached the executive office building. Then he stopped, and Ellin did too, turning toward him.

"This brain trust—do you really think I'd put it at risk?" Merak asked.

She opened her mouth, closed it again, and finally answered, "I trust you, Mr. Merak. I don't think you'd ever deliberately put us at risk."

"But I might do it accidentally?"

Ellin shrugged, then squared her shoulders and gave him a firm nod.

"I trust you too." Merak's gaze, somber and sincere, locked with hers. "Your mind can keep up with any of our researchers; I'm convinced of that. I want to know why you're concerned."

Ellin's breath exited her chest in a relieved sigh. She pointed at the warehouse. "I left my flex in there. Can I run back and get it? I can use it to show you what I found."

"Since we're here already, why don't you use the deskscreen in my office? I assume your research is on the company network?"

Not all of it was, but Ellin certainly wouldn't risk losing his trust by showing him her secret flex. It was in the pocket of the jacket she'd left in the warehouse office. There was more than enough information on the Merak research network for her to make a convincing case. "Thank you."

He took her to the back of the building, where he inserted his finger into a scanner. The door clicked, and he held it open for her.

As Ellin entered into a short hallway, she looked back at the scanner. Fingerprint technology seemed so old-fashioned for a place like this.

Merak must have seen where she was looking, because he said, "DNA verification. It brushes dead cells off my finger and analyzes them."

"Oh," Ellin said. "Fancy."

Merak smiled and followed the same process at a scanner next to the door on their left. He opened the door, and they entered his office.

"Have a seat, Ellin," he said. "Show me what you've found."

She walked to his desk. He had a hover chair, and it looked insanely comfortable, upholstered in butter-smooth faux leather. Ellin picked up a chair on the other side of the desk and started carrying it toward the workstation.

"You can use my chair," Merak said.

Still holding the other chair, which was faux wood with a small cushion in the seat, she said, "Oh, that's not necessary."

"It's right in front of the deskscreen already. Have a seat. I'll use this one."

He took the chair from her, and she walked around the desk. She couldn't help the small laugh that escaped her throat as she lowered herself into his seat. It molded itself to her like it had been waiting for her arrival.

When Merak was seated next to her, he placed his finger in yet another scanner, this one built into the front of his workstation. The deskscreen lit up. "It's all yours."

Ellin logged on to the company research network and pulled up charts of the daily radiation levels. Intending to explain the data to Merak, she turned toward him.

He was leaning forward, watching her with a strange expression. The fervency of his gaze stripped the words from her throat, and she pressed her back against the chair.

Is he about to hit on me?

No, it wasn't that type of expression. She didn't think so, anyway. He merely looked fiercely interested. In her? In the research? She couldn't tell.

He looked away from her, fixing his eyes on the screen. "What are we looking at here?"

He's interested in the research. Ellin let out her breath, nearly laughing with relief. She spent a few seconds enlarging the first chart and collecting her thoughts. Then she explained the rising radiation levels to Merak.

His eyes lost none of their earnestness, but it was all reserved for the data they were discussing. He asked smart questions and nodded at her ready answers.

Next, she delved deeper into the most recent daily readings, comparing them to the data from two deadly radiation accidents. The similarities were clear, but she still walked him through it, emphasizing the pertinent details.

When that was done, Merak silently examined the graphs and tables on the screen, flipping through them with quick gestures. Then he sat back, crossed one arm over his stomach, and gripped his chin with his other hand. His solemn gaze shifted to her. "I can see why you're concerned, Ellin."

"You can?" She'd been ready to defend her findings. Hearing his words, a smile tugged at her lips.

Merak, too, smiled. He rested his hands lightly in his lap, abandoning his thoughtful pose. "I may be stubborn, but I also love data. These aren't the figures I want to see, but this is reality, isn't it?" He released a sigh. "There are a couple of scientists at the dig site who are all too aware of the risks of working with radiation. I'd like to share your analysis with them."

Ellin sat up straighter and leaned forward. "You'd do that?"

"Of course. They need to know what you've discovered. They're probably too bogged down in all their data to see the patterns you've identified. Before I talk to them, however, I need to make sure I have the details straight."

Merak gestured at the screen, bringing up the first figures Ellin had shown him. He began explaining the research, as if he were talking to the on-site scientists, but he got the terminology all wrong. Ellin corrected him, and he started over, but then he made another mistake, this time in his description of a graph.

After Ellin's fifth correction, Merak threw his hands up and laughed ruefully. "I don't know what to tell you, Ellin! I'm a visionary guy, not a detail guy. Everything you're telling me makes sense, but when I try to explain it, I can't measure up to your clarity or accuracy."

Ellin was glad he'd said it, because she'd pretty much been thinking the same thing. "Why don't we call the on-site researchers? I can go over it with them, just like I did with you."

"It's worth a shot." Merak pulled out his flex, firmed it, and started navigating it. A couple of minutes later, he collapsed the flex and said, "They're not responding, and honestly, I'm not surprised. They're usually too focused on their work to realize I've emmed them. When I need to talk to them, I go there directly. This is time sensitive; I should probably head over there now. I just wish I had a better handle on the research."

Ellin bit her lip. Merak could talk to the researchers, but they'd never take him seriously. If it weren't for the radiation at the site, she'd offer to sit down with the scientists herself. Just the thought of breathing the air at that place made her heart beat wildly. She took a deep breath. "I know you wear an antirad at the dig site. How effective is it?"

"It blocks out one hundred percent of harmful radiation. I wouldn't settle for anything but the best, for myself or my employees."

You can do this. She forced a smile to her lips. "Do you have an extra?"

"Sure, I keep a few in my glidecraft." His eyes widened. "Are you offering to talk to the researchers yourself, Ellin?"

"Well, only if you think it would be helpful."

"It's a fantastic idea! I don't know why I didn't think of it myself. In fact, I can't wait to see their faces when they realize how well you understand their research!" He chuckled.

Ellin was still nervous about the radiation, but if Merak trusted his antirad, she could too. "How will I get to the site?" she asked. "On a hov?"

"I'll take you in my glidecraft. I'll need to introduce you to the scientists."

Ellin's mouth dropped open. *This day is turning out so weird.* A couple of hours ago, she'd seriously considered the possibility that Merak had ordered the deaths of two of his employees. Then she'd seen the empathy and grief in his eyes, and when she'd followed her gut and asked to talk to him, he'd further confirmed his trustworthiness by validating her concerns. And now he wanted to personally take her to share her data with the scientists? She'd hoped he'd listen to her, but she'd never dreamed the conversation would go this well.

Ellin realized she was staring at Merak like she'd lost her senses. She cleared her throat. "Sorry, I just—if someone had told me a couple of months ago that I'd be sitting in Alvun Merak's ridiculously comfortable desk chair, getting ready to take a ride in his private glidecraft to talk to his top scientists, I would've thought they'd lost their mind." They both laughed, and she said, "I guess we should go. Like you said, this is time sensitive."

He stood. "My glidecraft is out back."

21

SATURDAY, CYON 23, 6293
-14 DAYS

Trett joined Rena at a small table in the dining hall.

"Where's Ellin?" she asked.

Trett's sandwich halted halfway to his mouth. "I was going to ask you the same thing."

Rena chewed a bite of her own sandwich, swallowed, and shrugged. "She emmed me hours ago. She was going to help with memorial prep. She must still be busy with that."

"Yeah, she was in the same warehouse as me. They had her doing something in the office. She left almost an hour ago, and I haven't seen her since. Could she be in her room?"

Rena shook her head. "I knocked repeatedly. She doesn't sleep through something like that. And she's not answering ems."

Trett set his still-uneaten sandwich on his plate. He swallowed, but his throat was tight. "She left right after Merak."

Rena's wide eyes fixed on him. "Merak was there too?"

176

"He was helping us set up. He kept looking back in the office, like he was keeping an eye on Ellin. Do you think—" He leaned forward and waited until Rena did the same. Then he whispered, "Do you think there's any way he found out what we're doing?"

"I didn't think he'd find out what Nomi and Sep were doing, but now . . . I'm wondering. About a lot of things."

Trett sat up straight and forced a smile. Voice at normal volume, he said, "This sandwich is disgusting. Want to go eat in Krenner?"

Rena smiled back. "Sure, let's go."

Trett hoped his grin didn't look as fake as hers.

As soon as they sat in the café, Rena pulled out her secret flex.

"What are you doing?" Trett asked.

"Checking my IDMs. My hacker friend emmed me before dinner telling me she'd sent me something."

"I don't really care what your hacker friend is doing." It took a great deal of effort for Trett to keep his voice down. "I care about finding Ellin. Can't you track her or something?"

Rena looked up. "Sorry, Trett, I don't think she wore her tracking collar today."

He rolled his eyes. "You know that's not what I'm asking. Can you track her flex?"

Rena blinked. "That's actually a good question. I can't; we've locked down location detection on all our flexes. Maybe my friend can get past that. I'll em her."

Her fingers danced on her flex, and after the longest two minutes in history, she looked up at Trett. "Good news. Remember when my friend helped us with the security settings on our flexes? She still has access to them. She's tracking both of Ellin's devices now."

The server came up, and Trett curtly ordered two coffees, just to get her to leave.

"She located the devices," Rena said. She paused to examine the message, and her shoulders visibly drooped. "Both of Ellin's flexes are in the warehouse."

Trett squeezed his eyes shut and rested his head in his hands. "Tell your friend to wipe Ellin's flexes. Both of them."

"What?"

He lifted his head and clenched both fists, resting them on the table. "I have a bad feeling, Rena."

"I'm supposed to be the one with bad feelings."

"Yeah, well, let's hope you get something more concrete than that. Soon."

Rena nodded, and he saw her throat compress in a swallow. He supposed that was the most emotion he'd get from her.

"I'll ask her to wipe Ellin's devices. Then I need to check my IDMs." Rena returned her attention to her flex. A couple of minutes later, she met Trett's eyes, and though her expression was still blank, her chest rose and fell with rapid breaths. She handed her flex to him.

Trett took it and silently read the IDM.

I finally found out who Merak's father is. It shouldn't have been so hard, but apparently his mother changed her name, and it took me forever to track her original identity.

Like he told Ellin, his father was a legislator. Wallum Ekrid. Merak's mother worked for him. She quit about halfway through her pregnancy.

You've probably heard of Ekrid. He had the second-highest seniority in the national legislature until he died suddenly fifteen years ago. His private solarplane crashed.

I looked into the crash, and it's very strange. The government always investigates such accidents, and the records are supposed to be public. For some reason, this investigation is sealed. The only public information is a statement attributing the crash to a software failure.

Other than this incident, there hasn't been a solarplane crash due to software failure in fifty years.

I'll continue looking for more information, but I keep reaching dead ends. The people who set up the encryption on those records have more talent and more resources than I do.

-Kizha

Trett's eyes snapped up, meeting Rena's gaze. "Would the greatest philanthropist in the world be capable of arranging his father's death?"

Rena's mouth barely moved as she responded, "Would the greatest philanthropist in the world be capable of taking out two rebellious employees?"

"And Ellin—" Trett had to force the words through his tight throat. The world was ending in two weeks, and as torturous as the three days since their breakup had been, he couldn't tolerate the thought of not spending every possible remaining moment with her. *"Where is she?"*

Rena just shook her head.

Trett looked around. They'd often seen other Merak employees at this café. People knew it was *their place.* Awareness overwhelmed him—of how vulnerable they were here, how public this place was, how easy it would be for someone to find them.

Trett shoved his chair back. "Em your friend and have her wipe your official flex. Mine too. We'll leave them here." He took both devices and shoved them behind a potted plant near their table. "We can't go back to our rooms. And we can't stay here."

Rena stood, her fingers dancing across the screen of her secret flex. When she was done, they hurried to the door. As they exited, Trett murmured directly in her ear, "You'd better start having some visions. Fast."

22

Merak walked Ellin to his private glidecraft behind the office. She stepped in, then flashed him a smile. "It's nice in here!"

He laughed. That smile, the way she talked—so much about Ellin Havier reminded him of his Ellin. He stepped in after her and grabbed two antirads from their charging ports. After slipping one in his pocket, he handed the second one to her. "Put this in your pocket. It'll block all harmful radiation at the dig site. It even prevents sunburn."

She eyed the small device, then did as he'd asked. "How do I turn it on?"

"It'll already on. It's sensing your body shape right now."

He watched her, and he could tell the moment the antirad activated. She flinched, then gave him an uncertain smile.

"It feels like my skin is cold . . . but it's not," she said.

Merak chuckled. "That's normal. You'll get used to it."

"How does it work?"

"I have no idea. I'm surprised you're not currently explaining that to me." He gestured to the button next to the door. "If you're ready, just close the door, and we'll be off."

She pressed the button, and the door slid closed.

The ride to the dig site at the base of Cellerin Mountain only took a couple of minutes. Instead of landing immediately, Merak hovered above the site. "Care for an aerial tour?"

"Sure!"

He pointed to a relatively flat expanse with tents and buildings. "That's the staging area for the archeologists and their crew."

"Those people outside—are they working on the weekend?"

"We have crews working every day, sunup to sundown. Of course, they get breaks and days off." He pointed to the right. "That's where they're digging—or, rather, moving rocks."

"Are they moving those stones by hand?"

"Partially. The government wants us to do as much by hand as we can to protect the grounds, but eventually we'll need to bring in heavy equipment. The workers are trying to find the best path to the cave so we don't have to disturb the area any more than necessary. See? Two of the workers are using a mechanically assisted lever to move one of the larger stones right now."

Merak took a step back. As Ellin watched the scene below, he studied her. If she were any closer to the window, she'd be pressing her nose against it. She was fascinated, just as he'd known she would be.

Back in his office, as soon as Merak had realized how convinced Ellin was of her misguided conclusions, he'd realized she needed to visit the dig—not to convince the scientists of anything, but to soak up the excitement of the place.

So as they'd discussed her research, he'd overplayed his ignorance. When she'd suggested a video call, he'd pretended he couldn't contact the scientists. Right on cue, Ellin had offered to visit them in person, convinced she'd thought of the idea herself. *Oh, dear girl, I don't like all this subterfuge, but it'll be worth it once you see what I see—the world-changing potential of this project.*

Ellin continued her examination of the area for another couple of minutes before asking, "What are those?"

Merak looked where Ellin was pointing. "The portable structures? The one on the left is an administrative office. Next to that is a lab. The large building holds the kitchen, dining hall, and bathrooms. See those tents? They're climate-controlled, and all our workers stay there. Any other questions before we go down?"

She turned around. "If we have to shut this down because the radiation is too dangerous, will you make sure all these people get jobs somewhere else?"

He didn't shy away from her probing gaze. "I always take care of my people, Ellin. They're like my family."

She stared at him for a few more seconds, then said, "Let's go down."

Merak set the glidecraft down gently onto a dirt landing pad. "The scientists are probably in the lab," he said as they disembarked. "I don't think they take any days off. I have my doubts as to whether they even sleep."

He was right. A middle-aged man was hunched at a workstation, typing furiously, and a young woman stood before a massive wallscreen displaying some of the same data Ellin had shown Merak.

"Good afternoon," Merak said.

Both scientists looked up and greeted him tersely before turning back to their work. Merak barely prevented himself from rolling his eyes. He led a company full of sycophants, but the on-site researchers treated him like dirt. *No, not like dirt. They actually value dirt.*

He smiled at the thought, then said, "Ellin, this is Dr. Pranav and Dr. Toma." He gestured to the male and female researchers in turn. "Doctors, Ellin is our press representative for the Cellerin Project. I'd like for you to spend a few minutes showing her some of your data. I know you're busy, and I promise we won't take too much of your time."

Both scientists turned and stared at him and Ellin.

"You'd like us to share data with your press representative?" Pranav asked.

Merak stepped closer and clapped the man on the back. "She's sharp. She'll understand more than you think. Can you explain your hypothesis about the rising radiation levels?"

"Of course," Pranav muttered.

Merak took another step toward Pranav's workstation.

"Mr. Merak?" Ellin's voice reached him from where she still stood near the room's entrance. She beckoned him over, then spoke quietly. "I thought you wanted me to share my findings with them."

He placed a hand on her shoulder and smiled down at her. "I do. However, we need to respect them in their space by letting them explain their interpretation of the data first."

"Oh—sure."

He led her to Pranav, who started talking without even looking at them. The man spoke in a monotone voice and used vocabulary no one outside his field would understand. When he'd been talking for fifteen minutes straight, Ellin interrupted him.

"Pardon me, Dr. Pranav, but may I ask a question?"

"Of course." His sour expression belied his words.

Pranav's churlishness didn't deter Ellin. "I'd like to make sure I'm getting this straight. You think the digging is shaking things up, causing air to enter the chamber where the isotope is. The isotope is reacting chemically to one of the elements in the air, and that's why the radiation keeps getting stronger. Once you have the isotope in hand, you'll be able to contain it and control that reaction. Did I get that right?"

"That's our best hypothesis right now."

"But sir," Ellin said, "My understanding was—"

Merak interrupted her. "I told you she was a smart one." He squeezed Ellin's shoulder. "Let's see what's up on this wallscreen, shall we?"

Dr. Toma repeated most of the same information as her colleague.

"Your graphs look great," Ellin said when Toma stopped talking. "I have to admit, I'm interpreting them differently." She turned to Merak, eyebrows raised as if asking permission. He nodded, and she continued to question Toma.

Merak watched her. Deep down, he hadn't really expected Pranav and Toma to convince her. They loved data, not people, and they had no charisma or persuasive power. Still, he'd held out hope that she'd see beyond the numbers.

Whenever Pranav and Toma explained their findings to Merak, he saw *possibilities*. Patients cured of rare diseases. Lifespans extended. Ellin couldn't see past her own interpretation of the data, her own fear. Again, she reminded Merak of his daughter: intelligent but stubborn.

He interrupted her earnest questioning. "Ellin, hang onto that point you were making, okay? There's one more piece of evidence you should see. It may affect your analysis of this research."

"Can't I just—" Ellin began.

Merak was already walking toward the door. "It won't take long," he said over his shoulder.

He heard her footsteps following him.

Outside the building, Merak stepped close to Ellin and gave her a conspiratorial grin. "I don't want this to get out publicly, but I know I can trust you. We have a small sample of the isotope. We found it in a little hollow in a stone we moved. It's stored in the safest place we could find near the dig site. I didn't want to mention it in front of Dr. Boring and Professor Long-Winded in there; they'd be furious I'm showing you. I think you need to see it, though. We've already stabilized it."

"Oh, you . . . you've already stabilized it?"

Merak shrugged. "Well, I'm not the one who figured it out, of course. Good thing I hire researchers smarter than me, right?"

Ellin opened her mouth, closed it, licked her lips, and said,

"That's . . . wonderful. Really. All the research I've done led me to believe it couldn't be stabilized."

"You know I read that article you wrote back at headquarters," Merak said. "I'm sorry we couldn't publish it, Ellin, but I took your concerns seriously. I instructed a team to start working on advanced stabilization techniques that very day. Come see what we've done, and if you're still concerned, we'll come back here for a long conversation with the researchers."

Ellin blinked and let out a short laugh. "Mr. Merak, I . . . thank you for trusting me."

"Of course I trust you. You've earned it. Now, let's look at this isotope. It's this way."

Ellin had expected Merak to walk her to another building at the dig site. Instead, he led her all the way past his glidecraft and kept going along a narrow road.

"I like to run along this road," Merak said. "It's very peaceful."

Ellin nodded, but her thoughts were elsewhere. If Merak's scientists had figured out how to stabilize the isotope, maybe the prophecy was already void. It sounded like Merak wouldn't have pushed for new stabilization techniques if he hadn't read Ellin's unpublished article. Could something she'd written weeks ago have been the key to stopping the prophecy?

But if that were the case, why would Rena have continued to experience apocalyptic visions? *Maybe the article was just the first step. What else still needs to be done?* The answer was just ahead; Ellin was sure of it. Anticipation tingled in her chest.

She looked around, realizing they'd been walking for perhaps ten minutes, longer than she'd expected. The mountain was beautiful— and entirely deserted. She turned her attention back to Merak. "I didn't realize you were taking me on a day hike."

He laughed. "We're almost there. I didn't want anyone to stumble across the sample."

They turned past a stone outcropping, and Merak pointed at a faded, green building. "That's where we're headed."

"What is it?"

"It used to be a gift shop and café. The trailheads are nowhere close to here, and the place was never profitable. It wasn't open long."

They approached the building's back entrance. Ellin frowned at the chipped paint on the door. "You stored the isotope sample here?"

"It's close enough to access quickly but secluded enough to remain confidential. Plus, there's an old freezer in here that keeps the isotope at the proper temperature."

"It has to be frozen?"

"No, the climastat allows us to keep it cool but not too cold, just like the cave." Merak pulled his flex out of his pocket and held it up to a reader next to the door. There was a *click*, and he pushed the door open and turned on the light. "It's in the back."

Ellin followed him through a dim room, nearly sneezing from the dust. Hopefully the freezer was more sanitary than the stockroom.

Merak stopped at a large, metal door. "Here it is. Our future." He pulled at a sturdy bar holding the freezer door closed, then swung the door open, gesturing Ellin in. "The light panel is on the right-hand side."

She entered the freezer and felt around for the panel. When her fingers found it, a small square of lightfilm in the ceiling lit up. She was standing in a cube, perhaps two-and-a-half mets to each side, made entirely of metal and smelling of old dampness. Cold air blew in from a vent overhead. The room was empty.

"Where's the sample?" Ellin asked, turning back to Merak. Then her eyes left his face, flicking down to the item he was holding: a small, sleek handgun, pointed at her.

Ellin stumbled backward, nearly falling. She'd never seen a real gun. They were artifacts of a violent past, relegated to scary films and campfire stories. She drew in a frantic breath. "Where'd you get that?"

He gave her a rueful look. "It isn't hard for me to get things like this."

She coughed out a sob.

"Oh, please don't be frightened." Merak held out his empty hand, though she wasn't within his reach. "Have a seat, darli—Ellin."

Ellin obeyed, sitting against the back wall and pulling trembling knees into her chest. She couldn't take her eyes off the gun.

Merak sat in the doorway and pressed his lips together in a smile that looked oddly remorseful. "I won't be able to bring you blankets or food until tomorrow, but I did take this from the glidecraft." He pulled a water pouch from his pocket and slid it to her. It was emblazoned with the Merak Technologies logo.

Ellin took a drink, though her shaking hands spilled as much as she consumed, and her frenzied breathing made swallowing difficult. She forced herself to ask the question on her mind: "So, you're not killing me today?"

He ran his free hand over his forehead and cheek, sighing. "I don't want to kill you, Ellin. I want to make the world better with your help."

Her mouth dropped open, but she recovered quickly. She gulped another breath. "I do too! I know I'm scared about the project, but I'm loyal, Mr. Merak, and I'm a hard worker. I won't say anything else about my concerns. Just please—"

He held up his hand, and she snapped her mouth closed. "Ellin, we anticipate reaching the isotope within two weeks. You'll have to stay here until then. Please understand. I can't risk you stopping the project. You're so very intelligent and driven and"—he laughed, shaking his head—"and so misguided, but that's not your fault. You're young.

"I must take some of the blame for your line of thinking. I knew you were spending time with Nomi and Sep. I should have stopped that as soon as it was reported to me. I was just glad you were connecting with other employees. It was too late by the time they . . . left us."

Ellin's tongue darted out, moistening her lips. She swallowed before asking, "Did you kill them?"

He looked down. "Do you truly think me capable of that?"

"I think one of the richest men on Anyari is probably capable of a lot of things."

He sighed, his shoulders drooping. Then he met her gaze again. "Ellin, what I'm about to say is the absolute truth. Every decision I've made as the head of Merak Technologies has been for the betterment of our world. Every single decision."

She stared at him, still trembling and again fighting back tears. "Why don't you shoot me?"

Not taking his eyes off her, Merak moved the gun behind his back. He must have put it in his waistband, because he held both hands out, empty palms facing her. "The last thing I want is to hurt you. Can you move closer, Ellin? You look so frightened. You don't need to be scared of me."

She obeyed, scooting halfway across the little room, then bringing her knees back up to her chest.

Merak looked at her with the same warm gaze he'd given her so many times, and though Ellin didn't trust it a bit, it somehow calmed her. Her breaths slowed, and her trembling stopped.

He smiled. "Ellin, your name caught my eye before I ever met you, because nineteen years ago, my wife and I named our daughter Ellin. The two of you have more in common than your names. From the time she was tiny, anyone who met Ellin could see her intelligence and determination. Just like you."

She stared at him, trying not to betray her fear.

"I won't hurt you, Ellin. I promise. I could, of course. I could keep you quiet in any number of ways, but that's not what I want. You're too valuable. I can't lose you."

Merak's eyes had taken on that strange intensity again. Ellin drew in a shuddering breath and looked away.

He cleared his throat. "Merak Technologies can't lose you, because you're an excellent employee. We just need to change what you want. Redirect you."

She dared to look at him again. "How—how do you plan to do that?"

"I'll set you up here as comfortably as I can. When we retrieve the isotope, I'll bring you evidence of how it's changing our world for the better. And then, oh, Ellin." His expression softened, turning supremely gentle. "I have such high hopes for you."

Ellin started to tremble again. Merak leaned forward, reaching out a hand, and she recoiled.

His smile faltered as he pulled his hand back. "I know you don't trust me. I understand why. When I prove to you the value of what we're doing at the dig site, you'll come around. I know you will, because, Ellin, *I* trust *you*. Once you realize the good of what we're doing, you won't stay in the Press Office for long. For you, Ellin, the sky's the limit."

He gave her a closed-mouth smile. When she didn't return it, he stood abruptly. "I'll see you tomorrow." Merak stepped out of the freezer and swung the door shut.

Ellin heard the metal bar drop into place. She stared at the door, pressing her knees even tighter against her chest.

Merak stood outside the freezer, expecting to hear Ellin cry once he left. But whether it was because of the strength of the door or the girl, all was silent.

He placed both hands on the door and pressed his cheek against the cool metal, trying to keep his own tears in check. *Ellin, I never wanted to hurt you.*

His flex vibrated, and Merak stepped away from the door, wiping wetness from both his cheeks before pulling out his device.

There was an em waiting from the compound's chief of security.

We've been monitoring those three interns like you asked. Their flexes were just wiped. We pulled their last known locations. One was in the warehouse, and the other two were at a café in Krenner. I'm at the warehouse now, and nobody's here.

Merak gritted his teeth. Ellin's friends probably suspected something. He typed a response.

I'm concerned they may have stolen confidential information. Go to the city with as many staff as you can spare. Bring caynins too. Find them and bring them to my office.

The chief replied,

A couple of my guards are already in Krenner. I'll alert them and head that way with two more. I'll personally pursue the fugitives with caynins, and I'll send the other guards to public transportation centers and the airport.

Merak was about to collapse his flex when another em popped up. It was from Arisa.

Just wanted to say hello. I'll be in the chapel for an hour or so, but I'd love to chat later.

The chapel. Kind, good Arisa—how he envied her simple faith. She never had to choose between multiple horrific options, never had to compromise herself for the greater good. He was glad for that. With all they'd been through, at least one of them could live in peace.

He read the em again, then typed his response.

Pray for me, Arisa.

23

RENA AND TRETT set off on foot, abandoning their Merak-owned hovs in front of the café. It was dark, but the streetlights were bright enough to illuminate other pedestrians. Trett couldn't stop examining every person on the street, certain he and Rena were being watched or followed. *That guy. He's looking at us.*

"Trett!" Rena grabbed his arm, and when he looked at her, she was glaring at him. "I'm as aware of the danger as you are, but you look really suspicious."

He nodded, pulled his arm away, and kept walking, gaze straight ahead, jaw squared.

"Where should we go?" Rena asked.

"I don't know." His voice was tight, barely controlled. "We have to get off these streets and find a place to stay. At least we still have access to our money on our secret flexes."

"Yes, but if we use it, any decent hacker can figure out where we've been."

Trett released a quiet groan.

"We need new identities," Rena said softly. "Again."

"How long will that take?"

"I have no idea. I need to contact my friend."

"Once the IDs are set up, can she transfer our money and make sure Merak can't trace it?"

Rena ignored the question. "Don't turn around." Her voice was calm. "One of Merak's security guards is following us."

"What?" Trett resisted his instinct to turn. "How do you know?"

"He's on the other side of the street. He's on foot, probably didn't want us to notice him on a Merak hov. But I recognize him."

Breathing far too quickly, Trett scanned their surroundings. The street was lined with long buildings, each containing several businesses. *There—a restaurant.* Restaurants always had back doors, right? He grabbed Rena's arm. "Come on."

He dashed into the restaurant, pulling Rena with him. No one payed them too much attention as they rushed through the crowded dining room, then charged into the busy kitchen at the back. Warm air, noise, and spicy scents greeted them.

"I'm sure he followed us into the building," Rena said as they squeezed between cooks and equipment, ignoring the staff's exclamations.

"I know. Hopefully it's dark out back." Trett shoved the back door open. They were in a long parking lot that backed up to the businesses on the street they'd just left. Across the lot were similar buildings from the next street over. Hundreds of hovs, glidecrafts, and solarcars were parked in the lot. Way too many bright lights illuminated the area.

"Run!" Trett turned left and broke into a sprint. Rena followed.

They turned between two of the long buildings. Just then, a man behind them shouted, "Stop!"

Trett cursed.

"Your plan . . . didn't work!" Rena panted as they ran through the narrow alley.

Trett led her back to the street they'd just left. "Faster!" he hissed.

They made it past the next strip of connected businesses, garnering stares the whole way. "In here!" Rena said. She grabbed his arm and pulled him into another shadowy space between buildings. They dropped into low squats. Several seconds later, their pursuer ran past them on the street.

"What do we do now?" Trett whispered.

"I don't know." Rena's breaths were ragged. "I'm sure if one guard found us that quickly, there are more." She stood. "He's bound to double back when he realizes he lost us. Come on." They scurried back to the parking lot and resumed running. "I can't—do this—for long," Rena said.

Trett was short of breath too, as much from panic as exertion. He was just about to suggest they cross the parking lot to the buildings on the other side when Rena grabbed his arm and pulled him to a stop. In a voice that sounded weaker than usual, she said, "Trett?"

"Don't stop!" He pulled his arm free and frantically beckoned for her to continue.

The parking lot lights shone off her eyes, which suddenly went blank. Trett couldn't catch her before she fell to the ecophalt at their feet.

Of all the bad times for a vision . . . He picked up Rena like a baby and straightened with a low groan, then stepped between two hovs, determined to reach the other side of the parking lot. His attempted run was more of a lumbering walk.

Footsteps sounded behind him. Trett turned his head to see the same guard as before, dashing toward him.

"Damn it!" He tried to increase his pace, but Rena's dead weight was already taxing him. There was no way to avoid their pursuer.

"Stop!" The guard slowed to a jog as he weaved between vehicles. "I just need to talk to you."

Suddenly the burden in Trett's arms stiffened. He looked down to see Rena's eyes, wide and alert.

"Put me down," she snapped.

Trett complied as fast as he could. The guard was maybe thirty mets away; they could still escape. "Come on!" he said, turning to run.

"This way!" She beckoned and ran in the opposite direction.

As the guard turned to intercept them, Trett followed Rena, shouting, "The other way! We need to go the other way!"

Rena ignored him, even when Trett got so close that he was pleading directly into her ear.

Suddenly, she stopped. Trett pulled up short, nearly running into her. "Go!" he shouted.

She shook her head and stood stubbornly in a narrow parking spot, sized to fit a hov. It was one of five open spots, all near each other. The area was brightly lit by a nearby light. Rena had brought them to the most exposed place in the entire parking lot.

"Why?" Trett asked.

Rena didn't answer. Seconds later, the guard ran up, halting in an empty spot close to them. He held up his hands in a calming gesture and flashed them a friendly smile. It didn't compensate for his intimidating muscles. "I'm glad you stopped. Like I said, I just want to talk."

Movement caught Trett's attention as a dubhov emerged from between two nearby buildings. The vehicle was going much faster than it should have, and the two young men riding on it were laughing wildly, probably drunk.

The guard glanced over his shoulder and rolled his eyes, then returned his attention to Trett and Rena. "We were concerned about you. We noticed your flexes went offline . . ."

He kept talking in a soothing voice. The dubhov continued to approach, hovering dangerously high and weaving between other vehicles.

"Open spots! Right there!" one of the young men shouted.

"Where did you think I was going?" the other one replied.

The guard's expression was still calm, but his hand was creeping behind his back. Trett didn't doubt the man was reaching for stundiscs, the preferred weapon of private security guards. If Trett and Rena didn't comply, the guard would throw the palm-sized discs at them, incapacitating them long enough to restrain them. *Why are we just standing here, waiting to be attacked?*

In the distance, several staccato *uh-uh-uh* sounds traveled through the air. It was a distinctive noise—the call of angry caynins. The guard's eyes briefly flicked in that direction, and the corner of his mouth turned up as he pulled the stundiscs out.

Trett's heart pounded even more urgently. The stundiscs would paralyze him in seconds. Reinforcements, both human and beast, were on their way. And Rena was still standing there like a calm statue.

Suddenly, the approaching dubhov driver lost control. His vehicle tilted to one side at a dangerous angle, then careened into the guard, knocking him to the ground. The hov wobbled then dropped, landing on the prone guard's chest. A *crack* filled the air, the sickening sound of bones breaking.

"Now we go!" Rena cried, already running.

Trett followed, his eyes feeling like they'd bug out of his head. His stomach churned. *I think Rena just lured that guard into a crash.*

Rena seemed to know just where she was heading. She dashed all the way across the parking lot and led Trett between two buildings, slowing to a walk.

"We'll be safe on that street," she said, pointing ahead.

"For how long?"

"Long enough." Her next two words were so quiet, Trett almost missed them. "I hope."

***

Rena tried to ignore her pounding headache—*stupid PVS*—as she led Trett down the street. It was even busier than the previous street. She scanned the signs and pointed. "We'll get a table at that restaurant."

"We're going out to eat?" Trett asked incredulously.

"No one will find us there."

"We can't use our money!"

Rena hesitated, then said, "Just order water."

Trett sighed and followed her in.

About a dozen people were crowded in the tiny lobby, waiting for tables. At least that would make it easier for them to go unnoticed. They found a corner to huddle in, and Rena pulled out her flex.

"What the hell happened out there?" Trett asked, keeping his voice low.

She shifted her gaze to him. "Which part?"

"The dubhov crashing into the guard. You saw that in your vision?"

She nodded. "It was the only way to get rid of the guard that found us and the one who was tracking us with caynins." As if on cue, the distant *uh-uh-uh* of caynins rang through the air again.

Trett's eyebrows shot up. "They sound closer than before!"

"They probably are. Likely, the guard with the caynins found his colleague. It'll take time to arrange medical assistance."

"But our scent—"

She interrupted him. "Caynins are great protectors. They can recognize individuals by scent or voice. They're not great trackers in heavily populated areas, however. Our scents will be too faded by the time they come after us again." She saw more questions in Trett's expression and held up her flex. "We can talk more later. I need to work on these new IDs."

"Did you see anything else useful in your vision?" Trett pressed.

"I saw the restaurant we're sitting in. Like I said, it's safe. My vision ended here; we'll have to figure out the rest on our own."

Trett sighed, then pulled out his own flex. "I'll check to see if Ellin emmed me."

"Once we're using our new IDs, we won't get any messages from her," Rena said. "If she didn't em you, you should post in the reading group."

Trett nodded and firmed his flex. He cursed under his breath, then muttered, "No ems. I'll try the reading group."

Kizha had suggested they set up an alternate contact method, in case they got separated and couldn't communicate through ordinary channels. They'd all joined a public chat group that centered around books. Their logins weren't linked to their real or fake names, and they had a code to communicate with each other in case of emergency.

Rena sent Kizha a message about the new IDs. As she waited for a response, she watched Trett. It wasn't long before he angrily collapsed his device and wadded it up. She didn't have to ask whether he'd found a message from Ellin in the chat group.

Just then, Rena's flex buzzed. Kizha's em said,

I'll have the IDs to you in a few minutes. The money will take an hour or so.

Rena's jaw dropped.

That fast?

She stared at her screen until Kizha's reply popped up.

Back when you first asked me for fake IDs, you requested two for both you and Trett. Remember?

Oh, now she did remember that. She'd wondered why the nudge for two new IDs was only applicable to her and Trett. She slowly shook her head. Why had her prophecies prepared her for this, but they hadn't prevented whatever had happened to Ellin? To their parents?

Rena tried not to dwell on those unanswerable questions. She sent a quick thanks to Kizha then updated Trett on the new IDs and money. "We need to get on the local network and browse ads for cheap, short-term rentals. No hotels; Merak might have them watched."

Twenty minutes later, Trett held out his flex. He'd pulled up information on a tiny apartment not too far from there. "It says they're open to any length lease."

They reached out to the landlord, offering to pay her for three months in advance if she met them at the apartment immediately. She agreed with an eagerness that made Rena wary of the place's desirability.

No one pursued them as they walked to the apartment. Sure enough, it was old, stinky, and painfully small—but it was furnished and cheap.

"We'll pay twenty percent extra if you don't take it off the market," Rena said.

The landlord gave her a confused look.

"If anyone calls about it, tell them you're remodeling it and forgot to remove the listing," Rena instructed. "Do not under any circumstances show the space to other tenants."

"Okay," the landlord said. Questions blazed in her eyes, but she kept her mouth shut.

Rena pulled out her flex and saw that her money was in a new account under her new name. She paid for three months' rent, plus twenty percent, and the landlord left.

Still fighting a headache, Rena sat heavily on the couch and lay her head back. Despite her exhaustion, she didn't close her eyes. It would be useless to try to nap with these PVS symptoms and her anxiety about Ellin. "I'm going to order some groceries and supplies," she said. "I'll have them delivered."

"Good idea," Trett replied.

Rena had just found the nearest delivery service on her flex when pressure filled her head. Moments later, a vision overtook her consciousness.

It was Merak, sitting on a bed, flexscreen in hand. Through the large window over the bed, Cellerin Mountain rose in the distance.

Rena's perspective zoomed in, centering on Merak's head and upper torso. His face was somber as he examined whatever was on his flex. The top two buttons of his shirt were open, and he reached up and pulled out a necklace.

As Merak caressed the pendant with his thumb and fingers, Rena examined it. It was made of silvery metal molded in the shape of an eight-pointed star. At the end of each point was a teardrop-shaped loop. In the center of the star was a round, yellow gemstone, its facets glinting in the light.

Still within the vision, Rena pondered what she was seeing. Why would Merak be wearing a Rimstar, the symbol of the Rimorian faith? He wasn't religious. There was something familiar about that pendant, though, besides just the recognizable shape.

All at once, it struck her. When a person died, sometimes their loved ones had diamonds made of the carbon in their ashes. These *ash diamonds* were often placed in a setting shaped like a Rimstar.

Was that what this was? An ash diamond? If so, who was Merak remembering?

Again, Rena's perspective changed, shifting so she could see what Merak was looking at on his flex.

It was a picture of a little girl.

Merak coughed.

No, not a cough, Rena realized when the sound repeated. *A sob.*

He gestured at his screen, moving the photo down and revealing the title of the page. Rena read the heading as Merak traced it with his fingertip:

In Memory of

ELLIN MERAK

Underneath was his daughter's birthdate, over nineteen years ago, and the date of her death, seven years later.

The vision faded, and Rena's shoulders slumped in renewed exhaustion. Her breaths came quickly, and her eyes were wide as she turned to Trett.

"I've been wondering," she said, her voice quiet and level, "why

Merak seemed so interested in Ellin. Yes, she's smart, but other interns are smart too."

Trett looked up from his flex. "I've wondered the same."

Rena swallowed. "I think I know the answer."

As she related the vision to Trett, his eyes grew wide, and sharp breaths caused his chest to rise and fall rapidly. When he responded, his voice was quiet, but harsh. "You're telling me he's attached to Ellin because of his dead daughter? What does that even mean? Did he kill her because he can't stand to be around another Ellin? Or abduct her to somehow replace his daughter?"

"I don't know."

"Damn it, Rena! How are we going to find her?"

"We're living in a new place, and I don't have any routines here. Hopefully that'll provoke some visions about her."

Trett's hand slammed down on the bench beside him with a loud *whack*. "That's not enough!"

"It'll have to be."

Trett glared at her, his jaw muscles visibly clenching along with his fists.

Rena reached out and placed a hand on his shoulder. She'd never so much as shaken his hand before. He flinched at the contact but didn't pull away. "Trett," she said, "I love her too. More than you know."

She felt his shoulder relax a little. His mouth fell open, and he closed it and swallowed. "Good." His head dropped, and then his body started to shake. Snuffling sounds escaped his mouth and nose.

Rena kept her hand on him, not sure what else to do. Without warning, another vision began.

Ellin lay on a mattress in some sort of metal room. She wore a hooded jacket and was wrapped in a green blanket. Rena's perspective zoomed in, and she saw Ellin's torso moving with her breaths. The vision ended.

Rena sent up a wordless prayer of thanks, then gathered Trett into a hug and whispered in his ear, "She's alive."

24

I DIDN'T EVEN TRY *to run.*

After a long bout of silent, violent trembling, that was the thought that finally brought Ellin to tears.

She'd sat there, huddled up like a frightened animal, watching Merak. She'd seen him put his gun away. Sure, he was blocking the doorway, but she might have managed to push past him. He was decades older than her; she might have outrun him. If he'd grabbed her, well, she had nails and knees and fists. She could have fought. She could have grabbed the gun, maybe even figured out how to use it.

Instead, she'd fallen into her default mode. She'd given her boss obedience and respect, as if that could win him over.

And he'd left her here alone, in a freezer just cold enough to be terribly uncomfortable, with no blankets or food and no way to communicate.

Nobody knows I'm here.

NOBODY KNOWS I'M HERE!

She screamed, knowing the freezer's thick walls probably blocked her voice from exiting. Even if some sound got through, there wasn't a soul within earshot.

The sensation overtaking her was one she hadn't felt since the early years after the Skytrain accident. It was like some sadist had planted a line of stones inside her, sharp and heavy, beginning at her esophagus and ending in her intestines. She hugged her stomach, still crying, surprised her tears could make it past the solid fear inhabiting her throat.

You have power over this.

The thought pressed its way through her tears. It was a statement her favorite therapist had made, a mantra he'd insisted Ellin repeat to herself every time panic gripped her.

She couldn't stop the fear entirely; she knew that. What she could do was *breathe.* So she did, beginning the process of converting her sobs into deep breaths. In. Out. Repeat.

In an effort to calm herself, she closed her eyes and pictured Trett. She tried to think about him smiling, but instead all she could see was the confused, pained expression he'd worn when she broke up with him. That made her heart beat at an even more frenzied pace, so she replaced Trett's face with Rena's. The image of her stoic sister comforted her just enough to stop her tears, though she still couldn't seem to draw enough air into her lungs.

This panic isn't going to kill me.

That was another truth she'd learned. She whispered it to herself, then examined the panic, acknowledging its grip on her airway and heart. The pressure began to let up.

She repeated the phrase, out loud this time. "This panic isn't going to kill me." The irony of it slapped her in the face: *But Merak might.* A chuckle escaped her mouth. Laughter was completely irrational, but it sure beat crying.

The anxiety still had her in its grip, but now she was calm enough to partner it with logic. *I can't just sit here. If I want to escape from Merak, I have to act, even though I'm afraid.*

So she stood, drying her cheeks with her palms. She paced and planned, drinking from the water pouch, allowing her panic to subside one breath at a time. Just as she swallowed the last of the water, she realized what a mistake she'd made. She had to pee. And she was trapped in a metal cube.

Ellin sat. She could hold it until Merak came back tomorrow. Maybe he'd let her go behind the building. It would be the perfect opportunity to escape.

She'd been sitting in the back corner for perhaps an hour, huddled against the chill and trying to ignore her screaming bladder, when she came to the conclusion that she couldn't wait to pee.

This is just a problem to be solved, nothing more.

She didn't exactly have a lot of experience relieving herself outside of a bathroom. The last time she'd done it, she was four years old. She'd decided to water her mother's flowerbed. Pants around her ankles, she squatted, but her balance wasn't the best, and somehow she got more pee on her pants and shoes than on the flowers. Since then, toilets had always been sufficient for her needs.

While she probably had better balance now, she wasn't about to risk the same results, especially without any extra clothes. *Pants and shoes off, then.*

She pulled off her shoes and socks. When the soles of her feet contacted the cold metal floor, her entire body released a shiver. She ignored it and, after moving her antirad to the pocket on her shirt, took off her pants and underwear.

Then she started crying again. How had she gotten to this point—standing half-naked in a cold, dimly-lit freezer? It didn't matter that there was no one to see her; she could see herself—the goosebumps on her legs, her bare thighs squeezing together to prevent an accident, her trembling knees.

Her weeping increased her urge to empty her bladder, and she darted to the front corner of the chamber, where it was a little more shadowy. It was a silly concession to modesty; there was no hiding in this place if Merak returned.

Ellin squatted against the corner, the metal walls shockingly cold against her bare butt. Her whole body shook with sobs as she released the muscles in her aching pelvis and felt the relief she'd been waiting for.

The floor of the freezer, it turned out, wasn't quite flat. Pale yellow liquid streamed toward her left foot. She scooted her foot out of the way but immediately lost her balance, landing in the puddle of warm urine that was still growing wider.

Her cries turned into wails. She continued to sit, wiping her running nose with the back of her hand, until her bladder was finally empty. Then she stood and screamed every curse word she could think of as she rubbed her wet butt against the cold wall, trying to dry it off, aware of how absurd the action was.

Ellin's humiliation turned to fury, and she took great gulps of air, forcing herself to stop crying. She gave up her pointless wiping and stepped away from the wall, eyeing the floor.

Her discarded clothes and shoes were in the path of the still-spreading urine, so she moved them to the back corner. She'd wait to get dressed until she was dry.

"Stop feeling sorry for yourself!" Her words echoed in the metal cube. "Think, Ellin!"

Merak's treating me like an animal. I won't let him see me acting like one.

Ellin paced, arms folded against the cold, trying to convince herself she was calm, controlled. Strong. At last, her legs and thighs felt dry, and she eagerly pulled her clothes and shoes back on. The fabric was cold on her skin, but it was better than being bare.

She didn't want to sleep, but if she was going to fight back when Merak came, she had to be rested. She lay on her side in the same corner where she'd put her clothes.

The floor made her entire body colder, so she brought her knees to her chest and lay her chilled hands under her head. She shuddered, though she was unsure whether she was reacting more to the cold, her fear, or the smell of stagnant urine. The room was too bright to sleep, but she couldn't bring herself to turn off the light.

She lay, imagining every way she might fight Merak, remembering self-defense moves she'd learned in school. *Knee to his groin. Fingers in his eyes. Kick his knees. Stomp his toes. Choke him until he passes out.*

At last, she drifted into a light sleep, waking often. Her plans for Merak filled her waking moments, but it was Trett and Rena who populated her dreams.

* * *

SUNDAY, CYON 24, 6293
-13 DAYS

The next morning, Ellin was doing stretches on the floor when she heard the squeak of the door's metal bar being lifted. She leapt up and pressed herself against the wall, right next to the door. As soon as Merak entered, she'd attack. The electric buzz of adrenaline filled her limbs.

The door cracked open beside Ellin. Her muscles tightened.

Something slid in through the narrow gap. Merak's voice followed: "Put those on your hands and feet. When they're properly in place, they'll send a signal to my flex."

The door slammed close. Ellin pressed against its cold metal, but she heard the bar come down, rendering her efforts useless. She reached down to pick up whatever Merak had slid into the room.

There were two identical objects, thin figure-eights made of Flexen, the same pliable material used in flexscreens. She wasn't sure what they were officially called; everyone just referred to them as *eights*. Once placed on her ankles and wrists, they'd tighten, restraining her.

She threw them across the room and stood next to the door again.

It cracked open, and before Merak could speak, she shoved the door hard. It didn't open any farther.

"Ellin, I admire your tenacity, but I know you've had all night to come up with escape plans, and I've had all night to consider how to stop you. There's a gravity-amplified shelving unit in front of this door. I'm also here, holding a gun and watching through the gap. Put the eights on, please. I have blankets and food."

She kept pushing.

Merak didn't say anything else. He didn't have to. The door wouldn't budge.

Ellin looked down at the empty water pouch and shivered from the chill of the room. She could refuse to do what Merak said, and by the next day, she'd be weak from dehydration.

Or she could accept his offerings, keep her strength up, and attack when he dropped his guard. Bound hands could still turn into fists.

She retrieved the eights and sat in front of the crack in the door, meeting Merak's gaze. Keeping her expression blank, she placed the restraints on her ankles. They tightened, and she repeated the process on her wrists.

Ellin watched Merak push a button on the shelf. With a *shhh* sound, it hovered off the ground. He moved it out of the way and pressed the button again, lowering the shelf back to the floor. Only then did he open the door and enter.

"I'm sorry, Ellin." Merak knelt, out of her reach, his eyes oozing sympathy. "I didn't want you to have to wear those, but as I told you yesterday, I can't risk you leaving. Things will be better when you see what I've brought you. I promise." His eyebrows drew close to each other, and one side of his upper lip curved up. "What is that smell?"

Ellin raised an eyebrow and stared at him. It was a stupid question; the odor could only be one thing.

Merak's face slackened in realization, and then he brought a hand up to cover his mouth. He looked down, and his gaze quickly found the puddle from the night before. "Ellin, I didn't even think about your need to relieve yourself. Oh no, I'm sorry. That must have been—I'm . . . I'm genuinely sorry I didn't think of that."

Ellin had never seen him so perplexed. She felt the sting of tears wanting to sprout, and she blinked several times. His regret looked so real, and his voice sounded so kind. After less than a day in this place, she was already craving human empathy. *But not from him!* She swallowed and hardened her expression.

"Before I leave, I'll find something you can use as a toilet," he said. "I will. But first, I'll get you the other things I brought."

Merak exited and came right back in, carrying a large versabox. He set it next to her and pulled out a pale-green blanket. He ran his hand lightly along its surface. "We redid my daughter's room recently. This was hers." His voice was quiet. "It's very soft."

He handed the blanket to Ellin, following it with a pillow and an item she didn't recognize. "This is a mattress. Push the button in the corner, and it'll fill with heated foam. Here are a couple of changes of clothes and a jacket. I'm sorry it's cold in here; the climastat won't go any warmer. I brought these wipes so you can give yourself sponge baths, and this container will sanitize them for reuse. There's plenty of food and water. Oh, and—" Merak reached in and pulled out a flex. "This is set up with games, books, and films. It doesn't have a network connection, but it will keep you occupied."

He arranged the food along one wall, glancing at her frequently as if expecting her to waddle away with her eights on. When he was done, he sat in front of her. "Is there anything else you need, Ellin? I want you to be as comfortable as possible in this place until you're ready to join me in the world again."

Ellin looked pointedly at the stinking liquid on the floor, then raised her eyebrows at Merak.

"Don't worry, I haven't forgotten. I have an idea." He pulled out his flex and set to work on it. A couple of minutes later, he pushed one corner of the versabox.

Ellin watched as the box lost its firmness. One piece fell off, turning into a flat disk. The rest molded itself into a bowl with smooth, rounded edges, like an upside-down bell with a flat base.

"Best bowl design I could find on short order," he said. "I hope it works. You can keep the lid on it when you're not using it. You'll have to use the wipes since this bowl doesn't have a sprayer. Of course, I'll clean the bowl daily."

"*You* will empty my chamber pot every day?"

They were the first words she'd spoken since he'd arrived, and he chuckled. "Yes. I have two children. It takes more than a chamber pot to deter me." He gestured to the eights on her wrists and ankles. "I hate to make you keep those things on any longer, but there's one more thing I want to do before I go. I'll need to head back to the glide-craft first. I promise I'll be quick."

With a smile, he left, bolting the door.

Ellin was hungry, but she wouldn't debase herself by letting Merak see her eat with her hands bound. She watched the door, trying desperately to think of a way to stop him. She was still at a loss for ideas when he returned.

He bore a spray bottle, a towel, and a sheepish expression. "I really am sorry I didn't provide a way for you to relieve yourself, Ellin. The least I can do is get this place cleaned up for you."

He knelt on the floor and cleaned up every bit of dry or wet urine he could find. As he worked, he tried to start a few conversations with Ellin, but when she didn't respond, he gave up.

After a few minutes, he stood. "Now that's an improvement." He stowed the spray bottle and dirty towel under his arm and pulled out his flex. "Ellin, I have to go, but as soon as I bolt the door, I'll loosen the eights. From now on when I visit, I'll knock, and I expect you to put them on." He nodded at her and gave her a small smile. "I'll see you tomorrow."

"Wait!" Ellin blurted.

"Yes?"

"My antirad—how do I make sure it protects me when I'm getting dressed?"

"Oh, Ellin, you don't need to worry about that. The radiation doesn't travel this far. You'll be safe." He pulled out his own antirad and pressed a button on it. "See? I'm turning mine off."

He smiled at her, but Ellin didn't feel any better. His words reminded her of how far away she was, not just from the dig site, but from everything else too. *I won't let him see my fear. I won't.*

Merak left. The bar on the door clanged back into place, and Ellin's bonds loosened. She slipped the eights off and tried to ignore the heavy tightness that filled her core when silence settled over her again.

She squared her jaw and put on the jacket, which was branded with *MERAK* in huge letters across the back. Then she used the chamber pot and scurried over to the food. It was delicious, a fact she resented.

25

Ellin quickly fell into a routine in her metal prison. She woke early, thanks to the alarm on her flex. For fifteen minutes, she meditated, drawing air in and releasing it, developing a calming rhythm as she pictured herself on a beach or atop a mountain. Next, she rose and ensured she'd washed up, dressed, and fed herself before Merak arrived. He wouldn't ever see her weak if she could help it.

She watched films or played games on her flex in the morning. Then she ate lunch, exercised, and spent more time on her flex in the afternoon. After dinner, she read books and went to bed early. It was monotonous, and she had way too much time to think and worry. She'd chewed her fingernails down so far that her fingertips were sore, and she'd caught herself pulling out eyebrow hairs too.

For the first few days, she tried desperately to think of a plan to escape and stop the dig. Merak, however, was too consistent. Every morning, he knocked on the door and entered once she'd put the eights on.

She wanted to trip him with her bound feet or hit him in the eye with both fists, but he never got close enough. Then, horrifyingly, she found herself looking forward to his visits. He was unfailingly friendly, and after days of near-silence, she responded to one of his questions, then couldn't stop talking.

She wouldn't answer his questions about her family, but she did tell him about her goals—to become a surgeon, or maybe a journalist. He smiled at that, then updated her on the dig, which was progressing according to schedule.

On the sixth full day of her imprisonment, Ellin woke from a dream in which Merak had been holding her tightly, rubbing her back. It wasn't romantic in any way; rather, it was the type of warm, comforting hug she'd never been without. Her dad had given her hugs like that every day, and after her parents had died, her friends' parents sometimes wrapped her up in tight embraces. Then there was Trett. He'd always been a great hugger.

Ellin shut her eyes, hoping to return to the dream, craving the fatherly comfort she'd felt in Merak's warm arms.

She sat up fast enough to make herself dizzy. "This is not okay!" she shouted, determined to push the dream out of her head. When she realized she was hugging herself, she flung her arms out, shaking them off as if Merak had contaminated them.

Ellin's flexscreen was next to her bed. She picked it up and looked at the date. Cyon 29th. *Eight days until the end of the world.*

She realized she'd never bothered to look at the date the day before. She'd spent the entire day worrying about whether she was talking too much to Merak, while also planning what their next conversation might be.

The man whose hug she craved was responsible for her living in a cold, metal box that always smelled of human waste. Because of Alvun Merak, Ellin was isolated from the world, and Rena and Trett were surely frantic with worry.

Trett. How she wished she'd brought him with her to meet with Merak. Maybe together, they would've avoided capture. Or—and she knew it was a terrible thing to wish for, but the desire remained—maybe Merak would have thrown them both in this cold room. They could've made up and waited for the end of the world together. If one of them got anxious, knowing their time was short, they could have kissed or joked or read together—something, anything, *together*—to distract each other.

Her continued desire for Trett had compelled her to consider an uncomfortable question: *Why did I break up with him?* After days of chewing on it, she thought she'd figured it out.

Her relentless drive to achieve had always carried her along like a massive ocean wave. It was thrilling, to be sure. It was also exhausting, the constant effort to keep from drowning in ever-higher goals.

Trett had come along in a boat, offering to pull her up and travel together, but she'd been thrashing in the waves for too long, all alone. It was all she knew. She'd panicked at the thought of depending on him, afraid she'd lose herself.

I gave up the person I loved the most so I could save the world. That would've made sense if he were trying to stop me . . . but all he wanted to do was help me.

As Ellin was mulling over that terrible truth, the alarm on her flex sounded. Time to get up.

She hadn't cried since her first morning in the freezer, but with Trett's face and laugh heavy in her mind, she was having trouble holding back the tears. Meditation would help, but this morning, she couldn't bring herself to do it. She clenched her teeth and blinked repeatedly as she washed up, used the chamber pot, and got dressed. Breakfast was next on her schedule, but none of the food looked appetizing. She crawled onto her mattress, buried her head into her pillow, and gave in to loud sobs.

That was her position when Merak's fist pounded on the door. Ellin retrieved her eights, still weeping as she put them on. That done, she sat on the edge of the mattress, face buried in both hands.

She heard the squeak of the door opening. Then Merak's voice reached her ears. "Oh no . . . What happened?"

Ellin tried to laugh at the ridiculousness of the question, but instead, she cried harder.

Then it was just like her dream. Merak came over and knelt in front of her and gathered her in his arms, holding her just tight enough, one hand on her head, the other rubbing her back. She melted into the hug, crying into his shoulder.

"I'm sorry," he said, "I know this is hard. It'll be better soon, I promise. I know you can't see it right now, and I wish you could. It'll be beautiful, Ellin. You just need to hang on."

Those words, *You just need to hang on*, snapped Ellin out of the perfect peace she'd found in his arms. He was hanging onto her, controlling every bit of her life, from what she wore to where she pissed. Now he was hanging onto her physically, taking full advantage of the vulnerable position he had put her in.

No more hanging on.

Ellin gently pushed Merak's chest with her bound hands. When he pulled back with a questioning expression, she formed her hands into fists and thrust them up, smashing them into his jaw. With a grunt, he fell back, his backside hitting the metal floor hard. He jumped up and turned away before she could see his reaction.

After grabbing her reeking chamber pot, he left the room without a word. When he brought the pot back, she'd stopped crying.

"I thought we were building trust, Ellin." Merak turned away, but not before she saw the same blaze in his eyes she'd spied the first night they'd met. He strode out of the room without another word.

When she heard the door bar come down, Ellin waited for the eights to loosen from her wrists and ankles. They remained tight.

She spent the rest of the day hopping or scooting on her butt whenever she needed anything. Most of the time, though, she stayed in bed, fantasizing about beating up Merak and having world-class make-out sessions with Trett.

As days in this metal box went, it was a good one.

SATURDAY, CYON 30, 6293
-7 DAYS

Trett took a big bite of a Vegebar, chewed, swallowed, and took a second bite.

He hated Vegebars. They were made of dried elbow leaf, a variety of lettuce native to Anyari. It was as appetizing as it sounded. Fortified with protein, vitamins, and minerals, the bars provided a convenient alternative to real food.

Rena claimed to love them and had stocked the kitchen with them. That was a full week ago, on the day Ellin disappeared. Trett had been too distracted to argue with her choice.

Even now, he didn't think it mattered what he ate. Nothing would taste good. He just needed calories and nutrition so that if—no, *when*—Rena had a vision leading them to Ellin, he'd have the strength to go get her.

He glanced at his flex. It wasn't his normal breakfast time yet, but he'd been awake for hours. The little bit of sleep he'd gotten had been restless, and he'd finally given up all chance of getting comfortable. He'd offered the single bedroom to Rena, and he couldn't help looking longingly in the room whenever her door opened. Her bed was narrow, but at least it was long enough to stretch out on—unlike the tiny sofa Trett was using.

Groaning, he stood and walked into the cramped bathroom. He splashed his face with water from the tap and dried off on a cheap towel they'd bought. He turned around, leaned back against the sink, folded his arms, and stared at the wall. Had Ellin willingly gone somewhere with Merak? If so, why hadn't she told him or Rena what she was planning?

Because she's stubborn.

He shook his head. He'd had this conversation with himself countless times over the past week. It was true; Ellin was stubborn.

But so am I.

How many times had he avoided telling Ellin he was hurt by her single-minded pursuit of one goal after another? How often over the last couple of years had he covered his resentment with smiles, jokes, and kisses?

He'd waited to tell her how he felt until the world was about to end . . . and he'd expected her to take it well?

Squelching a desire to punch the wall, Trett turned and left the little room. Back at the sofa, he threw his fist into a pillow instead. He wanted to go back to that conversation with her in the café and redo the whole thing. *No, I want to go back to a million other conversations and redo those.* Maybe if he'd trusted her more, she would've told him whatever crazy plan she'd come up with a week ago.

Trett ate the rest of the Vegebar with his eyes closed. It tasted a little better when he didn't have to look at the blotchy, purply-brown color.

"I had a vision."

Trett's head snapped up. He hadn't even heard Rena's door open.

She walked in and sat next to him. Judging from the dark skin beneath her bloodshot eyes, he guessed she hadn't slept much either.

"About Ellin?" he prompted. She'd had several visions confirming Ellin's safety in that weird, metal room. She'd even seen Merak there. Infuriatingly, the prophecies hadn't revealed Ellin's location.

Rena nodded. "You won't like this, Trett."

His breathing immediately quickened. "Tell me."

"Merak was holding her."

"What the hell does that mean?" His voice had taken on a growling intensity that scared even him.

Rena's eyes widened. "Trett—it wasn't anything sexual. He was holding her like a young child. Like she was *his* child."

Trett's breathing had only gotten faster, and he blinked against his lightheadedness. "That doesn't make me feel much better."

"I know. I saw something else too. When Merak walked out of the metal room, it looked like he was in a vacant store. I think she's in a walk-in refrigerator or freezer, Trett."

"A vacant store? Where?"

"I don't know; I didn't see any windows or anything. Maybe I'll see more next time."

"You've got to contact that friend of yours. Surely she can pull up a list of vacant stores with walk-in coolers."

"I already did. She said most government databases don't go into that much detail. She'll keep looking."

"There has to be something else we can do!"

Rena looked down for several seconds, then returned her gaze to his. "We can pray."

Trett let out his breath and looked down. He didn't know when he'd grabbed the pillow, but he was twisting it so tightly, one of the seams looked ready to break.

26

SATURDAY, CYON 30, 6293

-7 DAYS

THE DAY after she punched Merak, Ellin woke to the sound of the bar on the door lifting. Her jailer was early.

Merak entered and gave her a sad smile before taking her chamber pot out. When he returned, he sat on the edge of her bed, near her head, where neither her bound hands nor feet could injure him.

Leaning over, he gently took her hands in his, *tsk*ing at the chafing on her wrists. Then he reached into his pocket and pulled out a tube of medicated salve. He placed the tube in her palm and closed her fingers on it.

Without a word, he left. Seconds later, the eights released, and Ellin stretched, squashing down the rush of gratitude she felt toward Merak for bringing her the medication. *None of that.* She'd use his salve and eat his food, but she wouldn't allow an ounce of emotional dependence to develop. Not after what happened yesterday.

When she'd finished getting ready (a silly term; what was she getting ready for?), she sat on her bed and picked up her flexscreen. The IDM icon was blinking with a notification. It had to have come from Merak; he was the only one who could connect to this flex. She opened the message.

It was a confidential update on the dig. Ellin read that they were on schedule and expected to reach the isotope in six to ten days. *Seven, to be precise.*

The IDM described the experts' plans for working with the isotope. Engineers had retrofitted current machinery to tame and harness the radiation's power, and medical researchers had already planned their first round of experiments.

The sheer quantity of information was overwhelming. Ellin spent much of the day reading it. She dug into the complex material, sticking with it until she understood it. Her anxiety stayed more in the background than it had since she'd entered her metal cell. Lost in the thrill of learning, she had to repeatedly remind herself of the truth. *We have a week to stop this.* She went to sleep that night with the apocalypse on her mind, and the next morning, she woke with new motivation to beat Merak at his own game.

When he arrived, he was carrying a knitted hat. He'd guessed, quite rightly, that Ellin's ears were cold. She swallowed her pride and put the hat on. Then she met his gaze and asked, "What safety precautions will the archeologists take when they remove the isotope?"

At first, Merak looked startled. After her brief attack two days before, he must've expected more hostility. Then his entire face relaxed into a smile, and he sat next to her on the bed, pulling out his own flex and showing her the equipment and personal protection they'd prepared for the few people who might come in contact with the isotope. His voice was loud and warm, his gestures flamboyant. Alvun Merak loved this project.

"If it were me," Ellin said, when Merak finally paused, "and I know it's not—but if it were, I'd suggest additional eye protection. Just in case."

Merak's eyes left the flex and met Ellin's. "That's a good idea." He shook his head slightly, chuckling.

"So good it's funny?" Ellin challenged.

"No—I'm not laughing at the idea, Ellin. It's excellent. However, I thought you'd never come around. I'm glad to realize I was wrong."

She continued to ask questions and give suggestions. Merak seemed to enjoy the conversation immensely, staying for over an hour.

When he left, Ellin grasped the top of her new hat, intending to pull it off. It was soft and warm, but it was one more reminder of her dependence on Merak.

She stopped. *It's not a symbol of my dependence on him; it's a symbol of his misplaced trust in me.* Her mouth curved into a small smile, and she pulled the hat lower on her ears.

SUNDAY, CYON 31, 6293

-6 DAYS

Rena sat straight up in bed. She'd had a dream. Nothing prophetic, just an old-fashioned, why-didn't-I-think-of-that-before dream. She sent Kizha an urgent message and waited for a response.

Fifteen minutes and five unanswered messages later, she had to accept the fact that even Kizha slept sometimes. After trying unsuccessfully to go back to sleep, she crept through the living room, where Trett was snoring on the couch. She made herself coffee in the kitchen and returned to her room.

At last, when the sky was just starting to lighten, her flex buzzed. Kizha's message read,

I'm so sorry. I fell asleep on the couch, and my flex was in my room.

Rena replied,

Can you video chat?

A few seconds later, Kizha's face filled the screen. She was in her small living room, and her sleepy, green eyes lit up when she saw Rena.

Rena got right to the point. "Is there a way to send tracking software to someone's flex without them knowing it?"

Kizha bit her bottom lip and looked thoughtfully off to the side before turning back to Rena. "I can't embed software into an em or IDM; security scans would prevent delivery."

"Oh." Rena's shoulders slumped.

"But there's another way. If someone clicks a link in your message, the site they visit can download software onto their device. Still, it would take some sophisticated programming to avoid detection."

Rena gave Kizha a small smile. "You up for some sophisticated programming?

"I'd love the challenge."

"That leaves us with one more problem," Rena said. "We'll need contact information for the person I want to send the message to."

"Who is it?"

Rena took a deep breath. "Arisa Merak."

"Why don't we contact Alvun Merak directly?" Trett's eyes bored into Rena's, his half-eaten Vegebar forgotten on the couch armrest.

Rena swallowed a bite of her own bar. "We can send a message to him too. His IDM contact is public. However, he probably gets hundreds of messages a day. He's not likely to read an IDM if he doesn't know the sender. We probably won't even get past his filters. It should be much easier to contact his wife."

She watched Trett run his hand through his short, brown hair and shake his head hard. Poor guy; he'd been a wreck since Ellin's disappearance.

"So we're counting on Arisa to open our message and then send it to her husband?" Trett asked. "And we're counting on him to open it and click the link?"

Rena nodded.

Trett pursed his lips tightly and folded his arms. His voice was low and furious when he finally spoke. "We need a better plan, Rena."

"I know," she murmured. "I wish my visions would tell me how to find Ellin. This is the best I've got."

He drew in a deep, loud breath through his nose, then exhaled the same way. "Okay. What are we going to send her? What's she most likely to open and forward to her husband?"

"I was hoping you could help me think of an idea."

They were silent for a few minutes, and then Trett's back snapped upright. "Didn't you say she's religious?"

"Yes."

A grin filled Trett's face. "I hope your friend can help us digitally impersonate a Rimorian emissary."

When he explained his idea to Rena, she nodded sharply, gritting her teeth against the stab of guilt in her chest. She didn't want to use religion to manipulate someone, but she didn't see any better options.

She and Trett drafted two messages, one to Merak and one to Arisa. Rena sent them to Kizha, who confirmed she'd found Arisa's private contact information. Once Kizha finished setting up the tracking virus, she'd send the messages.

Rena grabbed two more Vegebars and tossed one to Trett. As she ate, waiting on Kizha's response, she mulled over her recent shrouded prophecies. She'd seen Ellin and Trett fighting Merak. Ellin had to break free to make those visions come true . . . right?

Doubts besieged Rena. *Ellin has been doing whatever she can to thwart my original prophecy. If she succeeded, she could have altered other aspects of the future too.* In getting captured, had Ellin altered an immutable prophecy? Was that how she'd saved the world? The thought sickened Rena. *I want her to succeed. But please, God, not at that cost.*

After six excruciating hours, Kizha at last confirmed she'd sent the IDMs with the tracking link. She agreed that Alvun Merak was unlikely to see the message. They were depending on Arisa to pass her IDM on to her husband.

In Vallinger, where Arisa lived, it was the middle of the night. Despite that, Rena and Trett both gathered around Rena's flex, hoping against hope that Kizha would tell them their message had been opened. They watched one news video after another, and after a couple of hours, they started a classic film marathon.

Hours passed. They ate Vegebars for dinner and hardly spoke to one another. Trett took to pacing through the tiny space. Eventually, they both sat in the living room, staring at their flexes.

At two-thirty the next morning, Rena jolted awake from a short, unplanned nap. "This is ridiculous," she told Trett. "If we find Ellin, we'll need to be rested to rescue her. I'll change my settings so that if Kizha contacts me, my flex will sound an alarm so loud, it'll wake the whole building."

Trett grunted in response and lay on the little couch.

Rena woke after several hours of sleep. Her flex was stubbornly silent. Somehow, she and Trett made it through that day. And the next. Kizha sent Alvun and Arisa more IDMs. According to her, the messages all remained unopened.

Three days before the prophesied apocalypse, Rena entered the living room. When Trett woke and she shook her head at him, he started sobbing. Rena was pretty sure he was crying too hard to notice she was weeping too.

WEDNESDAY, CYGNI 3, 6293
-3 DAYS

As soon as Merak entered her cell three days before the end of the world, Ellin burst into tears. It was easy to do; she'd hardly slept for two nights.

"Ellin," he said, coming close, but not too close, "what's wrong, sweetheart?"

She forced the words out, despite sobs and bone-deep reservations. "Please hold me."

She was standing in the middle of the room. Merak glanced at her bound hands and feet, then scooped her up and sat on her bed, holding her like a baby. He rocked back and forth and whispered assurances, his own voice cracking with emotion.

Ellin hated how wonderful it felt, hated Merak for bringing her to the place where she'd actually enjoy this. She stopped weeping, but her breaths still came quickly, fueled by fury. She buried her face in his chest, schooling it into a humble expression.

"Tell me what's wrong, please." Merak sounded desperate.

She wished he'd put her down, but he continued to hold her close. "It's silly," she said.

"I'm sure it's not. Please tell me."

"I've read everything you've brought me for days now. Most of it, I've read four or five times. It's hard being in here when I know how much good work is being done out there."

Merak finally removed her from his lap, sitting her gently on the bed next to him. He said nothing, instead pulling his flex out of his pocket. After firming it, he tilted it so Ellin couldn't see it. A couple of taps, and the eights on her hands released.

Ellin gasped and pulled the things off. Before she knew it, she was hugging Merak, whispering, "Thank you." She had to force herself to let go of him.

Merak put the eights in his pocket. "This is a symbol of my trust. If all goes as I expect, I think you'll be joining me 'out there,' as you put it, very soon."

Ellin smiled, blinking away more tears. "How soon?"

Mirroring her smile, Merak said, "Perhaps in a week or so."

Her face collapsed into hopelessness, and she looked away.

"Ellin." Merak's hand cupped her cheek, and he brought her face up to look at him again. "Just a week. It'll be over before you know it." He kissed the top of her head and left.

The restraints on her feet loosened. She took them off and threw them at the door.

Merak bolted the door, then darted outside. He fell to his knees on the dirt, buried his face in his hands, and wept.

Holding Ellin like that—it brought him right back to the hours he'd spent holding his little girl in the hospital. She'd been sick with a fever for a few days, complaining of a tummy ache, and had suddenly gone into a coma.

He could still picture the doctor's face when he'd spoken the words: *Extremely rare, extremely aggressive liver cancer.*

Relieved hope had flooded Merak's heart. He'd grabbed Arisa's hand and spoken through a throat swollen with tears: *Cancer—so it's curable?*

Not this time.

Merak insisted they do everything they could, and the doctors complied. As Ellin continued to decline, Merak read everything he could find on modern cancer treatment. He came across the same basic statement, over and over: *Cancer has essentially been cured, except for rare, aggressive cases.*

Those last five words relegated his daughter to a cruel footnote, destined for digital immortality in some doctor's case study.

Ellin died six days after her diagnosis.

In the year after her death, Merak grew his company from a small, successful firm to a world-class corporation. As soon as he could spare the funds, he and Arisa started the Merak Foundation. They threw money at researchers specializing in *rare, aggressive* cancers.

Within three years, the nation of Vallinger had the technology to cure every form of cancer. Four years later, every country in the world had the same ability. The Merak Foundation was, quite rightly, given credit for most of the advancements.

Now, Merak was on a quest to shorten the length of cancer treatments. Yes, every cancer was curable, but what if someone didn't get diagnosed in time? He wouldn't rest until it was possible to eradicate cancer in one simple treatment, or even prevent it altogether.

Looking back at the faded, green building, he was filled with an urge to run back in and hold Ellin close again. Then he could let her out of that dreadful room, bring her home, introduce her—no, he couldn't go that far. Arisa and Gil wouldn't understand. Instead, he'd mentor Ellin, keep her close by his side as he worked with the corporation and the foundation. She'd change the world with him. Just like his Ellin would have done.

No longer crying, Merak stood and took a step back toward the building, then halted. Something told him it wasn't time to release Ellin yet, not until they had the isotope and she could witness its magnificent potential. If only she knew how much it hurt him to leave her in there.

"Soon, dear Ellin." He kissed his hand and held it out toward the building.

WEDNESDAY, CYGNI 3, 6293

-3 DAYS

Arisa Merak wiped her eyes.

She'd just had a video chat with her husband. He was in his room at the compound in Therro. That was her first sign that he wasn't doing well; he was never in his bedroom in the middle of a work day. Then there were Alvun's eyes; they'd looked . . . grieved? No, that wasn't quite it; she'd seen him look grieved plenty of times through the years.

Haunted. Yes, that was it. He'd looked haunted, and he wouldn't tell her why. He said the project was going according to plan, and he seemed to be getting over the recent loss of two of his researchers.

What is it, my love? Why won't you tell me?

Arisa's eyes were drawn to a painting on their bedroom wall. It was of Ellin at six years old, a year before her death. The portrait artist had perfectly captured her stubbornness and vivacity. Twelve years after losing her daughter, Arisa could look at the painting and feel true joy, bittersweet though it was.

Her joy shifted to concern as Alvun returned to her thoughts. Therapists and emissaries had told Arisa over and over that there was no right or wrong way to grieve. Yet she'd always sensed that Alvun had never truly faced their loss. He rarely talked about Ellin's death or his grief.

That haunted look in Alvun's eyes—it must be related to Ellin. That would explain why he was unwilling to talk about it.

Arisa got out of bed and walked to her private chapel. She touched the panel on the wall. Soft light and soothing music filled the room. Ignoring the chair she usually sat on, she fell to her knees and brought her forehead down to rest on the thick carpet.

"God, how do I help him?" she whispered.

She waited in silence, not really expecting an answer. Almost immediately, an image entered her mind—a list of IDMs. She chuckled softly; she was terribly behind on her messages. Taking a deep breath, she gently refused the distracting thought, centering herself by whispering a phrase of scripture from the Sacrex.

The image returned. All those unread messages. "IDMs, God?" she asked. "Now?"

She couldn't get the messages off her mind, so she stood and returned to her room, where she sat on her bed, firmed her flex, and pulled up her IDMs. Three messages from Emissary Thyri Tolgen caught Arisa's eye. She opened the first one and read it.

Dear Ms. Merak,

I am on an extended sabbatical and believe I have received a divine message for your husband. While I am attempting to contact him as well, I am unsure whether he will see my IDM. Will you please pass this message on to him?

It is a passage from the Sacrex that I believe will encourage him in the good work he's doing. You are welcome to read it as well; it's in the link below.

There is no need to respond; it will be a month before I read any messages I receive.

Sincerely,
Thyri Tolgen

Following the emissary's name was a link. Arisa clicked it and read the short scripture passage.

When you help those who are hungry, you bring nourishment to their bodies and to your own character.

When you aid the sick, you bring comfort to their bodies and to your own soul.

Truly blessed are those who bless their world.

Arisa blinked away tears. The message was perfect. Alvun did more for his fellow humans than anyone else she knew, yet he always feared it wasn't enough. Perhaps she couldn't heal his fatherly grief, but she could assure him that he was making Anyari a better place, just as he wanted to.

She tapped on the screen and sent the message to her husband.

27

I HAVE *to get out of here.*

It was late, but Ellin's eyelids might as well have been glued open. She couldn't stop thinking. Judging from the roiling of her gut, that's where the thoughts were percolating, rather than in her brain. She paced around her small space.

Even without her flex, she could picture the countdown. *Two days. Making friends with Merak isn't working. What do I do? Beg? No, I might lose his respect. Should I fight? No, he'll win, and I'll lose his trust.*

Ellin stopped pacing and filled her lungs with air. *There aren't any good options, so I have to take risks. I'll beg, then fight. That's it. Beg. Then fight.*

She sat on the cold floor with her legs in front of her, and leaned over, grabbing her toes. The stretch made her tense stomach hurt even more, but she leaned over farther. She had to be ready for Merak.

The bar on the door rattled. Ellin jumped up. *Why's he here at night?* She tried to relax her shoulders. *Act like a trusting young girl. Beg. Then fight.*

As the heavy door swung open, a voice said, "Ellin?"

Ellin's mouth went slack. "Rena?" The moment her eyes confirmed what her ears had heard, she started sobbing, and she threw herself into her sister's open arms. As they held each other, one thought broke through Ellin's delirious cries: *We haven't hugged like this since I was a little girl.*

Then she saw that Rena wasn't alone. Ellin let go of her sister and nearly knocked Trett down with the force of her embrace. He laughed, and his arms encircled her, squeezing her tight. She breathed in his scent and said, "You came."

"We need to go," Trett said. "He's probably got cameras all over this place."

The second Ellin's feet crossed the freezer's threshold into the warmth of the store, she began crying harder. She ripped off the hat Merak had given her and threw it to the floor.

Trett grasped her hand, leading her to the store's back door. "It's okay, we're almost out of here."

Outside, they ran through the darkness to where two hovs—one single, one double—waited behind scrubby bushes.

"Strip down," Rena commanded her.

Ellin gaped at her. "What?"

"He's probably got trackers in your clothes. We brought you new ones." Rena reached into the cargo basket of the single hov and handed Ellin a bag.

Ellin changed as quickly as she could. The underwear were too small, the pants too short, and the shoes a smidge loose, but it would work for now. She was thrilled not to be wearing the clothes Merak had provided; she only wished she could burn them.

They all put on helmets. Rena took the single hov. Ellin sat on the dubhov behind Trett and held onto his waist. Both vehicles sped away, Rena in the lead. Trett rested a hand on Ellin's arm.

Ellin laughed softly. "Your hand is so warm."

His voice came through the speaker in her helmet. "Yeah, Merak set your climastat pretty low."

"He said that was the highest it would go."

Trett increased his speed, and Ellin barely heard his growled words: "He's a lying asshole."

They traveled over rough terrain, their hovs making automatic elevation adjustments to avoid rocks and small bushes. After perhaps a quarter hour, during which Ellin couldn't think of anything other than how glad she was to be free and be with Trett, they reached a gravel road.

"Where are we going?" Ellin asked.

"We have a little apartment," Trett said. "We haven't been back to Merak's camp since we realized you were gone. After what happened to Nomi and Sep, we were afraid Merak had taken you. We got new IDs and hunkered down in Krenner, trying to figure out where you were."

Just as Ellin was about to ask how they'd found her, Rena spoke again, loud and firm this time. "Lights off, go off road." She was already following her own instructions.

"Why?" Trett asked.

The dim light of a distant streetlamp illuminated Rena's raised arm, pointing at the sky behind them. Ellin and Trett both turned. A glidecraft with a spotlight was coming their way.

Cursing, Trett switched off his hov's lights. With a lurch, he accelerated sharply and followed Rena off-road. They stayed parallel to the road, far enough away to avoid the light pooling from streetlamps.

"I'm watching the glidecraft! You both focus on driving!" Ellin cried, holding Trett tightly as she wrenched her neck to keep her eyes on the sky behind them. "They're gaining on us!" We can't outrun them! We've got to find a place to hide!"

"We're almost there!" Rena pointed ahead. "Faster!"

They were in the outskirts of Krenner, passing behind occasional buildings. The city proper, with crowds and places to hide, was still ahead. Ellin tightened her grip on Trett's waist. "They'll get to us before we reach the city!"

Rena didn't respond, steering them back toward the road and turning her lights back on.

"What are you doing?" Trett cried. When Rena didn't answer, he followed her, and in seconds, they were again flying over the street, which had been crushed gravel before and was now paved with smooth ecophalt. They sped past a couple of solarcars.

Still looking back, Ellin cried, "They're right behind us—and I see a second one!" An instant later, light from the first craft illuminated them.

"Don't stop!" Rena yelled.

"They're coming down!" Ellin said.

The glidecraft was indeed descending, even as it passed overhead. They'd land and wait for their quarry. Behind, the second craft was closing in.

They were in the city now, with buildings all around. Rena kept her course arrow-straight. Ahead of them, the glidecraft set down in an intersection. The other craft was landing behind them, close enough that when Ellin looked back, she could see the "MERAK FOUNDATION" lettering on the front of the vehicle.

"Turn left!" Rena braked abruptly, and Trett did the same. They turned at a narrow street a block shy of where the first glidecraft had landed. Suddenly, they were among dozens of hovs and countless pedestrians.

They slowed down to match the creeping traffic. "Popular dance club on this street," Rena said. "I've seen it in visions lately. It's always crowded at night. Don't look behind you, but there are Merak guards following us on hovs. They'll try to get through all these people and reach us, but they won't succeed."

"Why not?" Ellin asked, trying to keep her voice as calm as Rena's.

"Because we're turning here—" Rena made a sharp right, and

Trett followed. "And here—" She turned left. "And here." They zoomed into a parking garage. "We lost them."

"Are you sure?" Trett asked.

Rena's odd little chortle came through the helmet speakers. "I'm always sure."

They left the hovs in the garage. Rena led the way to a narrow alley between two buildings.

"Someone divided one small apartment into two tiny apartments," Trett explained as Rena unlocked the door. "Ours is only accessible from the alley."

Ellin walked in. Calling the place *tiny* was giving it too much credit. The front room, which included the kitchen and living room, was perhaps three-and-a-half mets square, furnished only by a small couch and a chair.

Rena caught Ellin's eye. "I'm glad you're safe." Not waiting for a response, she turned and headed straight for a door at the back of the living room.

"I'd like to take a shower," Ellin said.

"I'm sure you would, after being stuck in that room." Trett gave her a sad smile and handed her a large bag. "There are more clean clothes in here, plus shoes in a few different sizes. I'll wait for you. We have a lot to update each other on."

The shower, while miniscule, boasted hot water, soap, and shampoo. After nearly two weeks of bathing with reusable wipes and not washing her hair, Ellin didn't think she'd ever felt a better sensation than that hot spray of water. She lathered herself up, rinsed off, and then stood in the warm current of air produced by the body dryer. When she used the toilet afterward and it actually flushed, she decided that was even more satisfying than the shower. She put on a pair of soft pants and a long-sleeved shirt. One pair of shoes was the proper size. She put them at the top of the stack so they'd be ready when she needed them.

As promised, Trett was waiting for her. The single couch was tiny. He scooted over and patted the cushion, and she sat. He handed her a glass of water.

"I'm surprised Rena doesn't want to be part of this conversation," Ellin said.

"She's exhausted. She's been having a lot of visions. Most of them are shrouded, so she can't tell me about them, but she admits they've been stressing her out."

"She admitted she's stressed?"

Trett laughed softly. "It surprised me too." His face turned somber. "I want to hear what happened, but I need to tell you something first."

In a low voice, he told Ellin what they'd learned about Merak's daughter.

Ellin pressed her lips together, shaking her head, determined not to cry. "That makes so much sense. He's—he's a terrible man, Trett. Still, there's this part of me that wants to feel sorry for him, and I hate that."

"I can't even imagine what you went through in that little room. Do you want to tell me about it?"

She related her conversation with Merak in his office. Then she described the dig site and the freezer and falling in her own pee. She tried to laugh at that part, but it was forced. When Trett didn't laugh, tears returned to her eyes. She took a deep breath and continued her monologue, telling of her monotonous days in captivity and her recent efforts to get Merak to trust her.

When she finished, Trett spoke, his voice hesitant. "Besides making you wear those eights, how did Merak treat you?"

"He—he treated me well, most of the time." Ellin closed her mouth, determined to keep some details of her captivity private. Then she remembered her unwillingness to tell anyone about her meeting with Merak. *Look where that got me.*

She moistened her lips. "Trett, he never hurt me, except one time he made me keep the eights on overnight. He actually made me feel . . ." She trailed off, swallowing tears, looking away. "Oh Trett, I let him hold me."

Despite her best intentions, one tear escaped. Then, all at once, she was crying uncontrollably, complete with snot bubbling out of her nose. She couldn't look at Trett.

A handkerchief found its way into her hand, and she wiped her nose and eyes, though it was a hopeless endeavor. Trett's hand rested on her knee, and she found the courage to look in his eyes.

He was holding back his own tears, which made her cry harder. "Rena saw that," he said, his voice breaking. "Ellin, I'm so sorry." He offered her his arms and held her in a hug that surpassed the perfection of the one earlier that night.

The touch was calming and cleansing, and after several minutes, her tears subsided. When she pulled back, Trett simply said, "I'm sorry we didn't get there sooner."

"I'm glad you got there at all. How'd you do it, Trett?"

He told her about the message to Merak's wife, and she nodded. "That was smart."

He laughed softly. "Between Rena and me, we had just enough brains to come up with it."

A comfortable silence fell between them. Ellin filled it with a tentative smile, which Trett returned.

"I guess we should talk about stopping Merak," he said.

"We should." Ellin took a deep breath. "But not yet."

Trett raised his eyebrows.

Ellin felt something in her break, something that had been there for years, and through the gap, she let the words flow as freely as her tears had. "I care about saving the world, and I want to move on after that and do something big with my life. Maybe I'll be a surgeon, or a journalist who won't bow to Merak. I don't know. And despite all those dreams, I'm well aware that we have almost no chance of stopping him, and we've probably only got a little over a day left to live."

She tentatively took Trett's hand, and he didn't pull away. The words still insisted on coming out, but now she had to push them past the lump in her throat. "Being in that room, there was one dream that filled my thoughts more than all the others. Even more than saving the world."

"What was it?" he murmured.

"Trett . . . I just wanted to see you again." She swallowed. He was watching her expectantly. Her voice came out in a whisper. "I don't want to follow my dreams alone anymore. However much time we have left—even if it's only a day—I want to spend it with you. Please tell me it's not too late."

His face broke into a smile so wide, the shallow dimple in his cheek turned deep. Pulling his hand from hers, he ran gentle fingers down both her temples and over her ears, making her shiver. Finally, he cupped her face in his warm hands. He leaned toward her, close enough for her to feel his words as distinctly as she heard them, and whispered, "It's not too late."

He kissed her gently. Clearly he was being cautious for her sake, knowing what she'd been through, and she loved him for it. But she didn't want tenderness. The same *something* in her that had broken open, making way for honesty, had also made way for passion. She pressed against Trett, her mouth telling him the wordless story of her pain and fear and, above all, hope.

Rena's door opened, and her pragmatic voice interrupted them. "Plenty of time for that later." It was a ridiculous statement, probably the most false thing she could say at that moment.

Ellin pulled away from Trett, annoyance overpowering her embarrassment. Or maybe the embarrassment had fled along with her reticence? The thought made her smile, and she kissed Trett once more, a deep, hungry kiss, simply because she could. Then she sat up straight and called out to her sister, who'd walked into the tiny kitchen. "Rena, I suppose you want to talk about the end of the world?"

"No. I'm just getting some water." Her voice sounded weary.

"We'll make our plans in the morning. We should really all get some sleep."

Ellin watched as her sister walked back to her room. Her eyes were red, and exhaustion made her face look years older. What was it like to be Rena? To be battered by prophecies, some of which she couldn't even share?

Rena glanced back at Ellin before entering her room. Ellin gave her a small smile. Rena blinked and nodded.

Despite the promise of sunrise in a few hours, Rena couldn't sleep.

Shrouded prophecies from the past few weeks tumbled around her brain. She lay back on her pillow, stringing the scenes together.

I know what tomorrow will look like.

She knew most of it, anyway. She knew what Trett and Ellin would do, where their plans would work and where they'd go wrong. Their facial expressions, gestures, and words played in her head like a film on a loop.

Rena just didn't know how she fit into it all.

She sat up, hunched forward, and rubbed her aching temples. What was she supposed to do with all these visions when she didn't see herself in them and couldn't share them with anyone?

What if I did know my role? My future? Rena chewed on the thought. Having foreknowledge of Ellin's and Trett's actions was infuriating. She knew if she tried to change even the smallest detail, she'd freeze up. If she were in the visions too, it would be even worse. She'd be an automaton, acting according to cruel predestination, unable to even scratch her nose unless it had been foretold.

I'm free.

The truth washed over her, and she sat up straighter, mouth hanging open.

She'd always thought of her gift as a type of bondage, tying her inexorably to a fated future. The falsehood of that belief nearly bowled her over. She didn't know her own destiny. That meant she was the only one who was truly free. No, she couldn't change the world, but she could control her interactions with it.

"I can do whatever I want." She whispered the words, and then a laugh escaped her mouth. Her eyes darted to the door; she didn't want to wake Ellin and Trett. *Oh, who am I kidding? They're not sleeping.*

For once, the thought of them making out in the next room didn't bring on queasy jealousy. They'd been under as much stress as her, far more in Ellin's case. They were as unsure of their own futures as she was of hers. Let them have their fun.

Rena's thoughts turned inward again. *I'm free. So what do I want?*

The answer was clear. She wanted to support her sister, making the most of the last day before the apocalypse. Maybe it wouldn't make up for eight years of coldness, but it would be something.

The decision washed over her like warm, soothing water. A small smile settled on her mouth and lingered there—until an image of Kizha's face intruded on her contentment.

Kizha. Her best friend who could've been more, who still had no idea what was going on but had helped her every time Rena had asked.

A month ago, Rena had seen Kizha die, seen all the color flee from her lovely face and dark, curly hair. Rena had watched Kizha's perfect green eyes turn into unfocused, lifeless orbs. That vision had replayed in her mind dozens of times a day since then.

Lately, she'd avoided Kizha, contacting her only when necessary. She didn't dare warn her of the coming apocalypse and couldn't tell Kizha her own fate, even if she wanted to. *What else is there to talk about?*

Everything. Rena clenched her fists, pressing them against her lips. She'd muzzled the truth for years, and now all the words she'd carefully restrained were begging for liberation. At this point, what was there to lose?

She turned on the light and picked up her crumpled flex.

Fighting off a silly, giddy flutter, she firmed the device, pulled up Kizha's contact, and pressed the icon for a video chat.

Kizha's face and shoulders filled the screen. "You're up late." She smiled, but even the expression was shallow, like all their interactions had been lately.

Rena opened her mouth, but it was so dry. She licked her lips. Swallowed. *Here goes nothing.* "Kizha, I need you to know something."

Kizha's eyes widened in concern. "Okay?"

Rena swallowed again. This was harder than she'd thought it would be. She opened her mouth, expecting to stutter and hesitate, but the words tumbled out, breaking through her reticence. "I'm in love with you. I think I have been almost since we met. Kizha—I love you. I do."

She took in air, ready to release more captive words, but what she saw on the screen halted all her logical thoughts. Kizha's smile was one Rena never seen on her face before, gleeful and tender all at once. Her green eyes glistened with tears, and then merriment overtook her, uncontrolled laughter bubbling from her mouth.

Rena stared at her. The smile had been promising, but the laugh? What did that mean? "Why are you . . . Kizha. . . ?"

Kizha held up her hands, shaking her head, gulping air and trying to control her laughter. "Sorry—sorry." She finally calmed, releasing one more childlike giggle. Then she brought her flex closer to her face. "Damn it, Rena, I don't care how long you say you've loved me, I swear I've loved you longer."

A loud laugh, almost a shout, burst from Rena's throat. She covered her offending mouth. But her laughter didn't last, because Kizha's eyes caught hers, and the intensity Rena found there captured her breath. She uncovered her mouth, touched Kizha's lips on the screen, and whispered, "I wish you were here."

Kizha swallowed. "So do I. Rena—do you think we can see each other soon?"

For a second, she saw Kizha with white skin and hair, mouth

gaping. Rena blinked hard, forcing the image away, and instead focused on the life-filled green eyes and joyful smile of the woman she loved.

Rena still didn't know her own fate, but she knew how many life-less bodies her prophecies had shown her. She wasn't arrogant enough to think she'd be one of the few survivors.

"Yes," she said, and her mouth relaxed in a genuine smile, even as tears filled her eyes. "I think we'll see each other very soon."

28

Ellin slept curled up on the couch, her head on a pillow in Trett's lap. He was seated, head lolling back against the cushion, his warm arm resting on her. It was the best sleep Ellin had gotten in two weeks.

Rena came in. "Good morning, you two."

Ellin sat up and rubbed her eyes. Rena looked just as tired as the night before, but something about her was different. It took a second for Ellin to identify the change. *She's smiling.* And it wasn't some self-righteous, I'm-the-older-sister smile. It was a happy smile.

"Good morning?" Ellin didn't mean for it to come out as a question.

Rena's smile got bigger. "Want some coffee?"

Five minutes later, they were seated in the little living room—Rena on the single chair, Trett and Ellin on the couch—with cups of surprisingly decent coffee, fresh from the beverage maker.

Ellin started the discussion. "Rena, Trett said you've been having visions about tomorrow."

Rena nodded slowly.

"So what's our plan?"

Rena looked down at the mug between her hands, and when she met Ellin's eyes again, she was sporting a helpless smile. "All my prophecies about you and Trett have been shrouded. You need to plan however it seems best to you. I'll be with you every step of the way, supporting you however I can."

Ellin's eyes narrowed. "Did something happen to you?"

Rena laughed, and coming from her, it sounded like a foreign language. "I think the approaching apocalypse has changed us all."

Ellin blinked and shook her head. She took her coffee cup to the kitchen and placed it in the sink. When she returned, she sat next to Trett but locked her gaze on Rena. "Are we still supposed to try to stop this thing?"

Rena's nod was emphatic. "Yes. I've known that since the first vision. I think part of me has known it for years. You need to do whatever you can—the two of you, together."

Ellin took Trett's hand. "Then let's figure out how."

When they finished strategizing, Rena went to her room. Ellin figured her sister was sleeping until laughter floated through the bedroom door.

"I think she's talking to her hacker friend," Trett whispered. He paused, then added, "I've been wondering if they're more than friends."

"Really?" Ellin smiled, a rush of warmth for Rena filling her. "I hope you're right." She leaned against Trett's chest. He wrapped his arm around her, and they alternated between talking and dozing.

Trett's voice woke her from a snooze that had threatened to turn into a proper nap.

"Hmm?" she asked.

"I'm sorry we can't spend our last—that we can't spend today drinking great coffee or riding too fast on hovs or climbing a mountain."

Ellin sat up. "It's not our last day." She kissed him, then rested her forehead against his. In a bare whisper, she added, "And if it is, I can't think of a better way to spend it than this."

They remained on the couch all day, breathing in sync with each other, sometimes napping, sometimes simply *being*. They talked occasionally, sharing words of love Ellin had long avoided and long desired.

Every time Ellin thought she should search for more information about the dig site or go over their plan one more time, she instead kissed Trett and snuggled in tighter. Rena came out of her room several times to get a drink, use the bathroom, or eat the food they ordered from a local restaurant. Each time she entered the living room, she smiled at her sister and Trett with a contented look Ellin had never before seen on her.

That night, Ellin and Trett slept in the same position as the night before. Trett's flexscreen chimed at one a.m.

It was time to fight a prophecy.

SATURDAY, CYGNI 6, 6293

0 DAYS

Ellin, Trett, and Rena drove rented hovs to Cellerin Mountain. Wary of tripping Merak's electronics-detecting sensors, they stopped more than a clommet from the dig site and abandoned their vehicles behind some brush. They got their bearings using a map on Trett's flexscreen, then left even the flex behind as they walked, their path illuminated by stars and a quarter moon.

After navigating over rocky terrain for about half an hour, they arrived at the dig site. Hiding behind large stones, they saw that the area was lit by several floodlights. One security guard patrolled the area, but he was on foot and would be easy to avoid.

The guard and floodlights were more for show than anything else. While Ellin was locked up, Rena's hacker contact had worked for a full week to get into the site's security network and had told Rena that most of the security was digital, primarily movement sensors and infrared cameras. Earlier that night, the hacker had disabled the equipment and set up a program to feed false data into the system. She'd even turned off alarm sirens connected to the project leaders' flexes. She'd found evidence of electronics sensors but hadn't been able to access that part of the system.

The three intruders approached the dig site itself and hid behind the large stones settlers had piled up thousands of years before.

"I thought they'd almost reached the isotope," Trett said. "I don't see any digging happening."

"They made a path through the rock," Ellin replied. "We can't see it from here." She looked around in all directions. "I think it's safe—let's go."

They skirted the man-made rock formation, dropping to their hands and knees when they came under the illumination of a floodlight. They weren't crawling for long when they arrived at the path through the stones. It was wide enough for three people to walk through it side by side. They halted.

"Ready?" Trett asked Ellin, his voice a low whisper.

She gulped and glanced down the path that led to the cave. *How much radiation is bombarding us right now?* By the time Trett and Rena had thought to purchase antirads several days ago, it was too late. No one could deliver them that quickly. The device Ellin had borrowed had lost its charge a few days after she'd entered the freezer, and Merak had taken it back to his glidecraft.

Ellin closed her eyes briefly. If they got out of this alive, they'd seek immediate treatment for radiation exposure. *Will it work? Can anything protect against the levels here?*

She smothered the thoughts before they could paralyze her. *This is worth the risk.* She turned back to Rena and Trett. "Yeah. I'm ready."

"You've got this, Ellin," Rena whispered.

Ellin blinked. "Thanks."

Rena and Trett crawled into the pathway, while Ellin continued past it. She nearly yelped when a sharp rock dug into her hand. When she left the floodlit area, she stood and walked.

It didn't take long to reach her destination: a rock-cutting machine. Merak had shown her a picture of the tall, narrow piece of equipment that would cut through the final barrier over the cave entrance, a massive stone larger than a man.

Disabling this machine wouldn't keep the archeologists from their prize. It would, however, slow them down. They'd have to repair it (since it was the only large piece of equipment approved by the government for this phase of digging), and Trett and Ellin hoped that would take longer than a day.

There was no handbook on how to derail a prophecy, but Trett had suggested that making the deadline impossible might nullify the whole thing. Then they could work to shut down the dig and neutralize the isotope.

Ellin was the smallest of the three of them, so she'd volunteered to take on this part of the mission. She crawled around a large tread, then slid herself underneath the machine's body.

Once in place, she flipped open the multi-tool in her hand. Its luminescent paint emitted a dull glow. She examined the underside of the equipment, which looked just like the diagrams she'd studied in a digital repair manual.

Her first step was removing a metal panel. The screwdriver on her multi-tool should do the job. It was trickier than she'd expected; the screws were tight, and getting leverage in such a small space was almost impossible. After several minutes of hand-cramping work, she had the panel almost off.

That's when she heard footsteps crunching on the rocky dirt—slow, methodical, and coming closer.

Ellin drew in a sharp breath. Her feet were sticking out behind the machine. She let go of the panel, which dangled from one loose screw. Then she scooted in farther, trying to do so quickly, sacrificing her silence in the process.

She'd just pulled her feet under the machine when she saw boots approach, stopping close enough for the dull light from her tool to illuminate their stitching.

The dull light from her tool. Cursing inwardly, she shut the tool. Had the guard looked down? Would he have noticed it? *Did he hear me?*

That last question quickly rendered itself moot when the final screw on the thin panel released, and the metal fell on top of Ellin with a dull *thud.*

The boots shuffled, stepping away from the machine. In the moonlight, Ellin could barely see the guard's silhouette as his knees hit the rocky dirt, eliciting a low, growly groan. Then light entered the space from the man's high-powered flashlight. Ellin squeezed her lips shut, holding her breath.

The man groaned again, shifting his body. Ellin waited for his head to make its way down to her level. Instead, the light disappeared, and the man made a few more pained sounds as he lifted himself back to his feet.

"Critters," he muttered. Then he said more loudly, "Get on outta there!" He kicked rocks and dirt into the space.

Ellin snapped her eyes shut, but not before a grain of dirt entered one.

The man's footsteps began again, receding into the night.

Ellin released her breath and took in a gulp of air, blinking and rubbing her eyes until the dirt made its way out. She waited several minutes, probably far longer than was necessary, before opening her multi-tool and again illuminating the area.

After that, her job was fast. Most of the machine's vital parts were only accessible at specialized repair facilities. However, it used an efficient fuel cell, fed by a small water chamber. Sometimes the machine's movements jostled the chamber loose, so it was positioned where anyone could access it and tighten the fittings.

Ellin unscrewed the metal tank, removed it, and replaced the panel. Then she scooted herself out, relieved to be in the open after huddling in such a confined space.

She crawled the entire return trip, afraid the guard would shine his light in the shadows. The journey was miserable. Her stomach cramped every time she thought about getting caught; her knees and palms were sore; and it was hard to crawl with the water chamber under one arm. Eventually, she made it to the dark path, crawling until she reached Rena and Trett, who waited beyond the reach of the floodlights. She stood, rewarded with a quick hug from Trett and a heartfelt "Well done" from Rena.

Next, they had to watch the dig site, just in case their first plan failed. They all crawled out of the passage and exited the floodlit area, heading for a grouping of boulders Ellin had seen on Merak's pictures and videos. It would be the perfect, shadowy hiding place. They arrived, finding a cramped space to sit and wait.

There was no way to know what time it was. More than once, Ellin thought the sky was getting a little brighter, only to be disappointed by continuing darkness.

Once they realized the night guard's rounds didn't take him anywhere near the boulders, they risked chatting in low whispers. Rena told Ellin stories of their childhood, tales Ellin had been too young to commit to memory. Many of the stories involved their parents. Ellin repeatedly wiped tears away, wishing they'd had the conversations earlier but treasuring every word.

At last, dawn spread over the sky. Workers emerged from tents, went to the dining building for breakfast, and made their way to the dig. Ellin, Rena, and Trett fell silent. They weren't close enough to hear the words spoken around the site, but they could detect laughter and an atmosphere of excitement.

They watched as workers removed more stones, large and small, from the path. After a couple of hours, Ellin pointed at an incoming glidecraft and whispered, "Merak."

The craft dropped out of view. Merak himself was soon walking around the site, shaking hands and having conversations.

Lunchtime came, and as shifts of workers took time off for their own meals, Ellin, Rena, and Trett drank water and ate Vegebars.

Their hiding place seemed to get smaller as the hours wore on. They all repositioned themselves when they got cramps, and eventually they each had to pee in a bottle they'd brought for that purpose. It was awkward in the tiny space, but Ellin couldn't complain. It beat relieving herself in the corner of a chilly freezer.

Early that afternoon, work at the site ground to a halt. The general aura of excitement around the site intensified. A film crew arrived and set up near the rock cutter.

Rena grabbed Ellin's hand. Ellin raised an eyebrow but didn't pull away. They watched as Merak spoke to the camera for a few minutes.

Everyone turned toward the rock cutter. A worker climbed up into the driver's seat.

Then—nothing. After a couple of minutes of silence, Merak himself climbed up to talk to the driver. They both descended. Merak kept his voice low, but he gestured wildly, pointing at the machine and the dig site. The driver held his hands up, palms facing out, as he responded. Merak's posture relaxed, and he gripped the driver's shoulder and nodded.

The driver got in his seat again, and a moment later, the entire body of the rock cutter rose half a met into the air. He lowered himself to the ground and pulled himself under the machine—a much easier task for him than it had been for Ellin.

A few minutes later, he scooted out and had another hushed conversation with Merak, who nodded and gestured toward the on-site buildings. The driver walked that direction.

"He's probably trying to get a replacement part delivered," Trett said.

Ellin wanted to believe that, but her twisted gut was otherwise convinced. "He could do that from his flex," she whispered.

The driver walked into the science lab. Ellin bit at one of her cuticles while she waited for him to emerge.

When he did, he lifted his arms victoriously in the air. In one hand he held a water chamber, just like the one sitting next to Ellin.

She, Trett, and Rena were silent until the driver arrived at the machine. As the man talked with Merak, Trett muttered, "They had extra parts."

They'd talked about the possibility of a spare water chamber, but it was lined with nanotechnology and was extraordinarily expensive to replace. It was supposed to last as long as the machine itself. Who would keep such a pricey part around, just in case?

A project funded by Merak would.

The driver returned to his spot under the rock cutter. Ten minutes later, he slid out, climbed to his seat, and lowered the machine back to its original position. It took a few minutes for Merak to record his introduction again, and then he stepped away. Almost immediately, the treads of the rock cutter started moving, propelling the vehicle ahead. The crowd cheered.

Ellin wanted to scream or sob. Instead, she took a deep breath and whispered, "Plan B."

Plan B would only work if they were patient. So they watched as the rock cutter entered the pathway workers had spent weeks creating. The machine made little noise, leaving them to wonder what was happening. The air in their hiding place stank of nervous sweat and nearly sparked with tension.

At one point, most of the site's workers, including Merak, were huddled around the pathway entrance. "Now?" Trett suggested.

"Now," Ellin confirmed.

Crouching, she and Trett exited their hideaway, followed by a quiet "Good luck" from Rena.

Plan B was what they'd called their "Plan of Desperation." There was no Plan C. Either this succeeded, or it didn't. If they got caught, they got caught. Ellin figured they'd all be dying soon, anyway.

They ran toward the border of the dig site as quietly as they could, and soon they rounded a bend in the mountain's perimeter and stopped to catch their breaths.

"So far, so good," Ellin said. "Let's go."

She and Trett began walking, skirting wide around the site. They made their way to the opposite side from where they'd been hiding, then crept up closer until the buildings were in view. There weren't any convenient boulders to hide behind, so they settled for kneeling behind thorny bushes. From there, they could see the bathrooms at the back of the multipurpose building. They watched and waited.

In the first half hour, several workers used the facilities. But they weren't just looking for any worker. They needed to find one of the archeologists, all of whom Ellin could identify thanks to videos Merak had shared with her when she was captive.

"Don't archeologists pee?" Trett whispered.

"They sure do," Ellin said. "Look to your left."

A petite female archeologist was approaching the bathroom. When she entered, Ellin and Trett rose into crouched positions and ran to wait for her, one on either side of the door.

The door opened, and the woman started when she saw Ellin and Trett. "Who are you?" she asked, her voice alarmingly loud.

"We're researchers," Ellin said. "Back at camp. We need to talk to you."

The woman pulled her flex out of her pocket, backing away as she did so. She carried hers in a wad, just like Rena. When she'd firmed the device, her fingers flitted over it. She continued to back up.

Then she stopped moving and stared at her flex. Her fingertip pressed it firmly once, twice. Eyes wide, she looked up at Ellin and Trett.

"I'm sorry, we've disabled the sirens," Ellin said. "We need to speak to you. What you're doing today is incredibly dangerous. Please, give us a couple of minutes of your time."

The woman stared at them for several seconds before finally saying, "I'm listening."

Ellin did the talking, explaining her concerns with the radiation at the site.

She hadn't gotten very far when the archeologist interrupted her. "Excuse me—I'm sorry."

"For what?" Ellin asked.

"Our emergency call—it doesn't just turn on the sirens."

Ellin furrowed her brow. "What do you mean?"

Hands grasped both Ellin's arms, yanking them behind her back so hard it took her breath away. She spun her head to the side, but she couldn't see who it was. A male guard was restraining Trett in the same way.

Her eyes flitted down. The man holding Trett was wearing hover shoes. That technology was less than a year old and still prohibitively expensive. Of course Merak's guards would have the best gear possible, including shoes allowing them to sneak up on intruders. With a short hiss, the guard's feet dropped to the ground.

Ellin heard the same hiss behind her. Then Alvun Merak spoke, his mouth next to her ear, his voice warmly sorrowful. "The emergency call doesn't just activate the sirens. It calls me too."

29

SATURDAY, CYGNI 6, 6293
0 DAYS

ELLIN FELT Merak's cheek press against her hair. "You'll pardon me if I don't trust you," he said. His hand encircled her neck, squeezing just tight enough to scare her.

He pulled his face away from her but kept his hand on her neck. Then she felt the unmistakable sensation of eights slipping on her wrists. Merak nodded at the archeologist, who returned her attention to her flex. A few seconds later, Ellin's restraints tightened, and Merak let go of her.

He placed eights on Trett's wrists, then walked around to face them both. "We're going to watch the dig together. Don't try to run. I have a weapon." He patted his pocket.

An image of his handgun, the muzzle cavernous and black, invaded Ellin's mind. Her breath caught, and she nodded.

Merak approached Ellin and took her arm. "Shall we go?"

They began walking. Merak murmured, "I take it you're not wearing an antirad?"

"No."

"Oh, Ellin. You haven't seen the radiation figures from the last couple of days. It's not safe, not until we stabilize it. But at least . . ." He shook his head.

"At least what?"

"At least I won't have to do something to you I would've regretted. Most likely, the radiation will take care of that." He released a deep sigh and spoke in her ear, genuine pain thick in his voice. "Ellin, this isn't how I wanted this to go."

Her breaths quickened. It wasn't a rational response; she'd be dead by the end of the day, antirad or not. Besides, Merak might be lying, just like his claims about the climastat. Still, his blatant threat brought a familiar tightness to her chest and throat.

Merak led them to a long, narrow canopy fifteen mets or so from the passage entrance. A muscular, female security guard waited for them. She was holding Rena's arm.

Rena's lips pressed together in a sad smile when she met Ellin's gaze. Her hands were behind her back too.

"Rena?" Merak asked.

"I found her hidden behind those rocks," the security guard said, pointing.

"I can't say I'm surprised."

"She's my sister." Ellin wasn't sure why she said it.

Merak's eyebrows shot up, and he gave Rena a sharper look, then turned to Ellin. "You told me she was your friend."

Ellin shrugged, holding his gaze. "I guess we all have our secrets."

The corner of his mouth twitched. "Indeed." Gesturing to a row of chairs, he said, "Ellin, Trett, Rena, please sit. I'm sorry, it will be uncomfortable with your hands like that. It'll be worth it though. You've got front-row seats to one of the greatest days in history."

Ignoring Merak's suggestion, Ellin turned to him. "Mr. Merak, I know you believe in what you're doing here, but please, listen to me."

Merak laughed softly, shaking his head. "I've heard what you have to say."

"Not this." She caught his gaze and held it. "You've already proven that you're better than your father. You don't need—"

"This has nothing to do with my father." Merak stepped right up to her, his eyes filling with a familiar fire.

Ellin didn't back down, but she brought her voice low, her words meant for Alvun Merak's ears only. "Today you can save the world, or you can destroy it. Please—do what your daughter would have wanted you to do. Make Ellin proud."

Merak's arms swept up like levers, and he grabbed Ellin's shoulders, gripping them so hard that she yelped. "You know nothing about my daughter." His words came out hoarse and sharp, and spit flew from his mouth, a drop landing on Ellin's cheek. "You're nothing like her."

He pushed Ellin hard. She stumbled and fell on her back, dirt and rocks scraping her bound hands. Merak turned and strode away.

Rena and Trett rushed up to Ellin. She stood, wiped her wet cheek on her shoulder, and assured them she was fine.

The female guard approached them. "Mr. Merak told you to sit in those chairs."

Ellin sat, leaning back against her bound hands. As Merak had predicted, it was uncomfortable. Trett and Rena joined her, one on each side.

The guard sat next to Rena. "I'll stay here and keep an eye on you."

Ellin turned to Rena and spoke in a low voice. "Did you know they were going to catch you?"

Still watching the dig, Rena murmured, "No. She sneaked up on me. Hover shoes."

"Rena, do we have a chance?"

Rena turned her body toward Ellin and Trett, away from the guard. Her eyes were wet, and as she moved, one tear slid down each cheek.

Ellin's breath caught, her own eyes filling. "Rena?"

"You and Trett—" Rena's voice was soft, full of vulnerability.

She took a shaky breath and began again. "So far, you and Trett have done everything exactly as I saw it. Down to the tiniest detail."

Ellin closed her eyes, and when she opened them, she caught Trett's gaze on her.

He spoke quietly, but his voice was strong. "Ellin, I wish you knew how much I love you."

A sob shoved its way out of Ellin's mouth, landing between them. "Oh Trett. I love you too."

He smiled—how could he smile at a time like this?—and said, "I keep thinking about how we almost didn't move to Stollton four years ago. My mom had accepted a position somewhere else. A few weeks before we were supposed to move, she got an IDM." He shook his head. "Did I ever tell you about that?"

"No." Ellin took a deep breath. "What did it say?"

It was Rena who answered. "It was an IDM from the City of Stollton, asking her to apply to work there."

Brow furrowed, Ellin turned to her sister. "How do you know that?" she and Trett asked in unison.

Rena stared at Ellin for several seconds, then turned her eyes to Trett before answering, "Because I asked my friend to hack into the city's system and send it."

Ellin's slackened mouth recovered just enough to whisper, "Why?"

"You two were supposed to meet. I've had visions of both of you since before you were born." Rena's gaze pierced Ellin's. "Remember that." She looked at Trett and repeated, "Remember."

"You tried to keep me away from him," Ellin said.

A short laugh escaped from Rena's mouth. "If I'd seemed too eager, you wouldn't have given him a chance."

Ellin couldn't argue with that.

From several mets in front of them, Merak shouted, "They're in the cave!" He rushed to the videographer.

Ellin turned back to Rena. The question that had been building in her chest burst out. "We weren't ever going to be able to stop this, were we?"

More tears escaped Rena's eyes. "No."

All the air left Ellin's lungs.

Trett asked, "Why did you want us to try?"

Rena opened her mouth, but neither words nor breath emerged. She closed her mouth, licked her lips, and said, "There's a lot I can't say. It's shrouded." She swallowed, then spoke slowly, like she was choosing the only words she was allowed to utter. "You needed to learn to trust each other."

"Are you saying—" Ellin stopped when she saw Rena shaking her head.

"Let me speak . . . if I can," Rena said. "Someone—" She halted, took a shuddering breath, and continued. "Someone must tell the story. Someone must protect the stone."

Ellin could barely see through her tears. She managed one word. "Who?"

Rena blinked her own tears away and shook her head, smiling helplessly. After another false start, she whispered, "I'm so proud of you both." Her focus shifted entirely to Ellin, and her words flowed freely again. "I haven't been a good replacement for our parents. With all the visions I see, I can barely hold my own mind together. I want you to know, I've always wanted what was best for you. And you were the perfect person to fight Merak."

"It didn't work," Ellin whispered.

"It did. In a way."

Ellin sniffed, trying to stop crying. "I wish I could hug you."

Movement caught Ellin's eye. She looked back toward the dig. The rock cutter was backing out of the manmade path. It exited and turned, revealing its prize: a huge piece of jagged rock, as tall as a person, gripped by four massive clamps.

The security guard was watching the dig too, excitement written on her face. She stood and took a few steps toward the mountain, away from Ellin, Trett, and Rena.

Ellin watched the woman, then leaned past Rena to look at the chair where the guard had been sitting. A rush of nervous, determined energy flooded her whole body. "I love you, Trett. I love you, Rena." She took a deep breath and locked eyes with her sister. "The guard left her flex unlocked on her seat."

Ellin stood and ran down a steep incline, straight toward the dig, pursued by gasps and hushed protests from Trett and Rena.

"Stop!" The voice belonged to the security guard and was accompanied by panicked footsteps.

"Let her go." It was Merak, his tone both commanding and amused.

Ellin kept running. It only took a few seconds to reach the rock passage. She slowed, instinct telling her the workers were more likely to listen to her if she was calm.

A few steps in, her eights released. Ellin let out a little gasp and turned around. Rena had turned in her chair so her back was to Trett. Her hands were still behind her back, and she was holding something. It had to be the guard's flexscreen. Trett was hunched over the device, talking. He must be guiding Rena's bound hands as she navigated the screen. As Ellin watched, Trett pulled his hands out of his own eights, then grabbed the flex and released Rena's restraints.

Ellin didn't take off her loose eights. Not yet. If Merak saw that she was unbound, he might send a security guard to grab her. She turned and walked to the end of the passage.

There were three workers in the pathway, all facing toward the mouth of the newly opened cave. One held up a bright light, illuminating the cave.

The cave itself was small, its ceiling low. Inside, two archeologists, a man and the woman Ellin had met outside the bathroom, hunched around an object as tall as their knees. They wore thick gloves and, as Ellin had suggested to Merak, goggles.

"This thing is really hot," the male archeologist said. "I don't understand how it hasn't burned holes in whatever it's wrapped in."

"They're animal skins," his partner said. "Look at the basket-weave texture; they're from some sort of reptid. Like you said, they're remarkably well preserved. I'm sure the researchers will figure out why."

A knife of fear twisted in Ellin's chest. She remembered Sep telling them how hot the stone was when the colonists hid it, and she knew the male archeologist was right. Reptid skin was tough, but it still should've disintegrated thousands of years ago.

Standing on her tiptoes, she squinted, trying to get a better look in the cave. Though the skins were dulled with age and unimpressive to look at, the object gave her an eerie feeling. *Otherworldly* was the word that came to mind, an apt descriptor for a supposed space artifact.

Even if it was from space, shouldn't it obey basic scientific laws? *The skins should've burned off. The stone should've cooled down. The radiation levels should be dropping.*

The thing in that cave defied explanation. Couldn't anyone see how frightening that was?

"I guess we should get it out of here," the man said.

Ellin took a deep breath, gathering her courage. *It's now or never.* "Please." Her clear voice bounced off the rocks. "Please stop."

The three nearest workers spun and gaped at her, robbing the cavern of its light. Both archeologists in the cave turned toward the entrance.

"What are you doing here?" the archeologist Ellin had encountered earlier asked.

"Merak knows I'm here. I came to ask you to stop." Ellin had a sudden urge to break down in tears, but she took a sharp breath, reining in her emotion.

The woman stepped out of the cave, straightened her back, and folded her arms. "Why would we stop?"

A surreal calm came over Ellin, and she spoke in an unwavering voice. "I've reviewed all the research. This radiation is different than anything we've seen before. That's why the radiation levels have been rising and the object is so hot. It's dangerous. If we bring this into the world, countless people will die. Please. It's not too late to close the cave. If you tell Merak it's too dangerous, he might listen." She directed her entire attention at the female archeologist. "Please put an end to this."

The woman stared at Ellin long enough for hope to spark in Ellin's chest. Then she rolled her eyes and said, "Get her out of here."

The second archeologist exited the cave. "Maybe we should just take a few minutes—"

"She's a conspiracy theorist." The woman's voice was dismissive. "Two of you, take her back to Merak. And get that light shining in the cave again."

As ordered, the worker with the flashlight pointed it into the cave. The male archeologist stooped and entered it again, but the woman watched, her expression hard, as the remaining two workers approached Ellin.

"Come on. Turn around," one of the workers, a middle-aged woman, said.

Ellin held her ground.

The other worker, a burly man, grasped Ellin's shoulders with rough hands and spun her around. Then he grabbed her upper arm, squeezing hard enough to leave a bruise, and tried to push her up the path, away from the cave.

Feet planted, Ellin cried, "Please, just stop! You don't know what you're doing! Stop!" She knew nobody would take her shrill warnings seriously, but she couldn't stay quiet.

She continued to cry her warnings even as the big man picked her up, threw her over his shoulder, and marched her down the path, straight toward Merak.

As they approached, Merak said, "Put her down."

The worker complied, setting Ellin on her feet in front of Merak. She still had her arms behind her back, held in the loose eights, and when her feet hit the ground, she stumbled.

"Whoa," Merak said, grinning as he grasped her arm to steady her. "I love your determination, Ellin. I really do."

Then his face fell, grief replacing amusement. The hand that had held her up moved to her face, cupping her cheek. He rubbed his thumb gently against her skin. "I hate to lose you." He glanced at the videographer nearby and dropped his hand, stepping back from her. "You'd better go back to your sister and your friend."

"Please stop them, Mr. Merak. Alvun. Please."

He reached out and took both her shoulders, gently this time. "Go. Sit."

Ellin stepped away but didn't return to her seat. Instead, she watched Merak and tried desperately to think of a way to convince him.

Suddenly, excited voices filled the area. Ellin turned to see what the commotion was.

The archeologists had just exited the path and were walking toward Merak. Before them hovered a thin shelf, on top of which sat the object Ellin had seen in the cave.

All the air exited Ellin's body. She looked over her shoulder and found that Rena and Trett were approaching her. Nobody was watching them now; every eye was on the object.

Rena stood on one side of Ellin, Trett on the other. Trett's hand found her wrist, and he slipped the eight off it and grasped her hand in his. She almost suggested they put the restraints back on; someone might notice. But she couldn't bring herself to let go of Trett.

The archeologists approached Merak. The woman pushed a button on the hover shelf. It descended slowly and landed, sending up gentle puffs of dirt.

The animal skins were tied on with narrow strips of the same material. Whatever was underneath was irregular in shape.

The whole camp was gathered, jostling for space. Merak instructed them to step back, and they complied. Ellin, Rena, and Trett stood several mets away, where higher ground gave them a good view. Once everyone got settled, the site was eerily quiet.

Merak pulled goggles out of his pocket and started to put them on, but then he looked at the videographer and replaced the goggles in his pocket. He turned back toward the object. "Unwrap it," he said in a voice of hushed awe.

"It's very hot," the male archeologist said.

"Good thing you have thermal gloves on."

Both archeologists began removing the ties from the object as carefully as they could. It didn't take long for them to pull the long strands loose. Then they stood and slowly, carefully lifted the skins away from their prize.

The crowd gasped. The object did appear to be a stone, but not like any Ellin had ever seen. It was shiny black, like obsidian. Thick veins of iridescent, glowing orange ran through it.

Merak stepped closer, then knelt in the dirt. He held his hands up, his palms near the stone's surface, and from her vantage point, Ellin could see his grin.

"You were right," he said. "It's hot." He reached out a hand toward the male archeologist. "Let me borrow your gloves."

"Mr. Merak, we need to test—"

"Just give him your gloves," the female archeologist said. "He's wearing an antirad, and if it's too hot through the gloves, he'll stop touching it."

The man complied.

Still holding Trett's hand, Ellin reached out to Rena, who'd taken off her own eights. When Ellin grabbed her hand, Rena squeezed it.

Merak eagerly ran his gloved hands over the stone, then began tracing the orange veins with his finger, letting out a low laugh as he did so. He took a moment to look up at the crowd, then at the videographer. "So much power," he said. "So much potential. Mark my words, this stone will change the world."

A *pop* emerged from the stone, and Merak paused his exploration of it.

"What was that?" the male archeologist asked.

"I moved it a bit when I touched it." Merak's face was calm, but Ellin thought she could hear a tinge of nervousness in his voice.

The popping returned, several bursts of sound this time.

Merak stood and stepped away from the stone.

POP. This one was louder, and several more followed.

Rena put her arm around Ellin's shoulder. Ellin put hers around both Rena's and Trett's waists and felt Trett's arm encircle her too.

The noise was getting ever louder, like someone was setting off explosive devices inside the stone. Then, with a crack that sounded like the planet itself breaking, the stone shattered along every glowing fault line, its pieces falling away from each other, some of them tumbling to the dirt.

Orange light burst out of it—but perhaps it wasn't light. It was somehow more tangible than light, and it didn't dissipate like it should have. It spread and strengthened, covering the entire site with thick, flame-colored rays that continued as far as Ellin could see. They spread over the land and into the sky, above the massive mountain and beyond the valley.

A collective gasp rose from the crowd.

Then Rena cried out in a voice loud enough to echo through the quiet valley, "I love you both!"

Ellin squeezed her sister's waist, but her eyes met Merak's. She couldn't look away as every bit of color fled from his face and hair, until they looked like bones bleached by the sun. His white lips gaped open, and Ellin thought he would have screamed if thick blood weren't pouring out of his mouth, matching the streams of red coming from his eyes, his nose, his ears.

The entire thing took just seconds. Then Merak collapsed.

That jolted Ellin out of her frozen state. She looked around. It was like a nightmare, except Ellin had never been tortured by a dream this grotesque. All of Merak's people were on the ground, their skin and hair pure white, marred only by the bright red blood flowing from their faces, creating slow-moving rivers of gore through the dirt.

When she realized Rena had let go of her, Ellin turned. She looked down. There was her sister—her infuriating, wonderful, brilliant sister—on the ground, a heap of white skin and red blood.

Ellin fell to the earth, kneeling over Rena, and screamed, her voice melding with the orange rays that still cleaved the cool air. She paused only long enough for a breath before screaming again.

Then warm fabric and hard muscle muffled her voice. Trett was kneeling with her, his arms tight around her, holding her head to his chest.

Ellin's screams turned to sobs, and only then could she could hear the words Trett was saying to her, over and over.

"I'm still here. I'm still here, Ellin. I'm still here."

30

SATURDAY, CYGNI 6, 6293

0 DAYS

Ellin and Trett rode hovs over the road leading into the city of Krenner, passing countless crashed solarcars, solarbuses, and hovs. At some point, Ellin's tears had stopped, smothered by unremitting horror.

She tried to avert her gaze from the bleeding corpses of drivers and passengers, but her effort was useless. There was always another body, or black smoke from a downed glidecraft in the distance, or carribirds swooping in to gorge themselves on the dead. Above, the eerie, bright-orange sky seemed to scream, "You don't belong here anymore."

They slowed when they entered the city. There were bodies everywhere, stinking of metallic blood and some other, awful scent Ellin couldn't put a finger on. Trett's choked voice reached her through her helmet. "Let's find a dubhov. I need to be closer to you."

"Yes," was all she could say.

They dismounted and left their hovs on the side of the road. All around them were crashed vehicles and drivers who'd been thrown from their hovs. Trett walked up to a dubhov that was scratched up but otherwise didn't appear damaged. "This one looks good." He gestured to several nearby bodies. "We just gotta figure out who has the key."

Hov drivers carried contactless keys, usually in their pockets. The repugnant truth struck Ellin: to use this dubhov, they'd have to steal the key from a corpse. She screwed up her face and swallowed against sharp nausea.

"Hey." Trett pulled her into his arms, their helmets pressing against each other. "Don't worry about it. I'll look for the key."

She let him hold her for a long moment before taking a deep breath and stepping back. "I'll help. I need to get used to . . . all of this."

"Okay. I'm guessing it's one of them." Trett pointed at two male corpses, both lying on their stomachs near the dubhov. He and Ellin checked the men's back pockets with no luck. "We'll have to turn them over," Trett said.

Ellin grasped one man's bicep and attempted to flip him. His arm was mushy, like the muscle inside had disintegrated. Trett helped turn the man to his back and set to work going through his front pockets. Ellin wiped her hands on her pants, but her skin still crawled with the memory of that squishy arm. She ran a few mets away, pulled off her helmet, and vomited, then returned to Trett.

He gave her a sad smile. "Got the key."

Ellin replaced her helmet, wishing the breathable membrane blocked out scents. Trett swung his leg over the dubhov, and Ellin sat behind him. He released a sigh as she put her arms around his waist and pressed her chest to his back. "Guess we should find some supplies." His voice was soft in her helmet speaker.

"Yeah."

They didn't have much of a plan. Ellin knew at some point they should check their flexes, which they'd retrieved before leaving the mountain. Every time she considered it, however, electric panic shot through her body. They hadn't seen one other living person. What if they were the only ones in the world still alive? She assured herself that couldn't be the case; Rena had seen a few living people in her visions. But what if all the other survivors were on the other side of the world?

She shook her head. *Supplies first. Then we'll try to figure out our status.*

They found an outdoor store and filled brand-new backpacks with dried meat and fruit, two water filters, tents made of a high-tech, all-weather fabric, and several other items.

"This is good, but we need more," Trett said. "We can't stay in the city with all these bodies, and I don't know when we'll have a chance to resupply."

"If we want to carry more, we'll need a solarcar," Ellin said. "And neither of us knows how to drive one."

"I can't think of a better time to learn." Somehow, despite the dead customers all around them, Trett smiled.

After half an hour of searching, they found a heavy-duty solarcar with large tires. They pulled a dead man out of the driver's seat, and this time, it was Trett who vomited when he saw the smeared blood the man left behind. They returned to the store for a tarp to cover the seat. Then, for the first time in his life, Trett drove a solarcar.

Ellin followed him on the dubhov. Trett seemed to figure out the controls quickly, but there was no way for his first drive to be a smooth one. The vehicle's big wheels bounced over crashed hovs and dead bodies. Ellin tried to look away from the smashed corpses and resolved to travel in front of the solarcar next time.

Back at the store, they loaded the car with as many supplies as they could manage. When they finished, they leaned against the car, their sweaty bodies smudging the windows.

"We need to check social media," Ellin said, blinking hard, "and I don't want to."

Trett's shoulders fell as he let out a long sigh. "You're right, we need to. But I've gotta get away from all these bodies, Ellin. I can't stay in this city a minute longer than necessary. Let's leave Krenner, then check our flexes."

"Good idea."

Ellin drove the dubhov, and Trett followed. Exiting the city was far more difficult than they'd expected. Many streets were blocked by crashed solarcars, which Trett couldn't just run over. Ellin went ahead in her hov to find passable routes, repeatedly doubling back for Trett to follow her.

Bodies, vehicles, and buildings still surrounded them when the orange sky faded to black. Familiar stars blinked into existence, and Ellin lifted her eyes to them. "It's odd, isn't it?" she murmured to no one. "Our planet is devasted, but the rest of the universe is as beautiful as ever."

It had been dark for at least an hour when they finally exited the stinking city. After a few more clommets, the road was mostly clear of crashed vehicles and bodies. Ellin stopped, and behind her, Trett brought the solarcar to a halt.

They sat together in the road. Ellin pulled out her flex, despite the anxious knots in her stomach. She and Trett held the device between them, and she tapped a social media icon.

For the first time since she'd started her internship at Merak Technologies nearly eight weeks earlier, Ellin signed into social media under her real identity. She was greeted with the faces and names of familiar friends, and for a second, relief blossomed in her chest.

Then reality set in. Nobody was posting about worldwide apocalypse; they were telling jokes and sharing pictures. These posts were hours or days old. "I'm going to get rid of everything more than six hours old," she murmured.

She did, and the page turned blank.

Trett released a long breath. "We need to look at public posts. Still from the last six hours."

Ellin nodded and, ignoring the frightened lump in her throat, expanded the filters to include people she didn't know. She hovered her finger above the *Search* button, closed her eyes tightly, and tapped.

"Oh, thank God," Trett breathed.

Ellin opened her eyes. Trett was scrolling through an endless list of posts from people who'd lived, all over the world.

Survivors.

Trett slowed his scrolling, and together, he and Ellin read one post after another, mostly cries for help from confused, grieving people. Invariably, they'd lost their entire families. Most of them were utterly alone, though some had encountered other survivors. They were all horrified and desperate, and while Ellin understood those reactions, the posts flooded her with renewed hope. It ran from her eyes in salty streams and escaped from her chest in harsh sobs.

She and Trett sat on the deserted road all night, huddled in a blanket, reading social media posts. By the time dawn colored the still-orange sky, they'd seen a few mentions of meeting places in various parts of the world. Before long, someone posted a link to a growing list of meeting spots, organized by location. Ellin clicked, and she and Trett found one a little over a hundred clommets away.

"Let's go," Trett said, standing.

Ellin reached up and took his hand. "Wait." When he turned a questioning gaze on her, she patted the ground next to her. Trett sat again, and she asked, "Do you remember what Rena said? About what we're supposed to do?"

He nodded slowly. "Protect the stone."

Before leaving the dig site, they'd hidden the pieces of broken stone in a research cabinet, not sure what else they could do with it. "Yes," Ellin said. "She told us to protect the stone. She also told us to *tell the story*. We"—she paused, swallowing a sudden influx of emotion—"we're the only ones who know what happened, Trett. There are so many scared people out there, and they need to know the truth."

So together, they wrote the story of a stone, a wealthy business-man, and a seer. They told of Nomi and Sep, heroes who deserved to be remembered. Ellin included links to radiation data, proof that this story wasn't some apocalyptic hoax. She and Trett passed the flex back and forth, taking turns writing.

It was nearly noon when Trett typed out the last of their story. He tapped the screen to post it, and then he set the flex on the road, stood, and pulled Ellin to her feet. He hugged her tight, his arms warm and firm.

Ellen felt Trett's chest rising and falling in a soothing rhythm. She adjusted her breathing to match his, repeatedly inhaling the wonder of their survival and exhaling grief over all they'd lost. In time, she let herself cry for Rena and her friends and even her long-dead parents, and she felt Trett's chest shudder with his own tears.

At last, they stopped weeping and pulled apart. Ellin picked up her flex. The story they'd posted was still open, and she gasped. "Trett—look."

His eyes widened when he saw the screen. Thousands of people were, at that moment, reading their words. Hundreds had already shared the post. Watching the numbers rise, Ellin shook her head in wonder. Rena had been right, again. People needed to hear this story.

"We need to get the stone," Ellin said. "Too many people know where it is now. We can't let someone else find it."

Trett's brows shot up. "What will we do with it? We don't know if it's still dangerous."

"I know." Ellin gazed out at the horizon. "Everything Rena prophesied was true. I don't know what it means for us to protect the stone, but we have to do it."

Trett nodded. "We'll go to the dig site, then to the meeting place. But first—I'm starving."

They ate some of the food they'd looted. Afterward, they brushed their teeth, a task that felt almost obscenely normal in this tragic, new world.

The road to the dig site was deserted, though Ellin and Trett did see one solarcar along the way. It had crashed into a tree. Ellin wondered how many years it would remain there. Would humanity ever recover enough to clean up the mess of the apocalypse?

At the research building, they found that the stone pieces were already cooling, though their broken, orange edges remained luminescent. Ellin used her flex to take pictures of the stone. With gloved hands, she and Trett moved the pieces onto a tarp.

Before leaving, they took pictures of the cave and the bodies of Merak and his employees. They added several photos to their story, which had now been shared thousands of times.

Once the stone was safely in the solarcar, Ellin instructed her flex to give her verbal directions to the meeting location. She drove away, followed by Trett.

A few hours later, as the sun dipped low in the sky, they pulled up to a small house, surrounded by evergreen trees. Seven people waited in the front yard, including a wide-eyed, young child. Trett and Ellin stepped into the street and linked hands.

An elderly woman approached them, her lined face creased in a gentle, sad smile. She stopped in front of them and grasped their free hands. "Welcome," she said. "You're not alone."

EPILOGUE

"Come lie in the hammock with me."

Ellin looked up from the corn she was shucking. "I've got to get this done."

Trett pulled out the chair next to her, sat, and took her calloused hand in his. "The kids are napping. The corn can wait. Just for a few minutes?"

It was a little chilly on the covered porch, and a slight breeze rustled the husks on the table. Ellin looked past the wooden awning, where the sun shone brightly.

"The sun is warm today," Trett said, like he'd read her mind. His gaze flicked down, and he shooed away a shimshim that was creeping toward the basket of corn on the porch floor. It scampered off, its blue skin shining in the sun. Trett moved the basket to the table.

Ellin stood, smiling. "I think I can spare fifteen minutes."

Trett took her hand and led her to the big hammock they'd tied between two trees. He got in first, then pulled her next to him, almost toppling them both.

Ellin let herself laugh hard. She'd been trying to laugh more lately. Her kids helped with that resolution, as did Trett. She settled close to him, resting on his arm, her head on his shoulder.

Above them, tree branches filtered some of the sun, but the leaves had already fallen, and plenty of the sky was still visible. Ellin gazed up at the pale-orange expanse. When the stone had broken seven years before, the merciless, orange beams had covered the globe, then gradually faded. But the sky had retained a slight coloration, like a permanent, pale sunrise. It was a lovely, heartbreaking reminder of the apocalypse.

Most people now referred to that terrible event as *The Day*. While the stone's effects were as horrifying as Rena had predicted, an estimated one in ten thousand people had been, for some reason, immune to the deadly radiation. In minutes, a global population of four billion shrank to less than half a million.

The small group Ellin and Trett had joined had rapidly grown as they'd connected with other survivors. About a thousand people now lived in their fertile valley east of Cellerin Mountain. They had a teacher and even a doctor, luxuries many other places didn't have. These days, everyone was a farmer—even the doctors and teachers.

"Has it been fifteen minutes?" Ellin asked.

"No," Trett responded in a lazy voice.

Ellin elbowed him. Trett had no idea how long it had been, and neither did she. They didn't have a functioning clock, since most electronic devices had stopped working years ago. For once, she decided her never-ending chores didn't matter. She cuddled in closer to Trett and kept watching the sky.

"What kinds of birds do you think those are?" she asked, pointing.

Trett watched for a few seconds. "Too far away to tell."

The things gliding in the sky came a little closer, and a jet of fire emerged from the mouth of the larger one.

They both laughed. "Not birds," Ellin said.

The world had changed in many ways since the day orange filled the sky. It hadn't taken long for the survivors to notice strange things happening, phenomena they could only describe as *magical.*

New creatures, similar to those described in pre-colonial human mythology, had appeared. Unlike the dragon figure in Trett's old fountain, however, these beasts seemed to belong on Anyari, with recognizable traits such as compound eyes.

A few times a year, Ellin spotted a dragon or two flying overhead. The basket-weave texture of their skin marked them as reptids. No one knew where dragons had come from, but Ellin wondered if the stone's radiation had spurred instant evolution in an existing reptid species.

In a nearby wooded area, several locals had seen creatures similar to the unicorns described in Trett's favorite stories. The most common hypothesis was that the cervida species had given rise to Anyarian unicorns. Cervidas were docile animals, about as tall as a person's chest, with four long legs made for swift running. They thrived in wooded areas.

Unicorns, however, were significantly taller than cervidas. And unlike a cervida, who had two small, blunt horns, every unicorn boasted one long, glossy-white, pointed horn.

While Ellin hadn't heard of any other magical beasts in their area, rumors abounded of ocean fishers and sailors encountering sea monsters. Perhaps other types of wondrous creatures were scattered around the rest of the planet.

Nomads and visitors from distant communities passed along other strange tales too. They spoke of rivers parting for them to cross, of meadows that gave peace to everyone who entered them, and of boiling rain. They even described young children with powers to create fire or move the earth.

Ellin didn't know what was true and what was embellished, but no one doubted their world had changed in fundamental ways. It seemed that the very stone that had caused the apocalypse had also ushered in a new era of magic that, in Ellin's opinion, belonged in fantasy stories, not reality.

Perhaps she'd be happier with the changes if she understood them. Surely Anyarians would eventually redevelop the world's technologies, and researchers would explore the world's new, supernatural qualities. Knowing such a day was far in the future, however, Ellin had resolved to laugh at dragons and find contentment in the miracle of her own survival.

The dragons descended low enough for Ellin to admire their awe-inspiring forms. One of them had gray skin. The sun's bright rays sent rainbows shimmering on its iridescent surface. It was stunning—massive and muscular. The second dragon, however, was even larger. Every bit of its black body, which glinted slightly yellow in the sunlight, exuded terrifying strength.

When the dragons flew away, Ellin pushed herself up on an elbow, shifting her gaze to her house, then to the street beyond. "The chapel's busy," she said, before settling back to her original position.

Trett didn't look. "Usually is."

The chapel sat a few dozen mets beyond their farmhouse. Inside was the broken stone that had caused the apocalypse. The strange artifact's iridescent orange surfaces still glowed, hinting at untapped power.

In the early days, Ellin and Trett had kept the stone hidden among their other supplies, unsure how to best follow Rena's mandate to protect it. Rena's other command, however, was easy to obey: *Tell the story.* Every person in their small group had been hungry to hear the truth of the apocalypse. Many of them wished they could see the stone, and Ellin and Trett at last revealed the mysterious artifact.

Immediately, Ellin realized how important the stone was to the grieving populace. Everyone gathered around the broken pieces. Survivors who'd shown no emotion knelt and wept. Others treated the stone as if it were alive, screaming their grief and fear at its black-and-orange surfaces. Some found strength by being near something that had killed so many but hadn't touched them. It was more than a stone. It was a symbol of what they'd lost and what they'd survived.

The group converted a small outbuilding on Ellin and Trett's property into a home for the stone. They agreed to take turns guarding it.

Within three years, a Rimorian emissary arrived and, with the community's permission, moved into the building. She guarded the artifact and comforted visitors. Soon everyone referred to the building as a chapel, and people traveled for weeks to visit the stone. Ellin and Trett often took their own shifts at the chapel, sharing their story.

They held a unique status in their community, not only as the bearers of truth, but as the only couple anyone knew of who'd survived The Day together. It didn't take long for their peers to treat them as leaders. Four years after The Day, the group had voted Ellin and Trett onto their new legislature. The older woman who'd established their community became the mayor, but everyone expected Ellin to eventually be elected to that position.

Ellin was thinking how nice it was that no one from the community had interrupted them all day when she heard the back door open. A voice called, "Mommy? Daddy? I can't sleep."

Ellin released a sigh. She kissed Trett and whispered, "Can we ignore one of our youngest constituents?"

"I can't sleep," the little voice repeated.

Ellin and Trett sat up and repositioned themselves, using the hammock more like a swing, their feet hanging off the edge.

"C'mere, baby," Trett said, reaching out to Liri who, at five, was the oldest of their three children.

Liri joined them, sitting on Trett's lap and burying her face in his chest. They spent a few peaceful minutes together, but Liri was an active sort, and she never cuddled for long. Soon, she jumped down and settled herself under one of the trees supporting the hammock.

"Back to the corn," Ellin said, standing and stretching.

Trett stood too. "I have more harvesting to do before the sun goes down."

Ellin returned to the porch. When she turned to check on Liri, she groaned at what she saw. She ran back to the tree and squatted next to her daughter. "Liri Abrios, spit it out."

Trett's warm laugh reached them from where he'd stopped on his way to the fields, and Ellin shot him a glare.

Liri kept chewing. Ellin tried to put her finger in the girl's mouth, but Liri moved her head back and forth, determined to ingest what was in her mouth. A bit of chewed, brown mush escaped her lips.

At last, Liri swallowed. She grinned up at her mother. "It tastes so good, Mommy."

By then, Trett was kneeling next to Liri too. "Honey, you can't eat tree bark. We've talked about this. Your body isn't made to digest it."

Liri stood, and her little fists clenched tight at her sides. "But it tastes good, Daddy! It tastes good!" She reached out to the tree and grasped a piece of bark, trying to pry it off.

Ellin put out a hand to stop her but was distracted by a sudden darkening of the sky. She looked up.

Green leaves had sprouted all over the tree—spring growth, in the middle of autumn.

"Trett . . . ?" Ellin breathed.

He looked up, and his mouth dropped open.

They both turned their gazes on Liri. She'd stopped trying to pull the bark off the tree. Now she was pressing both hands against the trunk, and the smile on her upturned face was full of wonder.

Ellin took Trett's hand, and they watched as vibrant green leaves continued to sprout off every branch and twig.

At last, Liri pulled her hands away from the tree. "That was really fun!" She pried off another piece of bark and popped it in her mouth, then giggled and ran into the tall rows of corn.

Thank you for reading *The Seer's Sister*! Reviews make a *huge* difference to authors and readers. Will you write a short review on Goodreads and/or the store where you purchased this book? I can't tell you how much I'd appreciate it.

The Magic Eaters Trilogy takes place two hundred years after the events of *The Seer's Sister*. Keep reading for a sneak peek of Book 1, *The Frost Eater*. Order it now!

I'd love to keep in touch! Become an Email Insider to get news about free and discounted books (plus updates on my life in Texas). Visit carolbethanderson.com to sign up.

THE FROST EATER: BOOK 1 OF THE MAGIC EATERS TRILOGY

SNEAK PEEK

Two years after the world ended, I was born.

-The First Generation: A Memoir *by Liri Abrios*

"Darling, your crown is crooked."

Nora turned to her father. "You're always telling me it's not a crown, it's a headdress."

"When it's just the two of us, it's a crown." His brown eyes twinkled as he pointed to the band of gold around his head. "One day, you'll wear the real thing."

Nora was only seventeen; she wasn't ready to think about the day when she'd become an orphan and a queen all at once. "That won't happen for a long time. Straighten the headdress for me?"

He grasped it with both hands, shifting it to the left. It scratched Nora's forehead, eliciting a wince.

"Sorry. Does it feel secure?"

"As secure as it gets." The headdress was crafted of fine silver, with delicate filigree extending high above Nora's head. She usually loved wearing it. But after weeks on the road, she had pimples from the molded metal that rested on her forehead. She couldn't be happier that they were approaching the last stop on their tour.

Unseen people began chanting, "Cell-er-in! Cell-er-in!" The open-topped steamcar was having a tough time making it up a steep slope. Beyond the hill lay the town of Tirra, where crowds awaited their king and princess. Nora wished they'd harness a couple of orsas to the car and let the beasts pull it up the hill, but that would ruin the effect of them rolling into town in the most modern vehicle available. Most rural residents had never seen a steamcar.

"Almost there!" the driver called over his shoulder.

"Thank you." Nora's father returned his gaze to her. "Chin up."

Before he could finish his admonishment, Nora did it for him. "Smile big."

Her father winked. A gust of chilly wind blew Nora's straight, dark-brown, chin-length hair into her face. She peeled a few strands off her glossed lips and curved her lips into a smile she hoped was sufficiently regal.

Windmills rose up on either side of the road as the steamcar puttered to the top of the rise. Chanting people came into view, hundreds of them, lining the road all the way down the hill and into town.

Nora and her father waved, and the chants turned into cheers. The rush of support filled Nora's chest and tugged her mouth into a wider grin.

Eight guards riding orsas surrounded the steamcar. Between them, Nora glimpsed a little girl perched on a man's shoulders, wearing a headdress made of—what was that, corn husks? Whatever the material, it was molded to look like Nora's. She blew a kiss to the cheering girl.

It didn't take long to arrive at the bottom of the hill. They drove a few blocks and pulled to a stop in a quaint town square. A wooden stage awaited them, decorated with large, fabric bows in blue and black, Cellerin's royal colors. A woman who introduced herself as Mayor Ashler showed Nora, her father, and several guards onto the stage. When the crowd calmed, the show began.

Nora awarded the town with a Cellerinian flag that had flown at the palace. Then King Ulmin began speaking, and Nora instantly grew bored. It was the same talk her father had given in every town they'd visited, except that somehow it got longer each time. He spoke of The Day, two hundred years earlier, when billions of humans on their planet, Anyari, had died. Then he looked up to the sky and said, "But we thank God that four hundred thousand people, one in ten thousand, survived. They were your ancestors and mine. And they rebuilt civilization."

Nora had to admit, her dad cut an impressive figure. He was tall, with a broad chest and slim waist. His beard, more silver than brown these days, was perfectly trimmed. Autumn sunlight reflected off the gold of his crown and the silver streaks in his hair as he continued his speech, extolling the nation of Cellerin that had risen from destruction. He praised his grandmother Onna, Cellerin's first monarch, who'd ended a terrible war.

At first, Nora's father's speeches had inspired her. Now, three weeks into their tour, she was sick of the stories. She tried to keep her face pleasant. At least her clothing was thick and warm, protecting her from the late-fall chill. Her blue-and-purple outfit—more of a costume, really—had belonged to her mother. The shirt and pants were crafted of high-tech, preday fabric that had been made to last for centuries. It was layered and molded into a structural wonder that hugged Nora's long legs, curvy hips, and slender torso. A massive collar of sorts, shaped like flower petals, extended up from her shoulders in front and back. The fabric was a visual reminder of the old days, and the collar represented Anyari's people, who had bloomed from devastating tragedy.

"Princess Nora."

Nora jolted but quickly recovered. Her father was facing her.

"The people of Tirra have a gift for you." He beckoned her forward, and Nora saw that Mayor Ashler had joined him onstage.

Nora raised an eyebrow. *Going off script, Dad? That's not like you.* The crowd cheered as she stepped to the front of the stage and waved.

"Princess Ulminora." The mayor had a closed wooden box in her hands. She was beaming. "We heard you ran out of ice on your journey. I'm an ice lyster too, and I just returned from the mountain last week to retrieve fuel for myself."

Nora's eyebrows shot up, and her gaze found Cellerin Mountain, which loomed in the distance. The mayor had climbed its icy heights herself, rather than sending someone else?

Mayor Ashler answered Nora's unspoken question. "I grew up climbing Cellerin's slopes, and I can't seem to break the habit." The people cheered, and the mayor continued, "Your Highness, we grow both grapes and bollaberries in our town greenhouse. I'd like to introduce you to one of my favorite things: shaved ice with bollagrape juice."

She opened the hinged lid. The box was thick, clearly insulated. Inside was a mound of shaved ice, colored with pale-purple juice.

The mayor handed Nora a silver spoon. "Care to try it?"

Nora grinned. "Thank you, Mayor." Year-round access to ice was one of the perks of being a princess. However, a few days into the trip, Nora had eaten the last of the ice from her personal ice chest. She'd then discovered that they'd left behind the large chest they'd meant to bring. It was the first time she'd ever gone two weeks without doing magic.

She dipped the spoon in the snowy concoction and brought it to her mouth. Instantly, she knew she'd have to beg the chef back home to find a source of bollaberries. The combination of the berries, which originated on Anyari, and grapes, which originated on Earth, was perfect. Like so many mixtures of Anyarian and Original produce, the flavor was complex and surprising, both sweet and tart.

Without thinking, Nora dipped the spoon in the ice again. She halted and flicked her eyes up to the mayor's. "I'm sorry—do you mind me going back for seconds?"

Laughter and cheers filled the square. The mayor's eyes crinkled. "Have as much as you'd like."

Nora ate several more bites, then turned to her father. She lifted her hands and wiggled her fingers. "May I?"

He nodded.

She took a step toward the edge of the stage, held her arms out wide, and turned her hands toward the sky. The crowd's murmuring stopped, the hush only broken by a baby's cry. Nora's arms, fingers, and throat started to tingle, the sensation delightfully chilly. She brought her arms in front of her and held her palms toward the crowd. With a bright smile, she pushed magic through her hands, shooting two puffs of snow over the front rows. The crowd cheered.

Nora took a deep breath, lifted her chin, and blew snow from her cold mouth. It arced into the air, then fell on a dozen grinning towns-people. She laughed, basking in the crackling energy of the masses. In a thousand ways, she dreaded becoming queen. But she savored moments like these, when she forgot the stifling responsibilities ahead of her and simply enjoyed the people of Cellerin.

Then, all at once, the crowd's gazes shifted. Fingers pointed high and to the right. Excited murmurs grew louder.

Nora lifted her eyes to the sky. When she saw what was distracting everyone, her focus broke, drying up the flow of snow. She dropped her arms to her side.

A man was soaring through the pale-orange sky, swooping up and down like a drunk bird. *This little town has a feather lyster? And he chooses this moment to put on a show?* She shouldn't be surprised; the feather lysters she knew were the vainest people in all of Cellerin.

Two royal guards were standing in front of the stage. One drew a pistol. The other lifted his bow and nocked an arrow. Both aimed at the flying man.

At the same time, the six guards who'd been standing at the rear of the stage rushed to surround Nora and her father. They faced outward, weapons pointed at the flying man. "Let's get you two off the stage," one of them said.

From outside the circle of guards, Mayor Ashler said, "I assure you, he's harmless. He's a show-off, but he won't hurt anyone."

"Let the mayor in," Nora's father said. Two guards moved apart, and the mayor joined the cramped circle. King Ulmin's authoritative voice boomed in the tight space. "I'm staying here. I want a guard on either side of me. The rest of you, take Nora off the stage."

"My office is next to the stage," Mayor Ashler said. "I'll take her there, and we'll lock the doors."

"Dad," Nora said, "the mayor said that man is harmless. He doesn't even have a weapon. Should we really run from him?"

"I'm not running. I'm keeping you safe."

Nora rolled her eyes as everyone followed the king's instructions. Two guards held her elbows. Another stood behind her, hand on her back, and the fourth positioned himself in front of her. Nora was tall, but the guard in front of her was practically a giant, his shoulders even with her eyes. His name was Ovrun, and he was the youngest guard, only nineteen. His muscular shoulders, clad in black livery with blue epaulets, distracted Nora as the guards rushed her across the stage, down a set of steps, and into a dark building.

Mayor Ashler locked the door. "My deepest apologies, Princess Ulminora."

"It's Nora."

"Pardon me?"

"No one calls me Ulminora."

The mayor flipped a switch. A light bulb came on, illuminating a small lobby with a large, curtained window.

Enough wind power for lights in public buildings. This town's doing pretty well. Nora took off her heavy headdress and set it down. She approached the window, but Ovrun and another guard were standing in front of it, their arms folded. A third guard stationed himself at the far edge of the window and pulled back the drapes just enough to look outside.

Nora gave Ovrun her most dazzling smile, and the corner of his lips quirked up. "I appreciate you trying to keep me safe," she said. "All I want to do is peek between the curtains. Please?"

The guards exchanged glances, and then Ovrun parted the curtains just enough for Nora to peer out with one eye. The lyster was still flying. Nora watched for any signs of his magic waning, but he was soaring in confident arcs. *Must've eaten plenty of feathers.* The crowd cheered as he flew in ridiculous figure eights, nearly hitting the tops of buildings every time he reached the bottom of the shape. Nora rolled her eyes. *Show-off.*

Finally, the flyer ended his flamboyant display. He stayed in the air, however, hovering over a three-story building that faced the square. Nora was close enough to discern a rough outline of his face. He looked like a teenager, but he couldn't possibly be that young. It took feather lysters decades to perfect their magical faculty.

His dark hair was long enough to cover his forehead, but the wind was lifting it into a messy mop. Despite how ridiculous this made him look, he beamed as he waved at the crowd. Then he alighted on the edge of the roof and dropped to his hands and knees.

Nora squinted, then gasped. A thick ribbon of smooth, white ice flowed from the man's hands, extending off the roof. *He's an ice lyster, too?*

The ice grew at an unbelievable pace. Within a minute, a gorgeous, curving ramp with banked edges extended from the roof to the ground. Nora's jaw dropped. Despite years of training (focused on one faculty, not two), she'd never made that much ice at once.

The young man sat on the ramp and grinned once more at the crowd. He pushed himself forward until the ramp grew steep enough for gravity to take over, sending him sliding at a dizzying speed.

Nora had just enough time to think, *I've got to learn how to make one of those ramps!* when the lyster reached the slide's halfway point, and everything literally fell apart. The entire slide broke into at least a dozen pieces. The young man's hands flailed in the air as he tumbled down, his fall cushioned only by massive, jagged shards of ice.

Nora's hand came up to her mouth. "Oh!"

The guards on either side of her tensed. Ovrun grasped her arm and tugged her away from the window. "What's wrong?"

"Nothing. The lyster just fell." Nora pulled away and stepped back to the window. It was clear what had happened. The man had lost focus, turning his ice brittle. She'd done it a thousand times, just never when she was depending on her creation to support her full weight.

"Come on, get up!" Nora urged under her breath. All the lyster's would-be rescuers blocked her line of sight. Her heart pounded and her cheeks grew warm as she tried to determine his fate. Sure, he was arrogant and lacked common sense, but he didn't deserve to die in a pile of his own ice.

The clock on the wall seemed to tick louder than it had before. Suddenly, the young man pushed himself up to stand atop his bed of ice. Nora couldn't see his expression, but his wave to the crowd was hesitant, his hubris gone. He dropped into a squat, then jumped into the air and flew again, soaring over the buildings of the square and dropping out of sight.

Nora laughed at the sight, then stepped back from the window and nodded at the guards. "Thanks for letting me watch."

"Is the feather eater gone?" Ovrun asked.

"Yeah. What a fool. He's lucky you didn't shoot him down." Despite her words, all Nora could think about was how fun it would be to make and use a slide like that.

Across the room, Mayor Ashler cleared her throat. "I'm very sorry about all this."

Nora grinned and crossed to the woman. "It's okay; this is the most fun I've had in weeks. Tell me, Mayor, what's that lyster's name?"

Start devouring The Frost Eater today!

Also available as a highly-rated Audible audiobook.

ACKNOWLEDGEMENTS

Publishing a book shouldn't be a solitary endeavor! I love the community aspect of writing as I get feedback from many people along the way.

I can't thank my alpha readers enough! They all waded through early versions of the book, complete with awful typos and undeveloped characters . . . and then they helped me make the book better. For this book, my alpha readers were Molly Norris, Ana Anderson, Eli Anderson (who also helped with one of Sep's poems!), Cathy Norris, Melissa Lavaty, Kim Decker, Becky Brickman, Sarah Joy Green-Hart, DeDe Pollnow, Alex Pollnow, Stephanie Lynn, Alain Davis, Brooke Hunger, and Kristin Newton.

My beta-reader team agreed to read a more-polished but still unfinished version of the book. Their feedback really helped me make it better. Massive, huge, heartfelt thanks to Alain Davis, Ana Anderson, Anastasia Forrest, Ashley McCartney, Becky Brickman, Brenda Elliott, Danielle Ancona. Danielle Carriere. Eli Anderson, Erinne Lansing, Jenny Fox, Kim Decker, Kristin Newton, Lisa Henson, Mackenzie Bitz, Michelle Sundholm, Nikki Tuggy, Phil

Gorski, Randi Rigby, Rebecca Odum, Robin Higham, Sean Norris Westmont, and Tracy Magouirk.

Thank you to @bcsayerlit and @KenzieMillar on Twitter, who gave me some much-needed feedback and encouragement as I developed Rena's character.

Speaking of Twitter . . . shout out to all my friends in the #WritingCommunity there, including the various groups of writers I connect with through frequent private messages. You know who you are, and I hope you know what an encouragement you are to me!

I've dealt with anxiety for years, so Ellin's struggles are close to my heart. Some of her coping techniques in the freezer came from the book *The 10 Best-Ever Anxiety Management Techniques: Understanding How Your Brain Makes You Anxious and What You Can Do to Change It* by Margaret Wehrenberg. I recommend it!

I ask newsletter readers and social media followers to contribute their name ideas for my books. Many of the character and location names in this book came from their suggestions! Here are the contributors, with the names they suggested in parentheses: Linda Pearman (Nomi, Arisa), Kris Adams (Septimus, Tyr, Stelios, Thyri, Tereza, Merak, Karel), Cheryl (Micha), Marie-Eve Mailhot (Toma), and Patrice Einsel (Pranav), and Cherie Osier (Rouven). Thank you all for sharing your creativity with me!

Mariah Sinclair (mariahsinclair.com and thecovervault.com), thank you for creating such ridiculously stunning covers for this whole series!

Thank you to God, who I hope to keep seeking my entire life. I love the love He gives me.

And thank *you* for reading! (If you made it this far, I'm truly impressed!)

-Carol Beth Anderson
Leander, Texas

She looks like an angel . . . acts like a human . . . and must risk her immortal life to save the faerie realm.

Order your copy of *Faerie Fallen* (Feathered Fae Book 1) now.

A spoiled royal hungry for excitement. A young man who hates nobles. Can they foil a kidnapping before they fall prey to an enemy's deadly magic?

Buy or borrow *The Frost Eater* and devour it today!

ABOUT THE AUTHOR

Carol Beth Anderson is a native of Arizona and now lives in Leander, TX, outside Austin. She has a husband, two kids, a miniature schnauzer, and more fish than anyone knows what to do with. Besides writing, she loves baking sourdough bread, knitting, eating cookies-and-cream ice cream, and spending way too much time on Twitter.

Find Beth on Facebook, BookBub, and Goodreads, all under the name Carol Beth Anderson. She's also on Twitter and Instagram as @CBethAnderson.